Fred and Jenny

Book I An Unbelievable Beginning

The Fields where Dreams Come From

Philip Sorant

ISBN 10: 0615871518
ISBN-13: 9780615871516

DEDICATION

In Memory of Barbara Elaine Christophel

Barbara was a Loving Mother, a dedicated teacher, and an encouraging inspiration that bolstered my ambition to write this book.

And a Very Special Thanks to Marshal!

CONTENTS

"How many footsteps of others have we crossed or walked along side of, only one hundred or perhaps two hundred years later?"

CHAPTER ONE
GOOD NEWS TRAVELS FAST

Claire, while just about dropping her cup of coffee, and almost choking on her last sip, gurgled out "That's fantastic . . . I'm so happy for you Jen. Have you told Fred yet?"

"No, I've been trying to call him since 10:00 this morning, right after I found out but he is either in a meeting or on the phone. He's not even answering his cell phone!" Jenny said letting out a discouraging sigh.

"Did you leave him a message or something?" Claire asked.

"I don't think that voice mailing your husband is the best way of letting a man know, he's going to be a Father." And with a chuckle in her voice Jenny went on, "Do You?"

"Of course you're right Jen, as usual. I guess that's something you should say to him in person and alone but please let me know when he knows, because I'm already dying to tell someone . . . You know me . . . So?"

Claire paused a moment and while scratching her head went on, "Why did you tell me first?"

Jenny blushing a little and with an embarrassing type of a grin on her face answered, "Well I guess, I'm kind of like you. I was so excited I just felt I would burst if I didn't tell somebody. When you just happened to drop by to leave off these flowers, I guess . . . I just couldn't help myself. I hope my secret is safe with you?"

"Ah don't worry about it Jen. Gosh, look at the time, I gotta run. With all the errands I have to do today, I'll be lucky to get home by midnight! . . . See you later, call me."

Claire jumped from her seat and scurried out of Jenny's kitchen door leading to the driveway, barely turning as she gave Jenny a quick wave.

Jenny took a position at the kitchen window watching Claire backing out of the driveway and with one hand tucked under her chin, she sighed out loud, "I hope I did the right thing by telling Claire? Ah, I guess it's okay . . . She's a good friend. Claire won't say anything till I talk to Fred. Think I'll try him one more time before I take care of all my running around!"

Jenny had known Claire for about a year now and they did spend a lot of time together. Claire was about the same age as Jenny and they appeared to share the same values but Jenny was always very cautious about trusting people. It was not easy for her.

Meanwhile, at Fred's Office . . .

"Knock, Knock, Knock!" A rather tall man stood in front of Fred's office and he quietly voiced out the sound of his light taps upon an invisible door which was open anyway!

Fred looked up quickly at the entrance to his office and saw Roger's large silhouette darkening the brighter fluorescence of the over lit hallway beyond.

Roger stood there once again pretending to be knocking on the door. "C'mon Fredster . . . Time for lunch!"

"Not sure I have time today Rogg." Fred continued shuffling through a stack of papers but entertained the conversation with his friend and associate.

"Besides, it's way too early for lunch Rogg . . . It's only 11:00!"

"Yeah, I know but I have to leave early for a Dentist and eye Doc appointment . . . C'mon let's go to Garlic Gala for a Pizza." Roger stood while motioning his hands hoping Fred would follow.

"What, Garlic Gala, are you crazy . . . You wanna go to Garlic Gala and then make the Dentist and Doc Olsen suffer through your exams?"

Fred started to laugh and looked up to his longtime friend and stated with a friendly note of sarcasm,

"Rogg, you're a bonehead, you know that don't you?"

"That's true Fred, but I'm also your bonehead friend." Roger replied grinning.

With that, Fred ceased with his paper search and leaned back in his chair. That was true. Roger was his friend and a pretty good friend at that. Fred pointed his finger to the office door and said, "Roger, shut the door a minute . . . I've got something to tell you."

Roger quickly closed the door and in a very animated fashion slid a chair up to the front of Fred's desk and placed his elbows on Fred's blotter, cradling his chin in his hands.

"Go ahead Fred, spill it. . . You know they say confession is good for the soul. What did you do wrong Bud?"

"Will you knock it off Roger . . . I haven't done anything wrong."

Although Roger looked somewhat disappointed Fred continued on, "I really should be telling Jenny first but I'm dying to share this with someone and I haven't been able to get a hold of her on the phone. The line is always busy or no answer, But it's very important you don't say a word to anyone! Got it Rogg."

Fred gave Roger one of his intimidating focuses while pointing his finger at Roger. Roger flinched backwards a little and gulped, "Ah, don't worry Fred

. . . You know me. I won't whisper a word to anyone."

Fred thought about Roger's remark for a few seconds and said, "That's right, I do know you and I mean it Rogg . . . This is big and if you blat this one out on me, I could be in serious trouble. Do I make myself perfectly clear . . . Rogg?" Fred now was shaking his fist at his somewhat stunned friend.

"Ah, yeah Fred, ah don't seem so angry." Roger retorted indignantly.

Fred now assuming his congenial relaxed demeanor leaned over and started whispering so he could not be overheard by any nosey passerby's in the hallway.

"Remember that job that was advertised over in Evansville . . . The one where they were looking for a new advertising exec."

"Yeah Fred but you told me it was a long shot and you weren't going to bother."

"Shhh . . . Not so loud Rogg. I know but I sent my resume anyway. I didn't even tell Jenny I was doing it because I never dreamed that today would happen."

"So what happened today Fred, cut to the chase?" Roger appeared anxious.

Roger perked up slightly in a childish like anticipation and while cocking his ear in Fred's direction, Roger waited impatiently for the news.

Fred started whispering again and talking slowly.

"They called me on my cell phone this morning and want me to come in for . . ." Fred instantly raised his voice while punching Roger in the arm and exclaimed, "For an interview!"

Roger, surprised by the sudden increase in volume from Fred's voice, jerked back to a normal seated position. Roger just kept raising his arms up to his side and up to about his shoulder height, with his palms flat out. He did this about three times bearing a large smile on his face and blurting out the word 'Fantastic' with each lift of the arms.

Looking speechless for a second or two, Roger went back to his primary passion in life. "Okay, I'm ready for lunch, let's go."

Fred shaking his head a few times responded to his friend's apparent lack of enthusiasm over the news.

"You're hopeless Rogg . . . You know that don't you? Just hopeless."

Fred laughed as he broke some terrible news to his friend as the good news, didn't seem to affect Roger.

"Sorry, I can't join you and share in your insidious appetite Rogg. I have to get this work done cause I have to leave early today as well. Got to get back to town and beat the traffic out of this city. I have to stop at Baker's Garage and the Printers."

"Something wrong with your car Fred?" Roger responded with a noticeable sullen voice.

Roger knew how to put on a forlorn look when for some reason or another Fred might not always be available for lunch.

Fred could understand it though. Roger was a nice guy but not very self-confident in social environments but Fred also knew Roger loved to make him feel guilty about it. Overweight, unmarried and generally a strike out with the women, Roger lived alone in a two room apartment over Doc Olsen's office and depended on Fred for his friendship and guidance with almost every aspect of Roger's life. Fred didn't really mind but Fred also knew that Roger couldn't follow him around like a puppy dog. Fred and Jenny did their best to try to get Roger more independent and involved with Church Groups or social events but Roger never ventured out unless Fred and Jenny were going to be there.

"Naw, just have to pick up some parts for the tractor. You'll be fine Roger . . . I'm sure you will not even give me a second thought after your first bite!"

"Yeah, Yeah, sure Fred . . . No Problemo, anyway I'll catch you later Fredster."

Roger left with sort of a no big deal kind of an attitude but Fred knew something was bugging Roger. Roger now had a different tone in his normal jokester kind of nature. Fred also knew that Roger's appearance of being an extravert and an outward going kind of guy, were just a facade to cover up his total lack of confidence in himself. Roger had a tendency to overcompensate for his low self-esteem by trying to talk cool and be the prankster about everything.

Actually, this act of Roger's could be, and usually was quite annoying to all the other associates in the office. But Fred knowing Roger for a long time could overlook this flaw and what was really interesting about all of this; Roger in fact was a very intelligent man. Fred actually had been instrumental in getting Roger to apply for the IT job available at the advertising firm Fred was working for. Nobody knew computers and the internet better than Roger, and that was for sure. Fred guessed that management put up with Roger's obvious obnoxious personality as a trade off to the tremendous advantage which Roger's skill provided to the Company's success. Fred finally snapped out of his wandering thought process and got back to his work at hand.

Much Later that Afternoon . . .

Jenny hurriedly finished putting the groceries away which she had strewn across the kitchen table when she returned from the market. As she turned to grab her purse and fly out the door to tackle the next set of errands, Jenny jumped with a frightening start!

"GOSH . . . You again . . . Why do you always do this to me Bailey?"

Jenny frowned and while picking up her keys and purse off the table, patted the huge Newfoundland on the top of his head.

Bailey was an inherited pet so to speak. Fred's Mom and Dad had retired and moved to Florida where unfortunately, the community had a restriction on dogs and cats. Fred and Jenny agreed to take in the humongous breed and Bailey turned out to be not just a great dog, but also a great friend.

The problem with Bailey was, he loved to sneak up on Jenny and scare the daylights out of her. You would think that would be an impossible task for a 150Lb. dog to do. But despite his size, Bailey could stealthily move up behind you, remain as quiet as a mouse, and just patiently await the unexpected discovery of his presence!

It was almost as if this was a fun loving game that Bailey loved to participate in with Jenny! Although you would think that Jenny would be accustomed and catch on to this playful tactic by the beast, Bailey was successful in almost every attempt. In fact this ritual turned out to be a regular challenge and contest between the two, pitting Jenny's intuitiveness against Bailey's sneakiness!

Often Jenny would counter strike with sneak attacks on her own, but so far, Bailey was too smart for her. Fred several times had overheard Jenny, after a failed attempt, jokingly warning Bailey, 'Don't you worry you overstuffed Poodle. One of these days I'm going to get even with you . . . I will. One of these days.'

Jenny's next stop was the florists. She wanted to send a bouquet to her sister for her 10th wedding anniversary. The jing-a-ling of the bells on the front door alerted Mildred's attention and she looked over to greet her next customer.

Mildred gave Jenny a big smile and said, "Hi Jenny, haven't seen you in a while! What can I do for you today Dear?"

Jenny proceeded to tell Mildred about the flowers for the anniversary, and while they designed a look for the bouquet, they managed to slip in all the normal type of gossip so typical to a small town culture. The order was finally completed and just as Jenny was trying to close the conversation, Mildred provided Jenny with a quick departing escape route.

"Oh my word Jenny, I have to run . . . Forgot I turned the sprinklers on for the annuals. Don't want to drown my Daisies do I?"

Mildred rushed to the back door which led to the greenhouse and turned once more to Jenny.

"Where's my manors . . . Thanks for the order Jen! And by the way, tell Fred congrats on the new job."

Mildred rushed through the door and left Jenny standing at the counter looking somewhat confused. And she was. What did Mildred just say to her? Jenny mouthed out part of Mildred's departing statement and shook her head mumbling, "New Job??" Jenny snubbed it off and left for her next assignment.

At just about the same time, Fred arrived at Baker's Garage . . .

"Hi Fred."

"Hi Dave"

"Here's the stuff you ordered . . . Comes to $137.80." Dave lifted a medium sized box to the counter.

Dave Baker had run this business since Fred was a kid and Fred always remembered coming here often with his Dad. Dave hadn't changed much, except being a little older. He was a large man who always wore the same thing ever since Fred could remember. Blue Jeans, about two sizes too large with cuffs about six inches high above his shoes, a white tee shirt, and red suspenders. Dave was the best mechanic around for miles and a joker but Dave was about to render Fred a jarring surprise!

"Congratulations PaPa . . . Hear your gonna be a Dad soon!" Dave exclaimed smiling ear to ear.

"Huh?" was the only response Fred seemed to manage. Obviously confused, Fred had to ask, "Where did you . . . I mean how did you hear this?"

Fred didn't want to sound like maybe he was one of these dumb guys who really didn't know what's going on or communicate with his wife very well, so he quickly changed the way he asked Dave the question.

Dave shrugged his shoulders a little and answered, "Tony told me when he got back from lunch. Went to Sally's Diner for a Burger . . . Came back with the news."

"Yeah . . . But . . . Who told him?" Fred queried.

"Not sure? Think he said he overheard Sally's sister, Claire talking about it . . . Or something like that?" Dave scratched his head while he answered Fred.

All Fred could say as he slowly walked toward the door was "Mmmm . . . And Thanks for ordering this stuff for me Dave and thanks for the . . . Ah . . . Thanks."

Fred was definitely taken back with what was probably just one of those notorious gossipy rumors which can run out of control in a small town like Oak Grove. Fred headed to the printers hoping to arrive before they closed.

The Bakery was unusually busy . . .

Jenny arrived at the Bakery to find that she would have to stand in line for a while! "Great" she mused to herself and to damper her already souring mood, Jenny noticed Ellen Crenshaw presently being waited on at the counter.

Ellen was the wife of the Dentist in town and as a matter of fact, the only Dentist in town. Jenny thought to herself, maybe just maybe, if she looked in other directions perhaps Ellen wouldn't notice her as she exited the store.

Of course Jenny felt slightly guilty about feeling this way towards the aging women. It was just that Ellen was always so snooty about her money and loved to show it off whether it was her gaudy expensive jewelry or bragging about the priceless art in her collection. Anyway, avoiding another one of Ellen's flaunting displays would suit Jenny just fine.

No such luck. Ellen Crenshaw no sooner turned around when she noticed Jenny.

"Oh my word, You Dear Sweet Girl. How have you been . . . Haven't seen you in ages!"

Jenny felt compelled to say something like, 'Ages my butt! Don't you remember you caddy women. It was just last week when you were showing you're new BMW birthday present from your husband over at the Dollar Store . . . A Store you wouldn't dream of shopping at. You only stopped by to show off your money!' But of course Jenny didn't, but she sure felt like it!

Ellen went on, along with her obnoxious raspy cackling noise interjected between each word.

"Jenny dear, that is terrific news about your husband's new career. Hope your new money won't change just how sweet you are dear?"

"Ah?" Jenny didn't quite know how to answer but manage to recover quickly, "Certainly not . . . Certainly not." And Jenny felt like adding, 'Certainly not you old bat' but of course, she didn't!

Gosh, Jenny mused to herself, that women would go absolutely insane if there was someone else in town that had more money than she! Then it hit her with a shock. This was the second time in two hours somebody had mentioned Fred and a new job!

13

Jenny jumped in her car and headed home. "Why that Fred" she said out loud to herself, "Why would he keep something like this from me. I don't understand? How could he . . . It's like lying. Fred's never lied to me before . . . I think? Imagine me having to hear this from Ellen Crenshaw of all people. How embarrassing!"

The more Jenny thought about this, the more upset she got and by the time she pulled in the driveway, Jenny was boiling mad. Jenny commenced with dinner but it resembled more of a demolition derby rather than the finesse of a fine culinary skill. She orchestrated a loud ensemble with the banging of the various pots and pans! "Just wait till that man gets home . . . Just wait!" Jenny repeated this over and over again.

Fred arrives at Perry's Printing Shop . . .

"Wow Fred, you just made it . . . I was getting ready to lock up." Ed Perry smiled as Fred entered.

"Sorry Ed, good thing I made it cause these sales reports have to be done by next Tuesday. You can look them over later, and then call me if you have any questions. Don't want to keep you from your lovely wife." Fred feigned an out of breath type of sigh so Ed Perry understood how critical the printing job was.

Ed took a quick glance at the report draft and chuckled at Fred's comment about his wife. Glancing back at Fred, Ed piped in, "Hey that reminds me Fred, how does it feel to be a Father for the first time? Or at least the prospects of being a first time Dad?"

Fred was heading for the door but stopped short and turned back to Ed Perry. Fred still very confused over the news responded, "Ah nothing is really official yet Ed. Is it too much of me to ask where you heard this news?"

Ed looked a little reluctant and said, "Well I guess she wouldn't mind . . . Carol Olsen told me . . . Doc Olsen's wife. Seems that Sally from the diner had an appointment there today and bumped in to Carol on her way out. And Carol was just in here picking up some photos and told me the good news. Ah I hope I didn't upset you Fred . . . I mean . . ."

Fred cut Ed off before he could say anymore realizing that Ed looked a little embarrassed.

"Noo, I'm not upset. I guess this is just one of those things you have to put up with in a small town? Thanks Ed . . . See ya Tuesday!"

Fred laughed as he headed out the door, maybe to make Ed feel a little better as Ed's face was still blushed.

But as soon as Fred got in his car and cranked the ignition he blurted out loud, "Am I mad he asks? What the hey is going on . . . Is Jenny nuts? Thinks it's more important to tell her good friend Claairre before she tells her husband? I don't count . . . Noooooo the whole damn town has the right to know before I do! After all who am I . . . Just the stupid Father that's who!"

Before he knew it, Fred was screeching up the driveway to his home and Jenny was already warmed up for the brawl.

A Showdown for Supper . . .

When Fred bolted through the back door which led to the kitchen, he definitely did not remember how much of a formidable opponent Jenny could be when she was angry. And of course he had no idea that Jenny was yielding a large club in her hands and quite ready to swing it!

Although Fred got the first opening words out by trying to assertively control the situation by saying with a slight sarcastic tone in his voice, "Jenny, I believe we have something to talk about . . . Dear."

Well, that was about as far as Fred got because Jenny immediately let her cannons loose entirely catching Fred off guard.

"We most definitely do <u>MISTER</u>!" and Jenny continued to fire her guns, "I thought I could trust you Fred Goodman . . . What's all this stuff about you getting a new job? Do you think I like to hear this kind of stuff from Ellen Crenshaw . . . You know I just about can't stand that women. Is this how you get your wife to trust in you . . . You, You . . . Jerk! What other things have you kept from me? "

Fred was stunned because he was flabbergasted over what Jenny had just presented to him. Silent for a second or two and while gazing down to the floor Fred finally responded, "I'm sorry . . . I tried to call you . . . And . . . And . . . I guess I told Roger. He promised not to say anything."

"What . . . You told Roger! How much of an idiot can you be Fred? It's more likely you could get a hungry lion with a piece of raw meat dangling in front of him to keep his mouth shut . . . Before you could get Roger to!" Jenny let out a disgusting grunt of anger.

But Fred recovered quickly from the first punch, "You should be the one to talk . . . D E A R! It is so very nice of you to let the whole Town of Oak Grove know that you're Pregnant! Guess I'm just your DUMB husband and there's no need to share this with him first . . . What do ya gotta say about THAT!"

It was Jenny's turn to stagger and she suddenly felt ashamed and embarrassed.

"Gosh . . . I'm sorry Fred. I've been trying to call you all day . . . And Claire stopped by. Gosh Fred I didn't even know about this until this morning . . . When the Doctors office called and asked if I could drop by . . . Said they had to go over something with me in person."

But before Jenny could get another word in Fred snapped in, "CLAIRE . . . And you talk about ROGER!"

With that, Jenny started pointing her finger at Fred but stopped quickly and the tone in her voice was much more noticeably calmer.

"This is your home town Fred, not mine . . . You know these people much better than I . . . I'm sorry. I shouldn't have trusted Claire."

Both Jenny and Fred appeared to run out of a little steam in their argument and seated themselves on opposite ends of the kitchen table, heads in their hands, occasionally looking up to see who would be the first to mediate the atmosphere back to a normal situation. This lasted for about 15 minutes and the young couple apparently realized how foolish they were being to each other.

Simultaneously they both came to the same conclusion. They were letting their petty self-righteousness obliterate the joyous significance of the events that had transpired that day.

And again, at the very same instance, both Jenny and Fred rose from their seats and began apologizing to each other. They spoke so fast and so loud, and both at the same time. Neither one of them really heard what the other had to say but they both seem to understand.

"Gosh I'm sor . . . Me too. I didn't mean to . . . Roger . . . Pregnant . . . You're going to be a . . . Claire . . . Interview . . . Father . . ." And for about two minutes they each tried to blurt out their apologies.

Well dinner turned out to be a success despite its spurious beginning. Fred helped Jenny with dinner and the two bubbled over with enthusiasm discussing everything from what room to turn into the nursery, all about the prospects of a new job and how they could really use the extra money. All the anger from just a short time before had dissipated to a state of utter elation!

Later that night . . .

Jenny crawled into bed propping a couple of pillows against the headboard, her knees bent as she cradled the book she had been reading. She waited for Fred to make the final rounds about the house locking doors, turning off lights, and all that security type stuff which guys are so obsessively compelled to do!

Fred finally came into the bedroom and seated himself on Jenny's side of the bed as he always did every night.

Jenny leaned over and gave Fred a kiss, "Again, I'm sorry Fred for today . . . I guess we are reminded of a very valuable lesson about being a husband and a wife . . . Huh."

Fred patted his wife on the hand and acknowledged her affection, "I'm sorry too. Although Roger and Claire are really not that bad. . . Some things are made to be shared between a husband and a wife. At least before others! We should learn when to shut our big mouths."

Jenny responded, "Yep, sometimes Fred you need only two fingers to count the number of people you can really count on in life!"

Fred nodded his head in agreement and sat quietly for a moment on the edge of the bed. Then with a sudden spurt of joyfulness Fred stood up and while pacing the floor in front of the bed, began burbling out the excitement which Jenny had expected to see earlier in the evening.

"Wow, this is great . . . Even unbelievable! I'm going to have a son . . . I can't wait . . . Think of all the things we can do. I can teach him how to fish, We can play ball together . . . We can work on cars together . . . Boys like that!" And Fred went on and on.

Jenny just smiled but decided it was time to reel Fred in a little because it was apparent that Fred had overlooked just one little detail!

"Ah Fred . . . Fred? Earth to Fred, Earth to Fred . . . Come in Fred!"

Fred finally realized that his lovely wife was trying to capture his attention and he ceased his jubilant prospects for the future.

"What sweetheart . . . Am I over reacting or something?"

"Well" Jenny replied softly. "It's too early to tell Fred and I don't want to burst your Bubble but . . . What if the baby is a girl?"

You should have seen the expression on Fred's face. He sat down instantly and for a few seconds, Fred remained speechless. Then he suddenly jerked his head toward Jenny and said with un-sureness, "Ah, a G I R L!"

Jenny laughed. "C'mon Fred, move over a little . . . Let me get up and get a drink of water. Why don't you crawl into bed and relax. I'll be right back."

Fred did as Jenny suggested and Jenny disappeared into the dimly lit expanse of their large old farmhouse to go to the kitchen.

A strange but comforting sereneness enshrouded Fred as he lay there and awaited his wife's return. Fred was ready for a good night's sleep when all of a sudden the peaceful silence was shattered with a loud scream from Jenny!

"AGHHHH! . . . BAILEY . . . WILL YOU KNOCK IT OFF!"

Bailey struck again. Fred couldn't help to keep himself from laughing out loud. Life was good indeed. He loved his life, he loved Jenny and yes, he even loved his Dog.

Thanks Folks for joining us here today at Goodman Stadium. We watched a tight contest today between these two competitive players and before we say goodnight, let me recap the score for you
Bailey – 2   Jenny – 0
Join us again next time for another grueling match up!

CHAPTER TWO
LIFE IS LOOKING GOOD

Life was about to take some twists and turns for this young couple as they were about to embark on a new journey called parenthood. Both were very excited and although it was little known to each of them, they would discover an ever greater bond and significance in their relationship with each other!

Fred returned to work the next morning at Fairbanks Incorporated where he was employed as a graphic design consultant for this well-established Ad Agency. And Jenny decided she should catch up with her working endeavors as well. Jenny was fortunate to have a lucrative part time job which she could work at from home.

After Fred and Jenny tied the knot so to speak, they remained in Columbus Ohio for about two years. This was Jenny's home town where she was employed as a full time editor of informational and technical publications. She interned at this firm during her last two years of college and Pearson Publications was impressed enough to offer her a full time position after she graduated. Unfortunately,

Pearson was forced to downsize their operations and cut her position to a part time status. When Jenny and Fred decided to relocate to Oak Grove, she was delighted to learn that her employer would allow her to continue her services to the company via the computer and internet.

Although Fred and Jenny did not perceive this situation to be optimal for their financial concerns at the time, it now would be a tremendous employment benefit for the expecting and future Mom. She would be able to continue work from home.

Both Fred and Jenny had remarked to each other, how funny it was that something which happened a few years back and didn't appear to be a great set of circumstances, now in fact would be fantastic. Fred use to always say to his wife, 'It's amazing how decisions we make today, or events which happen today, will greatly affect our futures!' Jenny was beginning to find more merit in Fred's logical and analytical approach to life as she always had lived for the moment. But Fred and Jenny were certainly in store for more surprises in their near future!

Roger appears to be among the missing . . .

Fred arrived to work just a little bit late due to the unusual events of the afternoon and evening before. Of course the first thoughts Fred had was to seek out his dear old friend Roger and lay into him a little about the sanctity of keeping your word and not having such a big mouth. But Roger was not in his office where you might normally find him selectively consuming a double cinnamon coffee roll.

Fred walked down the hall to the reception area and approached Lillian, the only receptionist this firm had ever employed. Fred could never quite understand how she managed to keep this job, let alone get it to begin with?

Done up in her 1960's beehive hairstyle which never changed, except the color now and then, and wearing bright red lipstick, Lillian glanced up at Fred, "Hiya cutie . . . What can I do for you this morning?"

Fred cringed as he thought to himself, 'Gosh, this women had the personality of an old pair of sneakers' and answered, "Where's Rogg . . . Have you seen him Lillian?"

"Nope . . . You won't either . . . He called in sick. That . . . Overgrown computer monitor you call your friend!"

"Did he say what was wrong?" Fred asked.

"Nope . . . Didn't ask and I don't care!" replied the receptionist as she pulled out her nail file to manicure her brightly colored 2 inch long nails.

"Okay . . . Thanks." Fred turned quickly trying to abbreviate the time he had to look at the bagged out skin under the decrepit women's chin.

"No problem handsome . . . Come and take me to lunch sometime!"

Yeah Right, Fred thought to himself as he sped up his gait down the hallway. "Thank the Lord it's

Friday!" Fred softly spoke when he was out of earshot of the receptionist.

As soon as Fred seated himself at his desk, he picked up the phone to call Roger at home but there was no answer and his answering machine didn't even come on.

"Mmmm?" Fred said out loud, "Guess I'll try him later. He's probably sleeping?"

Meanwhile, Back at the Goodman Farm . . .

Jenny took care of a few household chores, grabbed a cup of coffee and jumped right into a pile of work which was patiently waiting for her on her desk. Fred had converted this spare room, which was in the newer portion of this old homestead, for Jenny to use as an office.

Fred referred to this as the "L" addition, which was off to the side and rear of the main house. A long hallway led to the living area and finally adjoined with the main hallway of the older portion of the house. This new part of the house was also where Fred and Jenny's bedroom was and featured a huge master bath and dressing area. There were two other rooms in this annex which were heaped with artifacts and treasures left by Uncle Harry and Aunt Ruthie. Fred had not thoroughly rummaged through these rooms yet to sort it all out. Also one of these rooms would be converted into a nursery for the newest member of the Goodman Clan.

At the other end of the hallway was another staircase which led to the second floor with four rooms above. And of course there was the elaborate balconied staircase in the main house with five rooms on that part of the second floor.

Fred's studio was located over the kitchen and it had its own narrow staircase which led down to the kitchen. Fred, always spoke proudly of this house and explained to Jenny that his studio was once used as the servant's quarters back in the early 1900's.

Jenny was at first intimidated by the size of this Victorian home but soon had fallen in love with this old house, and the once proud eleven hundred acre farm.

Musing out loud while she read over a draft for a training pamphlet Jenny said, "Wow, these guys can design a jet . . . But they don't look like they even have a third grade education in grammar. What a mess . . . Ha!"

She started shaking her head and as she did Jenny caught just a glimpse of a black tail floating past the doorway to the hall. A mischievous smile spread across Jenny's face and she quickly but quietly arose from her chair and tip toed toward the door.

"Hah . . . I got you now you deformed sheep dog!" she quietly whispered to herself.

She peered into the hallway but Bailey was not to be seen. Quickly sliding across the hardwood floor, which was easy to do just wearing socks, Jenny poked her head into the master bedroom but Bailey wasn't in there either. Jenny peered down the hallway, first one way and then the other but there was no sign of Bailey.

Placing her hand on her hip she was just about to call for the monster when, "OOOOOHHH! . . . You beast!"

Bailey apparently had circled around through the spare room, and again through Jenny's office rather quickly, and he at 150lbs came sliding over the newly varnished floor with his nose burying itself right into Jenny's posterior. If it wasn't for the fact that Jenny's instinct's had her reach out with her hands to grab the door casings to the bedroom, Bailey would have knocked Jenny down with his out of control slide.

Jenny was a slender framed women only standing about five feet, six inches tall and weighing only 110 pounds. It wouldn't have taken much for Bailey to plow her over. Jenny turned and first, shook her fist at Bailey, and then she proceeded to burst out in laughter.

Jenny dropped to her knees and started rubbing Bailey's head and ears playfully, "I love you Bailey! I'm way too happy to be mad . . . C'mon mutt . . . Let's go get you a treat and let me get back to work."

Bailey accepted his punishment well, devouring the large dog biscuit in one gulp and followed Jenny back to her office. Bailey flopped down on the Oriental rug in front of Jenny's desk and that is where Bailey stayed while Jenny completed her work.

A few hours later . . .

With a pen hanging out of her mouth Jenny made her last changes to a draft and she peered above her reading glasses to see Bailey clumsily lift his frame from the floor. Bailey moved to the edge of the desk and sat down staring at the phone on the edge of Jenny's desk.

Jenny focused on Bailey's maneuver and just seconds later, the phone started ringing and caught Jenny by surprise.

It was Fred, "Hi sweetheart, how's it going?" Fred said with charm in his tone.

"Fine my handsome Husband . . . Hey did you hear anything about . . . About you know what?" was Jenny's first question.

Fred knew that Jenny was referring to the upcoming job interview and with a whispering tone in his voice answered, "It's all set . . . The interview is set for next Wednesday. I already asked for a vacation day and I'll tell you all about it later . . . Okay?"

"Great" Jenny replied.

Now in his normal voice Fred said, "By any chance did Roger call there?"

"Roger? . . . Why would Roger call here?" Jenny was curious.

"Well he called in sick and I've been trying to reach him all day . . . I'm kind of worried."

"That's not unusual . . . You say he calls in sick a lot. What's to worry about?", Jenny answered.

"Yeah I know but usually he takes my calls."

Jenny smiled. "Did it ever occur to you Fred that maybe this time . . . Roger is really sick and not faking it this time!"

"Mmmm." Fred answered, "That thought never occurred to me! Oh well, guess I'll try him later. Anyway, I'm starving . . . What's for dinner?"

Jenny now laughed and replied with enthusiasm, "Lasagna . . . You're favorite!"

"Fantastic, when did you make that?"

"This morning. Right after you left for work . . . It's in the fridge cooling and I'll cook it again right before dinner. Just the way you like it . . . Twice baked Lasagna."

Jenny laughed again and said, "Are you sure you're not Italian? Your culinary passions certainly supersede your English Heritage!"

Fred chuckled and said, "I just love Italian Food. Hey I'll stop by the Bakery on the way home and pick up some hot fresh Italian rolls . . . How's that sound?"

"Sounds like a good dinner Fred . . . And may I add, with a very special guy. Hurry home and drive safe. I Love you."

"Love you too Doll . . . See ya soon . . . MOM!" Fred laughed and hung up the phone.

Jenny was still smiling as she looked over to Bailey who maintained his stance next to the phone.

"How did you know Bailey? . . . You knew that phone was going to ring!"

Jenny shook her head, stood up, and motioned for the Mammoth to follow. "C'mon Sir Bailey, let's go prepare dinner for the King's Banquet!

Bailey listened and walked right alongside of Jenny all the way to the kitchen. This was unlike the canine's normal behavior. For the most part, Bailey would roam around the huge home barely visible, unless of course, Bailey was plotting another sneak attack on Jenny. Jenny was somewhat bewildered over Bailey's sudden change in behavior this afternoon.

"Mmmm!" Jenny muttered out loud as the pair approached the kitchen.

Dinner was fabulous as usual . . .

According to Fred, Jenny was a fantastic cook, even though Jenny did not share in his opinion over her own culinary prowess.

The couple leisurely ate their meal buzzing over their new adventure as parents, which color to paint the nursery, and what they would need before the arrival of the newest Goodman. Of course, Fred's upcoming interview, plans for the weekend, thoughts on the fast approaching summer were among the topics as well.

Lost in their conversation, neither Fred nor Jenny had noticed that Bailey had joined them in the kitchen at dinner time and lay on the floor in front of the pantry. Bailey had never done this before!

Two hours had passed before Fred and Jenny had finished the dishes and adjourned to the back porch which was located off the kitchen facing the rear of the main house. This was Jenny's favorite time of day and a special time to spend with her husband. The three season porch was comfortable in the spring, summer, and fall but Fred would close it up to save in heating costs over the winter months, as they also did with other areas of the home.

For about five minutes, Fred and Jenny sat silently in the glider together just enjoying the view out over the back pasture. Then Fred decided to ask, "So when should we tell the folks and the rest of the family about our new son . . . Ah!" Fred quickly cleared his throat and added, "Ahem, or Daughter?"

Jenny smiled, "I don't know? Maybe we should wait until after your interview and after my next exam? Just to be sure about things, if you know what I mean? And after our fiasco yesterday with Claire and Roger . . . Maybe we should be a little more patient. If you know what I mean?"

Fred broke out laughing, "Yeah, you're right. Besides with friends like Claire and Roger I wouldn't be surprised if half the country knows by now! Give it a few more days and everybody will know . . . Ha!"

"Speaking about those two blabbermouths, after I talked with you today on the phone I tried calling Claire . . . Several times . . . No answer or return call." Jenny stated as she put her hand on Fred's lap.

"Mmmm" Fred answered, "I don't know but maybe they're feeling guilty or something about spilling the beans and maybe they think that we know that they did. . . I don't know?" And Fred continued, "I'll try Roger again on the phone tonight and if I don't catch him maybe I'll swing by his apartment tomorrow. Have to run to Baker's again . . . Forgot one more thing I need to fix the tractor."

Jenny nodded her head, "Your amazing Fred! Not only are you a good talented artist and designer . . . You're quite the mechanic, plumber, carpenter and who knows . . . Maybe a future farmer? To be honest, I wasn't sure that either you or I were up to taking on the task of keeping this old place up, but you have proven me wrong Fred. And I just want to tell you again that I'm glad we came here and I love it here and I love being Mrs. Goodman. Just thought I'd let you know . . . Again!"

It was true, Fred had many talents, but he certainly did not give the appearance of being a Farmer. At Five foot Ten, and only a 160 pounds, Fred's frail frame along with the fact that often he threw on his glasses around the home instead of his contacts, suggested he may be more of the kind of guy who might be an accountant.

Fred smiled and took Jenny's hand. But Jenny wasn't the only one who had been a trifle apprehensive with the opportunity which Fred's Uncle Harry had bestowed upon them. Fred was slightly nervous and concerned as well. He wasn't convinced yet about whether or not they could manage this homestead. But he didn't want to let Jenny know! He knew Jenny was looking to him for security and confidence.

A Goodman History Lesson . . .

The Goodman's legacy on this farm started back in 1882 when a wealthy English businessman by the name of John Sebastian Goodman the First, traveled with his wife and two sons to this valley. Goodman purchased this farm from the Town of Oak Grove for the miniscule sum of $800.00. It's not clear how much John was worth or how John Sebastian came by his fortune, but he was filthy rich and some of his fortune is still around today. Yearning for a new life in America, the stout Englishman and his wife who bore him six more sons, reclaimed the over grown land and turned it into a thriving dairy farm.

Rich with longevity, the history of this land goes back far beyond the Goodman's arrival in America; back to 1705 to be exact when Dutch families settled in this then hostile territory. A small settlement actually flourished on this property, located in the back northeast corner which is evident by the ruins and remains of several stone foundations.

Fred's Uncle Harry even uncovered an Old Dutch cemetery when he was clearing and extending some pasture land back in 1955. Restoring the cemetery the best he could, Harry continued to maintain it and built a small road to it so that it was accessible to the public. Fred had taken Jenny back there a few times but she always referred to it as being spooky.

Again, the records and history of this property are vague and spotty but it was determined that sometime in about 1825, a French family took possession of this farm and worked it until just before the Civil War. The homesteaders disappeared or died off and the farm was abandoned for nearly 30 years until the Town of Oak Grove claimed the property. When John Sebastian showed up in town, the Elders were eager to sell it to the businessman in hopes of building up the economy of this small community.

Having the finances to do so, Goodman constructed a beautiful Victorian style House in 1886 which exists as the main portion of the house today. However, the Family was devastated with illness, disease and misfortune and in 1904; there was only one remaining Goodman.

John Sebastian Goodman the II, Goodman's only surviving son out of eight took over the farm and family fortune in 1905. He married a young woman from Philadelphia and she gave birth to Sebastian Goodman in 1906 who was Fred's Grandfather. Fred's Grandpa Sebastian lived to be 77 and Fred remembered him well. When Fred was a young boy he quite often played and hung around the farm. Fred could still remember the stories his Grandpa would spin about Indians, World War I, and working on a farm with no electricity, telephone, or even a TV.

Well, Grandpa Sebastian worked the farm well. Sebastian kept the family fortune going, and he built the second part of the house contemplating a big family with many strong grandsons to help work the farm. He and his wife Emily raised four sons, Fred's Uncle Harry the Oldest, Douglas who became a casualty of the Korean War, Fred's Dad Robert, and Michael who died in a car accident at the age of 16.

Sebastian was greatly disappointed in the loss over two of his sons and expected a lot from Harry and Robert. He was a tough hard man and Fred's Dad took about all he could stand and finally joined the Navy at age 18 leaving just Uncle Harry and Michael to help with the family legacy.

Sebastian hired a farm hand named Rube Gildman who was older than Fred's Dad. Rube and Harry carried the bulk of the burden in running the farm. The three including Grandpa Sebastian, were quite successful and manage to turn this farm into a thriving productive dairy farm.

The years between 1948 and 1965 were the most lucrative. With over 200 head of milkers, and 500 acres of corn, Sebastian expanded even further with the raising chickens and selling fresh eggs. In 1951 Sebastian purchased a Milk Truck and started delivering fresh Milk and Eggs to the residents of Oak Grove and neighboring Milburn. That old milk truck was still running and sat out in the shed area of the

Equipment Barn. Fred was very fond of this antique relic and so was Rube Gildman.

Fred's Dad returned from the service, married Fred's Mom but decided to buy a small Cape cross town away from the Farm and became a very successful car dealer in Milburn. Although Grandpa Sebastian loathed Robert for his dissertation of the Family duty as Sebastian put it, Fred's Dad and his brother Harry got along fine without any grudges. Despite Robert's estrangement from the farm.

Fred's Dad never talked much about the farm and Fred always got the impression that his Dad wasn't quite being honest about something?

Uncle Harry married Fred's Aunt Ruthie in 1942 and she was quite a tough women. She had no qualms with milking the cows, fetching the eggs, or even driving a tractor or spreading manure. She helped out wherever she could and Fred would remember her best for her homemade oatmeal cookies.

Unfortunately, Ruth was unable to bear children which hindered greatly the prospects of future Goodman's to carry on the legacy of the farm.

Fred loved to spend time on the farm and even though his Dad would not set foot on it, he would drive Fred over often. Fred would stay overnight on many occasions, especially in the summer.

Rube became sort of an older brother for Fred and even made a sketch of the farm so that Fred would not get lost when Fred was younger! And Fred just adored Uncle Harry and Aunt Ruthie. As Fred got older, he helped Uncle Harry on the Farm and Harry started to pay him wages when Fred turned fourteen. Fred had two older brothers, Daniel and Jeff, but they too patterned their Dad's dislike for the Farm and didn't spend as much time there.

   Both Fred's brothers were five and six years older than Fred so when Fred had turned fourteen, both his brothers had left for college. Fred stayed in close contact with his brothers as best he could but Daniel, the oldest, became a famous criminal Attorney and had a practice out in California. Jeff became an optometrist but he moved to Canada. Fred had not seen either of his brothers since the wedding which was now going on three years.

So how did Fred and Jenny end up here? Well it goes something like this . . .

   Sebastian finally passed away in 1983 but Harry and Rube had fairly well taken over the job of running the farm back in 1969. Harry was not quite the business brain that his father was and hard times fell onto the Goodman farm. Times had changed greatly in the dairy Industry as more modernized operations replaced the old ways of farming. New legislations for the pasteurization processes and the need for larger trucking operations to transport the milk and eggs to the Co-ops, forced smaller farmers to either invest into larger overhead operations or be forced out by the larger farms. They couldn't compete in the market place. Harry refused to change, wanting to depend on only the local trade; he soon realized that he was being pushed under.

Now the Goodman Farm was not the only Dairy operation in this Valley. The Shiff Farm and several others, had been around for just about as long as the Goodman's but Howard Shiff played the risk, modernized his farm, and started selling directly to the large distributors and Co-ops. Howard Shiff and Harry had been long time friends as well as competitors and the Shiffs soon found that there operation and ambitions had eventually out grown their own farm.

Fred's Uncle Harry and Howard Shiff entered into an agreement which allowed Harry to lease out 300 acres of his pasture land to the Shiff Farm. In return the Shiffs would pay a yearly fee including a small percentage of the profits yielded from Harry's land. This kept Harry from going under and Harry continued to grow corn and vegetables to stay afloat.

Harry and Ruth eventually abandoned the Dairy operations at the farm and sold their cows to the Shiffs and the Aristotle Farm nearby. With new legislation also affecting the egg industry, Harry also had to cease with the chicken operations. Ruthie and Harry planted other vegetables and ran a fairly successful Farm Stand and Green House at the corner of Pasture Lane and Route 16 which was a great location. Harvest time was busy and Ruthie was also pretty good at raising annuals and perennials.

But in 1984, Harry's health was failing and Harry and Aunt Ruthie were very concerned over the future of the farm. Fred would help out in the summer and Rube, aging as well, did his best to keep things going.

About 16 months after Fred Graduated College and married Jenny, Uncle Harry passed away. And it was no surprise that just 3 months later, Aunt Ruthie died suddenly of a stroke.

But it was a big surprise to Fred that his Uncle Harry had left the entire Farm to Fred with one major proviso. Fred could not sell off the Farm. Fred would have to take up residence at the Goodman estate, and maintain it as best he could. There was a considerable amount of cash in the family fortune and Fred's Dad, as well as Fred's brothers, inherited about $100,000 each. The remainder of the cash which was only about $160,000 was left in trust, to be used for taxes and major repairs on the Farm and House.

If Fred decided not to accept this gift, the estate allowed for the deed to the property to relinquish back over to the Town of Oak Grove, whence it originally came from back in 1882. Uncle Harry was a sly old fox; he knew Fred loved the farm, and Harry really wanted it to remain in the family.

The reality of it for Fred was really quite simple; take the farm or get nothing at all! Fred and Jenny would learn some day that Uncle Harry and Aunt Ruthie had given far more considerable thought about the future of the Farm, than most would have imagined!

Fred and Jenny obviously struggled over making this decision but Jenny knew just how much Fred had loved the farm. Besides, Jenny hated Columbus and the city life. Jenny decided to support her husband and they left Columbus and moved into the old homestead. Fred put his dream of being a full time free-lance designer aside and took on the Job at Fairbanks which helped considerably with the expenses at the farm.

Despite the trust and the lease income that Uncle Harry initiated, Jenny and Fred really had to fight to make ends meet. For the time being, all farming operations ceased except for the leased land and haying operations. Many acres of field were left to fallow and many were being overgrown and returning to wooded areas.

Fred and Jenny were getting tired and I imagine the readers are as well so let's just see how this evening ended . . .

Jenny crawled into bed and Fred came to her side and sat down. Fred rested his elbows on the top of his knees and placed one hand under his chin.

"Fred" Jenny said quietly, "Bailey has been acting a little funny today."

"What . . . Did he make you laugh?" Fred grinned!

"No . . . No, That's not what I mean . . . I mean he has been acting a little strange or something!"

Again smiling Fred answered, "Well maybe I should take him to see a Psychiatrist then."

"Quit being a smart butt . . . I told you how he knew the phone was going to ring today!"

"Yeah . . .Yeah." Fred retorted.

"No I'm being serious Fred . . . That dog got up and stared at the phone and seconds later . . . You called. Then later he followed me back to the kitchen and . . . And did you notice at dinner? He came in and sat in the kitchen the whole time we were eating!"

Fred thought about it and then looked to his wife, "Mmmm . . . Well, maybe he senses something?"

Fred didn't even get to finish what he was saying when Bailey sauntered into the room and walked over to Jenny and gently placed his head upon her stomach. Both Jenny and Fred cocked their heads in somewhat of an amazement.

"Like I was starting to say." Fred continued. "Maybe he is sensing your new condition . . . They say dogs can do that sort of thing." Fred ruffled the curly hair atop Bailey's head.

Fred got up and shut the light off, gently slipped into the bed alongside of Jenny and kissed her on the cheek, "Good night sweetheart, I love you."

Bailey remained standing nudging his nose into Jenny's hand.

Jenny made no response at first and then she spoke gently, "I love you."

Bailey groaned and you could hear him flop to the floor right alongside of Jenny. There was another pause and then Jenny mumbled "And I love you too Fred!"

Fred sat up quickly realizing that he had somehow fallen to the #2 position in the appointment of the nightly endearments by his wife and he could hear Jenny softly chuckling. Fred slapped his wife on her backside and he lay back down placing his arm around her.

Good Night and of course join us in the next Chapter when Rube and the Milk Truck prepare for their last Ride.

CHAPTER THREE
PREPARING FOR THE LAST RIDE

Saturday morning arrived much sooner than Fred would have preferred but he slowly got out of bed at the first sign of light.

He looked over to Jenny who was still quietly sleeping and he and Bailey softly crept out of the bedroom.

Fred had a big list of things to do this day so he thought he better get an early start. Quickly getting dressed, Fred made a pot of coffee and took care of Bailey who was ready for his regular morning routine. Bailey gulped down his four cups of dog food and Fred let him out for his 30 minute meander in the back pasture right behind the house. Fred sipped on his coffee and soon Bailey announced his return at the rear kitchen door by kindly barking twice, as he did every morning. Bailey scooted through the kitchen and disappeared into the hallway.

Fred was just a little curious as he leaned out the kitchen door into the hall but Bailey apparently took a left at the other hallway that led to the bedroom. Fred hurriedly walked to the junction of the two hallways and just as he peered around the corner, Fred could see Bailey vanishing into the bedroom where Jenny still lay asleep.

Fred smiled, shook his head and smiled saying, "That dog?" Fred poured himself another cup of coffee and headed over to the equipment barn.

Now this barn was the smallest on the Goodman Farm and it is where Jenny and Fred also kept their cars. This was the location of the earliest Goodman barn but it had burned to the ground once and rebuilt in 1926. And this structure was heavily damaged in a blizzard in 1948 and again rebuilt with an addition added on to it.

Fred opened the side door, flipped on the lights and walked to the center of the barn. Fred placed his coffee down on the trunk of his car, poked his hands in his jean pockets and slowly turned looking up and down as he completed a full circle. "Remarkable!" he said, "Just astounding!"

Fred was always awe stricken when he perused over the hundreds of items hung and placed throughout the entire barn. There wasn't a single inch of space left on the walls or the beams, or anywhere on the interior of this structure. Every possible space had something hanging from it. There were chains, antique scythes, cow bells, harnesses and saddles. Old milking machines were propped carefully in one corner of an old stall. Milk bottles, old carpentry tools, whips, and old horse drawn wagon wheels, were suspended throughout.

Everywhere your eye would fall, the scene would reveal an old treasure or artifact from the farming days of old. Some of this stuff was over 100 years old.

But this barn also had the tools of more contemporary times as this is where Harry and Rube did most of the maintenance on all their equipment. In one corner, was a strong work bench and tool boxes which held almost every type of mechanical tool you could imagine.

Uncle Harry and Rube were no doubt very self-sufficient farmers, who had to by necessity; maintain every piece of equipment or machinery in tip top running condition. They had all the proper tools to do so. Uncle Harry even had acetylene cutting torches and welding equipment. In another corner lay the woodshop with table and radial arm saws, band saws, clamps, hammers, and you name it; it was all here.

Among the new, were many old artifacts of the farming industry of yesteryear. What really astonished Fred however, was that all of these thousands of items were not just piled or stored in heaps or on top of each other. Rather, it appeared to Fred that everything which was in this barn looked as if it was purposely placed, like it was on display!

Right after Harry passed away, Rube had produced a detailed inventory list for Ruth of every item which was on this farm. To stagger Fred's thoughts even further, this was just the small barn; one out of five others and they too were loaded with treasure and all sorts of farming equipment.

Fred was obviously not a complete stranger to farming so he had looked over the list for Aunt Ruthie just before she died and assured her that Rube had been thorough and complete with his accounting. Rube had even counted the number of nails, screws, nuts and bolts that had been painstakingly sorted into bins throughout the years!

Fred moved to the rear of the barn where the Kubota tractor sat waiting for Fred to replace the plugs and power drive belt, plus give it an oil change and lube for the summer.

This was the last piece of new equipment Uncle Harry had purchased back in 1981 and it was equipped only with a mowing deck and a small snow plow. Its main function was to maintain the lawn areas around the house and barns and part of the back pasture directly behind the house. The Kubota was great for maneuvering those close cuts to the structures and fences so that weeds and tall grass did not overtake the Farm. And this is exactly what Fred used it for.

Jenny gets started for the day but the Milk truck doesn't want to . . .

Fred finished the work on the tractor and his coffee as well. He was delighted when he turned to see Jenny holding a fresh cup of coffee in one hand and juggling two donuts in the other. Bailey moved right alongside of her and sat down while keenly keeping his eyes on the donuts precariously held in Jenny's hand. Perhaps one may fall, Bailey was probably wishing!

"Good morning sweetheart . . . How'd you sleep?" Fred greeted his wife.

"Not too bad . . . I see you got an early start. Just like a farmer!" Jenny laughed and Fred rescued the two donuts from her hand.

"Myfavlit" Fred mumbled while stuffing his mouth with the two glazed donuts.

Fred took a sip of the coffee and said, "The tractor is all set . . . Well except the new belt which I'll get at Baker's today . . . Right after I stop at Roger's . . . Which I will do right after I get the Milk Truck going."

"Which I'll do right after I do this!" Fred set the coffee down, wrapped his arms around Jenny and gave her a long kiss.

"Why Mr. Goodman . . . What might I expect next!" Jenny flirted.

Fred just smiled and took his wife by the arm and guided her to the other side of the barn which led to the door for the shed area. He guided her down two steps and he switched on the lights and pointed his finger.

Jenny laughed and remarked sarcastically, "You guys with your trucks and tractors! . . . It is something else though . . . That's for sure."

Except for a coat of dust and the worn tires, the 1951 Divco Delivery truck looked almost new. Well, at least in pretty good shape for a 50 year old truck.

It was painted deep maroon with black fenders and trim.

Fred walked over to the side of the truck and gently wiped the dust while he blew a large breath from his mouth. He then stood back and read the words he exposed in white lettering, "Goodman Farm and Dairy . . . We Deliver Fresh Milk and Eggs to your Door every Morning."

Jenny sighed and said with a misty tone in her voice, "Wow Fred, this is a piece of Americana long gone by, and maybe even forgotten about!"

"That's for sure sweetheart . . . This ole girl stopped making its rounds long before we were even born!"

"Will it start hon?" asked Jenny

"I imagine . . . At least it has for the last fifty years. I charged the battery a day ago so I'll give it a shot in just a minute."

"You didn't cover it like Rube said to do Fred."

"I know . . . I know . . . I forgot . . . Guess I took Rube too much for granted for everything he has done around here. But I'll clean it up."

And that was true. Year after year, even after Harry and Ruthie had died, Rube would take care of the lawns and farm. Without fail Rube kept this truck washed, waxed, and ready to go. This was Rubes pride and joy.

When the delivery service was thriving, Rube would show up every morning at 3am and assist Harry with the loading of the milk and eggs. Then Rube, dressed in a grey uniform would head off before sunrise to insure that all their customers would find their fresh milk and eggs on their door step when they awoke. Except for a dent on the rear fender where Rube had backed into Elmira Mcginty's stone wall, there was barely a scratch on this classic.

Rube was fast approaching 80 and up until last year, Rube was still going strong but his health started to fail considerably. As a matter of fact, Rube had digressed so much that he had to be placed in a senior home and Fred and Jenny would visit him often. But that wasn't about to deter Rube Gildman from making his yearly appearance with this Milk truck in the annual Memorial Day Parade.

Since 1960, Rube would proudly drive his joy down Main Street, generally behind the National Guard Marching Band. They usually loaded the Divco with World War II vets, hanging out the back of the truck, waving and throwing out candy to the spectators.

"Fred I'm going to leave you with your toy . . . And before you go to Roger's, could you bring in the step ladder to the parlor so I can get started on the dusting." Jenny smiled and left for the house, with Bailey right behind her.

Fred nodded his head while he watched Jenny's newly acquired sidekick follow her out of the barn.

"Sure sweetheart . . . Shouldn't be long?"

Fred lifted the keys to the old Divco which hung on a ring dangling from one of the main posts of the barn, where they have been for nearly fifty years.

Positioning himself on the seat and fondling the worn steering wheel, Fred turned the key . . . 'Yun, yun yun yun yun' . . . . Nothing. . . Fred tried again but the old engine would not start. "C'mon sweetheart, you can do it."

Fred encouraged the old truck. 'Yun yun yun yun yun' . . . And finally after several attempts, the engine came to life, for a short time that is.

It sounded terrible, coughing and spitting. The year before it started just fine and ran great. Fred should have listened to Rube and Dave Baker when they told Fred over and over again to start the truck often. Fred was negligent in heeding their advice.

Finally Fred got the truck to run without stalling and it was obvious that something was wrong. It was blowing black smoke and sounded like a bucking bull with asthma. "Hmm" Fred groaned out loud to himself and turned the truck off.

Fred grabbed the stepladder for Jenny and feeling dejected, brought it into the parlor where she was already engaged in the never ending battle of the dust.

"What's wrong Fred? . . . Heard the truck . . . Is it okay?" Jenny could see that her husband looked disturbed.

"Don't know . . . Something's not right and I'm not sure I have enough time to check it out before Memorial Day?"

"Fred, do you really think Rube can drive anymore? Sometimes things do have to come to an end." Jenny firmly stated.

Fred was quick to answer with a chuckle in his voice, "Of course he can't drive . . . He can't even find his glasses which are sitting on the top of his head most of the time! Rube's nephew Jeremy said he would drive this year. Thought I had mentioned that to you, but anyway I'll ask Dave Baker about it when I stop there today . . . A mechanic more talented, you will never find."

Jenny stood with one hand on her hip and pursed her lips a little then answered. "Fred, remember money is a little tight and . . ."

"I know. Nobody knows that better than me." Fred said.

Jenny realized Fred was saddened over this dilemma so she changed her tone, "Well, you're right, Dave is a genius and maybe it's something minor or something? We'll take it one step at a time I guess."

Jenny tried to relieve Fred's noticeable anxiety over the problem.

Fred looked around in the gigantic Parlor and said, "Are you sure you can handle this yourself Jenny? You know with your condition and everything."

Smiling Jenny answered, "Fred, I'm pregnant, not dying! . . . I'll be fine . . . Just get going and do what you have to do. I'll just take my time."

"Okay, I'll be back soon . . . Love Ya." Fred walked out of the Parlor and headed back to the barn.

As Fred drove into town he couldn't help but be concerned over the fact that he had placed his wife in a situation which required an awful lot of work.

Now besides being pregnant and with her still working the part time job, much of the burden in keeping the house up was falling upon her shoulders. Fred helped when he could but he had enough to do outside and with his job and all.

To conserve fuel, Fred and Jenny would close up the parlor and most of the rooms upstairs in the winter time, as Harry and Ruth did. Fred's Uncle and Aunt were very wise to modernize the electrical and heating system back in the late 70's and with the addition of separate heating zones, along with beautiful French doors, many sections of the house could be isolated during the colder months. Besides, it was a full time job just to keep all those rooms clean!

Jenny loved to open the Parlor in the spring and it was the premier part of this old house but maybe this was all too much for her? Somehow or another,

Fred knew the right answers would present themselves to him. "Hmmm" Fred said out loud to himself several times as he made his way into town.

Fred's first stop – Baker's Garage . . .

Dave Baker had the belt Fred needed for the tractor as Fred knew he would. Dave Baker was very attentive to the needs of the local farmers and generally kept a good inventory of parts and supplies which they often required.

Fred filled Dave in on the plight of the Divco, the approaching Memorial Day Parade, and Rube's desire to make the Parade yet another year.

Dave listened attentively and as he wiped off the Parts counter. Dave had already thought of a plan for Fred but was courteous enough to let Fred finish his plea for help before letting him in on his own ideas.

"See this counter Fred" Dave said.

Fred nodded and Dave continued, "Have you ever seen it so clean?"

Not knowing where Dave was heading with this question Fred answered, "No I guess not."

"It's because business is dropping off. Times are changing . . . Let Tony have the morning off . . . I may have to cut his hours. You know Howard Shiff's son Ben, who took over the farm up there, he built his own garage and hired his own mechanics! Can't say I really blame him but old Jake Aristotle . . . Well he isn't doing much nowadays and like I said things are changing!"

Feeling like Dave was preparing Fred for some sort of let down about the truck, Fred just slowly nodded his head.

But Dave was great at catching you off guard and just as Fred thought he was going to hear from Dave, 'Sorry can't help ya out' - Dave smiled and looked at Fred and said, "No sense towing it down here yet . . . Just so happens I have some free time today. Why don't I stop by this afternoon as soon as I close up here and I'll poke my nose into it."

"Ah, sounds great Dave . . . Thanks, I'll be home a little later . . . Few more stops . . . But Jenny's home and you know where the keys are. That's great Dave because I'm sort of dreading the prospect of telling Rube that I ah . . . Ah . . . Maybe I messed up his truck!"

Dave laughed, "Ah don't worry about it . . . I'm sure we can get one more trip out of her and hopefully Rube too! I hear he is not doing too good!"

Fred acknowledged Dave's concerns for Rube and left to confront Roger but feeling a little more optimistic about the truck.

A swing by Roger's . . .

Fred pulled into the long paved driveway which led up to Doc Olsen's home and office. This was also where Roger had been renting an upstairs apartment for years. Many of the residents in town were getting older and the Doc had no shortages of patients being as he was the only optometrist in this county. Business was booming for the Doctor with the demand for geriatric eye care!

Fred passed the small parking area for patients and continued up to the rear of the house. Roger's car was not there and the Good Doctor was out sitting on his rear porch sipping a cup of tea.

Fred turned his engine off and got out of his car. Doc Olsen immediately stood up from his lawn chair and came to the edge of the deck to greet Fred.

"Hi Fred, long time no see . . . Your eyes must be doing fine!" Doc chuckled and extended his hand.

Fred shook Doc's hand, "Where's Rogg, have you seen him?"

"Not lately. He left pretty early this morning. Saw him drive out at about seven . . . With fishin poles!"

Fred knew that the only time Roger went fishing was when he was really upset about something.

"Hmmm . . . He must be mad about something?" Fred stated.

"Well Fred, you know how Roger is . . . He did mention to me yesterday that . . . Well Jenny was pregnant. And you took on a new job over in Evansville. If you don't mind me asking, is that true?" Doc was grinning a little.

"Ah yeah . . . I mean yeah, Jenny is expecting but I haven't even had an interview for that job yet. That Roger, I should have known better than to tell him anything. Jenny and I got into a little fight over that."

"Again Fred, if you don't mind me saying, I wouldn't get too upset at Roger for all of that cause that's not what is really bugging him. Besides . . ."

Doc Olsen quickly nodded toward the house where Fred could see Carol Olsen through the kitchen window doing dishes or something.

"I heard about Jenny long before Roger came home! If you wanna spread something around this town fairly quickly there are two ways of doing it – Tele-phone and Tella - my wife!"

Fred laughed and said, "So what do you think is ailing Roger?"

"You" Doc said emphatically.

"Me, What did I do." Fred slammed back.

"Well it seems that Roger thinks you're deserting him with this new job of yours and . . . Well you have to remember Roger's past and how much he depends on you."

"So what am I supposed to do . . . Live my life around Roger?"

"Of course not Fred, you're first responsibility is to that wife of yours and of course your new family.

You just have to give Roger some time to get use to things and I know, he'll see you are still there for him. You remember how hard it was for him when you went off to college but he got use to it . . . Remember?" Doc replied with affirmation in his tone.

Fred looked down at the driveway a minute and a myriad of memories came to his mind in a flash. Fred had known Roger his whole life. They were in every class together all through school but Roger was different; sort of a nerdy kind of a guy and as a matter of fact, he still was. Roger always seemed to get picked on or bullied and things got worse after the fire.

Roger's Mom, Dad, and baby sister perished in a blaze that destroyed the family home back when Roger was thirteen. It was a severe tragedy for the town and Roger went to live with his Aunt and Uncle, not too far from the Goodman Farm. Roger, by the sheer stroke of luck was over at some other relatives spending the night when the fire broke out.

Fred kind of gazed up at Doc Olsen and the Doc could see that Fred was traveling through the past a little. The Doc gave Fred a few more moments to reflect.

Fred looked at Doc and finally said, "Wow what am I supposed to do about this . . . Any suggestions Doc?"

Doctor Olsen warmly smiled at Fred and answered Fred's question.

"You know, sometimes life puts us in funny positions . . . And we always don't like them but we have to handle it whether we like it or not! Fred, I know you will do the right thing . . . You always do. But don't ever forget where your first responsibility lies. Never forget that!"

Fred nodded his head in agreement with the wise Doctor's advice, climbed in his car, and rolled the window down to say goodbye to Doc as he backed down the driveway.

Doc winked at Fred and as Fred slowly started to back up Doc Olsen had one more thing to say, "Are you going to get corn planted in time this year Fred?"

Fred stopped and scratched his head, "Ah no . . . Was I expected to?"

Doc laughed, "Everyone in town misses the Goodman sweet corn!"

Fred smiled and laughed.

Returning home, Fred saw Dave Bakers van parked in front of the barn but Fred decided to go in the house and see his wife first . . .

As Fred walked through the kitchen he could see Jenny in the parlor with a rag hanging out the back pocket of her jeans and pointing to something on the wall.

She looked down at Bailey saying, "So what do you think?" Bailey was cocking his head like he was trying to understand what she might be saying.

Fred softly walked into the Parlor and surprised Jenny with his arrival, "Ah . . . So what's Bailey think!"

Jenny jumped and turned, "Fred what are doing scaring me like that . . . Bailey seems to have stopped doing that and now . . . Now you start sneaking up on me."

Jenny came over and gave her husband a warm welcome. Jenny gently spun her husband around and said with pride, "How's it look!"

"Fantastic . . . You did a great job!"

And she did. The curtains were open and all the covers were off the furniture and the parlor glowed and had the smell of fresh polish and wax.

"This place is amazing Fred . . . Look at all this history! Look at the amount of items in here, the old photos and paintings, all this antique furniture, all these artifacts, lamps and it looks like a virtual . . . Ah . . . Let me think about it . . . A sort of . . ." Jenny pointed with an admiring tone.

Fred cut her off, "A Museum?"

"Exactly, it looks like a museum in here . . . Upstairs too."

"Not to mention the Barns!" Fred added.

Fred and Jenny immediately stopped talking, quickly turned their heads towards each other and looked into each other's eyes. It was almost as if a thought, the very same thought, had entered into their minds, both at the same time. But before either one of them could say another word, the sound of a knock on the back door commanded their attention.

Dave Baker knocked again and this time hollered, "Fred . . . Jenny."

"Dave, come in." Fred hurried to the door but Dave was already walking into the kitchen.

Jenny smiled, "Hi Dave how's it going . . . Have a seat . . . Would you like a cup of coffee. . . Fresh pot!"

"No thanks on the coffee Jenny, but I will have a seat for a minute. Nice to see you and congratulations . . . On the baby and all."

Dave lowered his large frame onto one of the kitchen chairs at one end of table. Fred and Jenny sat on the sides across from one another.

Jenny smiled, "So how's your wife doing Dave?"

"Oh fine, fine . . . Listen folks, about that ole truck out there. It has definitely seen better days."

Fred broke in, "What's wrong with it Dave?"

"Well besides the fact that it's darn near fifty years old!" Dave started smiling. "I'm afraid the lifters are hangin up and the compression isn't so great. And let me see . . . You need to clean the carb and a few other minor things I guess."

Jenny looked nervous and her next question certainly reflected that nervousness in the way she asked the question, "How much do you think . . . To fix it?"

Fred put his head down expecting the worse cause he knew they probably couldn't afford this if it was too much over a couple of hundred dollars.

"Could be about a thousand or a little over." Dave answered.

Both Fred and Jenny sighed, looked at each other and Jenny took Fred's hand.

The first thing out of Fred's mouth was, "Oh my gosh, what will I tell Rube?" and Fred shook his head, "He's going to be so disappointed."

Jenny nodded and murmured, "I know . . . I know."

Dave folded his hands together on the table and then realizing they were still a little greasy, immediately dropped them down to his lap again.

For a few seconds none of them said anything and then Dave piped in, "Listen, I've got an idea, if you guys pay for the parts, about two hundred . . . And let me work on it up here . . . I'll get that old Milk ferry goin again for ya."

Jenny smiled, "Dave we can't let you work for nothing. That wouldn't be fair . . . But that's so nice of you to offer but . . ."

Dave waved his hand, "Get that thought out of your head young Lady . . . Let me tell you, if it wasn't for Ruth and Harry, I probably would of not made it. Why there was always one thing or another that needed repair up here and when things were bad during the war . . . Why they let me earn some money by helping out up here. Not to mention that Ruthie kept us well stocked with fresh corn and vegetables and of course her famous homemade pies and oatmeal cookies. So don't tell me what's fair. You know, Eleanor and I are thinking of getting out of the auto stuff. We have a pretty good nest egg. And as a matter of fact . . . I was going to ask you guys if you needed any help up here on the farm? When you got the farm going again."

Dave started looking out the window with a smile and a smirk on his face, "But it doesn't look like it this year anyway. The discussions is over. I'll get started on the truck this week."

Dave got up from the table, groaned a little, and waved goodbye as he strolled out the kitchen door.

The weekend whizzes by . . .

Delighted with Dave's offer, Fred and Jenny finished putting in a full day that Saturday. Jenny completed cleaning the parlor and Fred rode the Kubota around the farm and took care of some the first mowing of the season.

Fred and Jenny did get a chance to discuss Roger. Jenny explained that she continued phoning Claire but with no luck. Fred decided to wait until Monday and approach Roger at work and Jenny would give Claire's sister Sally, a ring at the restaurant, if Claire was still among the missing.

Jenny made a terrific roast for dinner which included a juicy bone for Bailey and the couple, very exhausted, retired early for the evening.

A Lazy Sunday Morning . . .

Both Fred and Jenny, along with Bailey slept in a little later this Sunday and arose to a gloomy day with the threat of rain. Usually, the couple enjoyed quieter days around this old farm on Sundays.

Today's plans however called for a visit with Rube Gildman over in Milburn where he resided at the Milburn Manor, a quaint community for the elderly.

They left the farm around 11am that morning and as they turned out of the farm entrance and headed for Route 16, Fred slowed down as he noticed the Shiff farm hands ushering about 50 cows into one of the pastures which Fred leased to the Shiffs. When he got to the corner of Route 16, Fred stopped and gazed over to the Farm Stand, then back to the cows crossing the Road.

Fred spaced out a little and Jenny said, "Is everything okay Fred?"

"Yeah, it's fine . . . It's just good to see cows on this farm, even if they don't belong to us . . . Cause they certainly belong here!" Fred answered with emphasizing the word 'Here!'

"What did Ruthie sell here Fred" asked Jenny.

"Well obviously corn, after it was pulled. But she had a lot of fresh vegetables as well . . .You know that grass pasture out behind the house?"

Jenny nodded and Fred continued, "At one time that was all veggies. Tomatoes, squash, cucumbers, broccoli . . . You name it . . . If it could grow well around here, Ruthie planted it!"

"Wow" Jenny mused. "Did it make much money?"

"Some years I guess but that's a lot of work. Crops like that have to be picked by hand and Ruthie slaved over that field. I miss those days though . . . Cows, the stand . . . I especially miss Uncle Harry and Aunt Ruthie." Fred closed with a smile and a sigh.

"You're so sentimental Fred but . . . I guess that's one reason why I love you so much!" Jenny reached over to grabs Fred's hand.

It took about a half hour to get over to Rube's new estate, as Fred referred to it. When they walked into Rube's room he was half way between the chair and the door. It looked as if Rube wasn't quite sure which way he wanted to go and Fred announced their arrival.

"Hey Rube, how's it going?"

Rube slowly turned to Fred and it took a few seconds for Rube to recognize his visitors, "Oh . . . Fred, Come in, come in . . . And Jenny, how you doing dear?"

Jenny patted Rube on the shoulder and helped him back to his chair where he fell into it rather than seated himself in it.

Fred didn't have to wait long for Rube's anticipated questions, "Is the Truck all set Fred, cause you know the Parade is in two weeks."

"Three weeks Rube . . . The parade is in three weeks. And Dave Baker is working on it."

"You always have to get so technical Fred. Three weeks, two weeks . . . Huh . . . What do you mean Bakers working on it? It was running fine. What did you do to it Fred?"

"Nothing Rube . . . It just needs some work that's all. It is Fifty years old Rube."

"Well Baker's a good man, he'll take care of it. Just see to it that it's ready for me to drive in the Parade. You know that truck is almost fifty years old."

Jenny smiled and looked over to the old farmer.

"Drive, you can't drive that truck Rube." Jenny thought that she better clear that notion out of the old gents head.

Rube looked up at Jenny like she had two heads or something, "Drive, are you crazy lady . . . I can't drive! My nephews going to do that."

Rube kept shaking his head but he was smiling.

Jenny slumped a little from probably some embarrassment over treating Rube maybe just a little too immaturely but Rube just continued.

"Pull the corn in yet Fred?"

"Ah no . . . Didn't plant it yet!"

Rube held one hand to his ear and Fred had to repeat himself just a little louder this time, "I SAID I DIDN'T PLANT IT YET!"

"Unh . . . Well when it's time to get it in . . . Call me and I'll help you get it to market. Just like old times, Hey Fred."

"Sure Rube . . . You bet."

Each visit with Rube was getting harder and harder for Fred. Rube was failing fast and while Fred watched Jenny carry on some small talk with Rube, Fred couldn't help but to be saddened.

This once proud tower of strength, this man who could lift bales of hay all day long and still get up at 3 am every morning to milk the cows, this invincible hero of Fred's who could outwork any other farmer in the county, was now nothing but skin and bones who could hardly walk from a chair to a bed. Fred sighed and Jenny could tell this was hard on Fred.

The couple visited with Rube for about an hour and when they left, Rube made Fred promise once again, that Fred would call him when it was time to harvest the corn.

Jenny sympathized greatly with Fred's emotion over watching this last patriarch of American History fade and about ready to disappear; as is his once proud profession was.

It was a quiet ride back to the farm and Jenny also understood how much it meant to Rube and Fred, to have that old jalopy of a milk truck running again. And Dave Baker must have known too.

Sunday Evening came very quickly and the two were very tired . . .

After nibbling on some left over lasagna, and already dressed for bed, Jenny and Fred shut the lights off in the kitchen and headed for the bedroom. They hadn't noticed that Bailey was nowhere to be seen?

Now that the parlor was open for the summer, Fred and Jenny walked arm and arm, through the parlor instead of walking down the main hallway. When they got to the doorway to the rear hallway, Fred took a look around the room and said, "Amazing . . . This room and this house is amazing!"

Jenny squeezed Fred's arm and they headed to the master Bedroom as Fred reached out and turned the light out in the parlor.

As they walked through the darkened hallway Jenny said, "By the way . . . Have you seen Bailey lately?"

In a deep ghostly type of voice Fred slowly answered. "Nooo . . . Hah . . . Hah . . . Hah! Maybe he is somewhere in this old house lying in waiting to STRIKE! . . . Hah . . . Hah . . . Hah!"

"Stop it Fred . . . Don't scare me . . . Its dark in this hallway!"

Now if you were a fly on the wall in this old house, this is what you would have heard when Fred and Jenny walked into the dark bedroom and Fred switched on the light . . .

"UH – UNH NO WAY . . . NOT A CHANCE . . . YOU ARE NOT GOING TO SLEEP ON MY SIDE OF THE BED! . . . OFF THE BED BAILEY . . . NOW!"

Jenny would continue to giggle and laugh on and off for several minutes and Fred continued to mutter indignant comments and remarks to his over exertive canine. Soon the lights went off and silence set in finally bringing an end to this day.

CHAPTER FOUR
FRED'S BIG DECISION

Like clockwork and without fail, Monday morning finally did arrive. This week was to bring with it quite a few obstacles and situations which Fred and Jenny Goodman certainly did not anticipate. These predicaments started unfolding the minute Fred arrived at Fairbanks for work.

Fred barely walked through the lobby door when Lillian, the receptionist barked orders out to Fred.

"The Boss wants you in his office right away Fred, Pronto he said." Lillian followed with an annoying chuckle.

Hastening to his office and plunking his attaché to the desk Fred murmured out loud, "Great, Roger told him about my interview . . . Great going Rogg. Now I'm probably going to get fired . . . Jeez!"

The door to John Fairbanks office was open but Fred nervously knocked on the door jamb. Mr. Fairbanks was a lean aging man who dressed very well and was always good to Fred, but he was a stern person to work for. He didn't tolerate too much and like now, he was always straight to the point.

"What's up with Roger, Fred?"

"Ahem . . . I'm not sure John. Haven't talked to him since last Thursday."

John could tell Fred looked a little uncomfortable.

"What do you mean you don't know? You're his best friend?"

Fred answered quickly, "Yeah I know . . . But he's been acting a little strange lately."

"What do you mean lately? Roger is always acting strange. Roger called in sick for the whole week. Says he's got the flu or something? Is that true Fred?"

Fred remained silent while shrugging his shoulders and John Fairbanks continued.

"Out of courtesy to you Fred, I'm going to let you try and talk some sense into Roger. The email system is down again and accounting can't link with sales. And you'll have to agree, I have been very fair to Roger. He has already missed 16 days of work since January and . . . And quite honestly I can't tolerate this anymore. I left a message on Roger's phone and if he doesn't get his butt in here pronto and fix these problems . . . He's through! If you want to try and talk some good judgment into him that's fine but I need to know something by noon!

Otherwise I'll have to call in some temp people and Roger is history. Sorry Fred and how's that lovely wife of yours, Glenda?"

"Jenny . . . My wife's name is Jenny and she's doing fine."

Fred was squirming because he realized that he hadn't been able to talk to Roger at all and if he didn't get through to Roger, John Fairbanks would fire him.

"Ah yes Jenny . . . Well give my regards and let me know if you have any luck with Roger?"

John Fairbanks looked squarely up to the clock on his office wall. Fred knew it indicated that time was closing in on Roger.

Fred hurried by Lillian's desk, completely ignoring the comments she was making. Fred flew down the hallway which led to his office and while mumbling to himself, went to his desk and picked up his phone.

While he was dialing he was still mumbling, "C'mon Rogg. Pick up the phone . . . You jerk . . . How could you put me in this position?"

Roger must have received Fairbanks message because now the phone just rang and rang. Roger must have turned the answering machine off. Fred raised his hands toward the ceiling, "What the heck am I supposed to do about this?"

Jenny encounters her own dilemma . . .

Jenny started early on her work as she had two deadlines to meet for the week but at about 10 o'clock she decided to call Sally down at the local diner. Sally was Claire's older sister and when Sally and Jenny did some fund raising together for the local Church, she was introduced to Claire.

Sally answered, "Thanks for calling Sally's can I help you?"

"Hi Sally, this is Jenny Goodman . . . How are you doing?"

"Oh Jenny, nice to hear from you but if you're looking for Claire, she's not here right now."

"Well yes I am trying to reach Claire . . . I have tried her for days but she doesn't return my calls."

"Well I can understand that . . . Claire says you're boiling mad at her . . . For telling your little secret!"

Jenny couldn't believe what Sally had just said.

"What . . . Ah . . . What do you mean mad?"

Sally with a slightly snooty tone in her voice answered, "Well Dear . . . Claire said you left a message on her machine which . . . Let me say it this way . . . Wasn't too friendly! If you know what I mean dear."

"Sally, all I said was thanks for letting the cat out of the bag but it was no big deal because Fred and I finally touched base."

Jenny all of a sudden felt like she was defending herself and was starting to get a little perturbed.

"Well that's not the way I heard it dear . . . But I'll give her the message that you're looking for her . . . When I see her. Got to run now . . . Five customers just walked in . . . Bye dear."

"What the heck is going on?" Jenny muttered out loud as she looked down to Bailey who had now joined her.

"Imagine that Bailey! Claire screws up and now all of a sudden . . . I'm the bad guy! Weird . . . I thought Claire was a real good friend but good friends don't act like that, do they Bailey?"

Bailey whimpered and tucked his head under Jenny's hand. Jenny was confused and hurt but she stroked Bailey on the head and had to get back to work, whether she felt like it or not.

Dinner time sounded more like a complaint department rather than a peaceful relaxing evening at home . . .

You might be able to imagine how upsetting and detailed Jenny and Fred's dinner conversation may have been as both were totally flabbergasted over the situation with Roger and of course, Claire's indignant attitude toward Jenny.

Fred tried his best to console his wife and Jenny attempted to convince Fred that despite Roger's past, Roger was a grown man and people were just going to have to cease their enabling of Roger; so he

73

could stand on his own two feet. Of course Fred knew that Jenny was right but Fred still felt guilty. And Jenny battled with her anger toward Claire.

When Jenny first came to Oak Gove with Fred, Claire was the only one who truly reached out to Jenny in friendship and now Jenny felt betrayed and hurt. Both decided that the best course of action was to do nothing, except to continue to try and phone their alienated friends.

Jenny finished up the dishes and sat down at the table and waited for Fred to let Bailey back in from his evening saunter outside. Fred leaned back against the counter and looked to his wife who was quietly contemplating something.

"Fred . . . Did I tell you . . . That Bailey talked to me today!"

"Huh!" Fred scrunched his face slightly and looked strangely at his wife.

"Bailey talked to me today . . . We had quite the conversation I might add." Jenny blurted.

Fred turned and started opening the cabinet doors one by one and peered into each cabinet closely.

Jenny crossed one leg over the other while folding her arms together and sarcastically asked, "What on earth are you doing Fred?"

"I'm looking to see where you hid the brandy . . . You must be drinking!"

Jenny laughed, "Fred don't be silly, I'm pregnant. I'm not going to drink! And I'm serious. Bailey came up to me when I was sitting at my desk and put one paw on my lap . . . And he started to kind of like growl but it wasn't a real growl . . . More like a half bark and a half growl!"

Jenny smiled and tried to mimic Bailey's conversation, "Rah, rah . . . Rah rah, rah rah rah . . . Rah . . . Rah!"

Fred threw his hands up and started to roar in laughter.

"That's great . . . Just Great . . . My best Friend is crazy and now my wife and dog are going stark raving mad . . . What's next . . . Maybe I'll show Bailey how to drive the tractor so he can start mowing the lawn . . . Hah!"

Jenny smiled and shook her head side to side a few times.

"Well . . . Don't believe me. But every time I said something to Bailey, he answered me back. Mmmm! We had quite the conversation . . . The two of us did indeed!"

Fred just frowned and went over to his wife who was still seated and offered his hand out, to help her up.

"Come Dear . . . I believe it's time for you to get your sleep . . . And it appears it is well needed!"

Fred smiled, shut the lights off in the kitchen and they took their evening stroll through the parlor to the master bedroom, arm in arm, as they did almost every evening.

Fred's big day for the interview finally arrives . . .

Despite the frustration over the concerns for Roger and Claire, Jenny was bound and determined to send her husband off to his interview in the best of spirits. Jenny made Fred a terrific breakfast, made sure his suit was in perfect condition and straightened his tie just before he walked out the kitchen door.

Evansville was only 30 minutes away from the Goodman farm so Fred's commute, if he should get the job, would actually be much closer compared to his drive into the big city with Fairbanks Advertising.

A straight shot down the Interstate with an easy on and off. Fred arrived at International Graphics in just 25 minutes. This was great but Fred was slightly nervous and somewhat intimidated by the ornate architecture of this fairly new four story building.

Once inside the lobby, Fred was further taken back by the elaborate and expensive ambiance which the lobby boasted. The highly polished marble floors had beautiful granite stones rising from it, with each of these stones featuring many of International's Customers and the graphics which apparently this firm had designed.

Fred, while clutching his attaché, slowly walked toward whom appeared to be a receptionist and as he meandered through the maze of stone, his head was turning constantly viewing all the displays.

Fred had never seen a set up like this. He was impressed but also very surprised at the way new modern businesses presented themselves to potential clients and the public.

Fred was not prepared for what was to happen next. A young lady, dressed in a very short dress arose from what looked like a small desk at which she was seated at near the center of the lobby.

Fred immediately caught sense of her perfume as she pranced, rather than walked toward Fred. Fred had to shake his head a little when he realized that this receptionists blouse was cut so low, that it would not leave much to the imagination. Fred blushing a little, tried to look anywhere except at the face of the young women approaching.

"Good morning Sir . . . How may I help you this morning?" The receptionist greeted Fred with a very soft and sultry tone in her voice.

Fred was obviously uncomfortable as he was trying to look everywhere but at this lady's mid-section. "Ah . . . I'm Fred Goodman . . . And . . ."

Fred realized he was starting to stutter slightly and the receptionist smiled and giggled but Fred managed to continue, "I'm here to see Mr. Gates . . . Ah, for an interview."

The receptionist continued to smile, "We're expecting you Mr. Goodman and if you would have a seat over there I'll inform Mr. Gates that you have arrived."

The young lady pointed over to a small sitting area decorated with two large leather sofas and high backed loungers. She then strutted, not walked, back to her tiny station and it looked as if she hiked up on her already short skirt rather than tug it down when she seated herself on her chair.

Fred nodded his head a little, out of disgust, and commenced looking over all the company propaganda spread out on the very expensive coffee table.

International handled some major accounts from all parts of the world. The clientele of this firm appeared to be mostly retail interests, including catalog designs, logos, and advertising graphics. 'Mmmm' Fred murmured and thought to himself, 'Right up my alley', but Fred was getting more uncomfortable by the minute and the atmosphere of this place certainly was not helping.

It wasn't long until Fred heard the ding of the elevator and looked up to see an older gentleman swiftly walking in his direction.

"Good morning Mr. Goodman . . . I'm so glad you could make it today . . . How was the drive . . . May I call you Fred?"

The well-dressed executive extended his hand to Fred and continued, "Gates . . . Bob Gates . . . And you may call me Bob. We try to break down the formalities here."

Fred glimpsed over to the receptionist who now had crossed her legs and was bouncing one leg up and down looking as if she was trying to attract attention to herself as two other men had entered the lobby.

"I see that Mr. Gates, I mean Bob . . . and Fred will be fine." Fred answered as he followed Bob Gates into the elevator and up to his office.

Mr. Gate's office followed suit with the layout of the rest of this building and it was lavishly decorated. Fred could see that this firm obviously was doing quite well.

Once inside, Gates handled the interview in the typical fashion by letting Fred give a quick biography and a plea, as Fred use to always refer to it, for this part of an interview. Fred commenced explaining to Mr. Gates as to why he should consider Fred for the job. Fred sensed that he was not presenting himself very well and he didn't know why, but he did know how uncomfortable he was feeling.

Gates looked over Fred's resume which was on his desk, cleared his throat and proceeded with his executive dissertation.

"Fred you have a very impressive resume and to be quite honest with you, we have only interviewed one other applicant for this job. You and one other fellow from Atlanta . . . But what I would like to do now . . . If it's fine by you . . . I would like to call in Mitchell, the exec you would be working with."

Fred nodded his head and Bob picked up his phone, "Hi . . . Bob here . . . Are you available to come in and meet with Mr. Goodman . . . Fine."

Fred was just thinking to himself, Gee I wonder what kind of guy this man named Mitchell will be, when suddenly a lean blonde women stepped into Gate's office. She too, looked as if she was dressed to go out to a singles nightclub or something and Fred suddenly realized that this situation was not probably what he expected.

Fred immediately stood and the attractive women, Ms. Mitchell extended her hand. Fred guessed that the style around here was for the women to dress as provocative and sensual as possible, as she too seated herself in a manor to attract Fred eyes.

Gates proceeded, "Here's the deal Fred. The job starts at 80 thousand a year, plus insurance, plus travel expenses. How's that sound for starters? But I do have to tell you this . . . You have explained to me that you have done some free lancing and you have a couple of active accounts but I'm afraid you would have to curtail those activities. International does require full rights to all your work and does not permit free lancing."

"Ah great!" Fred got taken in quickly with the salary. That was twice as much as he was getting at Fairbanks but it was something else Gates said which hit Fred very quickly.

"Excuse me Bob but you did say something about travel expenses?"

"Yes . . . Listen, a few things have changed with the scope of this job from what we had advertised and also from what we talked about over the phone. Let me explain . . . Corporate has made some changes and it has been decided that most of the operation which you would be involved with will be handled out of our New York office . . . Which means you would have to fly to the City and stay for two or three days a week. Of course we would pay for your transportation and lodging and you would be working directly with Mitchell. How's that sound Fred . . . What do you think?"

All of a sudden, it hit Fred square in the face; travel, leave Jenny home alone on the farm, leave the farm, what about spending time with his son . . . or daughter?

Fred was no longer nervous and he immediately stood up and held his briefcase with two hands in front of him.

"I appreciate your time and it sounds like a great opportunity."

He gestured to both Mitchell and Gates, "But the fact of the matter is that my wife is expecting our first child and I originally anticipated this job to be based here in Evansville."

Mitchell stood up and smiled and as she did, she slid closer to Fred and rubbed his shoulder, "That's terrific Fred . . . But isn't that all the more reason to join our team? Think of all the financial benefits you can provide to your family . . . Wouldn't you like some time to reconsider? I think we could work well together?"

Fred, being polite as he was, slightly chuckled.

"Well, with all due respect to you Ms. Mitchell, and to you as well Mr. Gates . . . There is a big difference between financial security and the welfare of your family. And a true man has to recognize that the time which you spend with your family . . . Can never be substituted or replaced with money!"

Fred could not wait to leave this building and go home to his wife. He politely shook the hands of the two executives and breezed out of the lobby totally ignoring the frilly, phony farewell from the receptionist.

As Fred unlocked his car he started imitating the attractive blondes comment to him with a exaggerated sarcastic ring to it, "I think we could work well together . . . Sure you do you . . . You sleaze . . . Jeez!"

Fred did feel good about himself. Fred started to remember the stories which Jenny had told Fred about herself as a child. Growing up with a Father who paid more attention to the dollar rather than his wife and daughters.

But he also knew that he was going to have to explain this to his wife very prudently when he got home. Jenny sure was hoping for this to be Fred's big opportunity and the first thing she would think of is, Fred declined the job because of Roger.

Fred has a lot of explaining to do when he gets home but of course, it will have to wait until the next Chapter.

CHAPTER FIVE
FRED'S BIG EXPLANATION

Fred draws a deep breath as he turns up the driveway to the farm.

Although Fred felt really good about his judgment and decision about turning the job down at International, he was also concerned about how Jenny was going to take the news. Not to mention that they certainly could of used the money which the position offered.

"Oh well . . . . Here goes." Fred sighed as he pulled up to the barn.

Slowly getting out of the car and walking very hesitantly toward the rear kitchen door, Fred noticed the back end of Dave Bakers truck poking out from behind the barn.

"Mmmm . . . Must be working on Rube's truck . . . Better get inside and deal with this thing with Jenny first."

I guess Fred knew his wife fairly well because, as he feared, Jenny was waiting for him. Jenny was standing up against the kitchen counter, with her arms folded, and anxiously tapping one foot.

"Why didn't you call me Mr. Goodman . . . I've been waiting for hours to find out what happened."

Fred thought to himself, great, Jenny never called him Mr. Goodman unless she was really perturbed.

"Hi sweetheart . . . I'm sorry . . . It's just that I guess I don't have very good news to tell you."

Jenny could tell that Fred was slightly dejected but Jenny also knew Fred very well, and surmised that there was an obvious reluctance on Fred's part to spill the details. Reserving any sympathy or compassion toward Fred, Jenny blurted out, "You didn't get the job did you?"

"Well . . . Sorta kinda something like that honey."

"What do you mean, sorta kinda . . . Don't play word games with me Fred. I'm your wife . . . Tell me straight out."

"Well they offered me the job for 80G's a year."

Jenny started beaming a big smile and figured her husband was feigning the disappointment with the intention of playing a joke on her.

She then rushed over to Fred and placed her hands on Fred's shoulders. "Wow that's fantastic!" Jenny let out a shrill and continued, "Gosh Fred, this is terrific! Can you imagine what this means?"

Jenny stepped back from her husband and spun around twice on her toes with her hands raised in the air but she suddenly realized that her excitement was a solo festivity. Fred was not smiling or celebrating in any way. She wondered why not?

Fred plunked himself down in his kitchen chair and remained silent. Jenny assumed her place up against the counter exactly where she was when Fred first arrived home.

Crossing her arms and resuming the tapping of her foot, Jenny glared at her husband.

"This better be good Fred . . . This better be good!"

Fred seeing no sense in trying to sugar coat the facts simply blurted them out, "I turned the job down Jenny."

Fred cradled his chin in his hands with his elbows securely braced on the table preparing for the blast.

"You WHAT . . . Are you out of you mind Fred . . . WHAT . . . What possible sane, reasonable, explanation do have for this pray tell?"

Bailey, who up until now, had been sprawled across the kitchen floor in front of the pantry, and not being able to resist intervention, arose and took a position right alongside of Jenny.

"SEE . . . Even Bailey can't wait to hear your excuse."

But before Fred could utter a single word, Jenny decided she was not ready for the explanation right as of yet and continued with her sermon.

"I know . . . This is all about Roger isn't it. Poor Roger . . . Can't leave him alone for a minute. Next thing you know you'll be begging Fairbanks to get his job back!"

Fred tried to interrupt, but Jenny was on a roll and wasn't about to yield the floor.

"Fred you have got to free yourself from this ridiculous loyalty you have for this immature adult, cause it's screwing up your life! How many weekends did you leave from college to come home . . . How many jobs did you get for him?"

"Jenny . . . Please this is not about Roger." Fred begged.

"I'm not done Fred Goodman . . . Do you remember how many dates you broke with me because poor Roger was having emotional trauma!"

Bailey looked like a spectator at a tennis match as his eyes shifted constantly, back and forth, between Jenny and Fred as they spoke.

"I'm telling you Jenny, this has nothing to do with Roger . . . Please will you let me explain."

"I understand and care what Roger went through but this is sheer lunacy when you put Roger ahead of your wife and child and chuck an $80 Thousand Dollar a year job out the window . . . Just for Roger!"

Fred just shook his head and was getting quite frustrated with the fact that he couldn't get his wife to stop for a minute so he could explain.

"I've been trying to tell you sweetheart . . . THIS DOES NOT HAVE ANYTHING TO DO WITH ROGER!"

"Well, then who does it have something to do with FRED?"

Fred paused a moment and sighed, "You Jenny . . . It's all got something to do with you."

Jenny looked bewildered. She went to the other end of the kitchen table and took her seat.

"Okay, so now it's my fault . . . Unh Fred."

"NO . . . It's not your fault but it is about you . . . And me . . . And our Son."

Jenny frowned and Fred added, "Ahem . . . Or daughter"

Knowing that he now had Jenny's attention, Fred proceeded with his story.

"Listen Jenny . . . The whole situation with the job was different than what they told me. For some stupid reason or whatever, the big execs decided to base this position which I would be involved with, in

New York City. It means I would have to travel. Be away from you and the home for three . . . Maybe four days a week."

"But for 80 Thousand . . . I could manage Fred or maybe we could move?"

"Yeah right . . . Sure . . . You know you hate City Life and I do too. And don't give me that garbage you could manage here by yourself! Aren't you the girl that did nothing but cry and complain about your own Father? All the stories you told me about how your Dad was never around for your Birthdays, Christmas, or anything you did at school? He was too occupied with money . . . What . . . Are you willing to trade off for the big money . . . Like your Mom did and be more satisfied with a luxury house and expensive furniture, then a loving family? Jenny you have to understand that this job was not right for me . . . Or you and our new family. Besides there was a BIG problem with the person I would be working with and traveling away from home with . . . Mitchell."

Jenny was looking very sullen and perhaps even embarrassed. "Why what was wrong with this guy, Mitchell?"

"Maybe nothing if in fact he was a guy . . . But Mitchell was a Super Model look alike! . . . And she dressed like a sleaze besides!"

Jenny's eyes looked quickly up at Fred with that remark. Fred could tell instantly that Jenny was about to cry. Jenny's face quickly overwhelmed with tears as she again realized, that she had over reacted and misplaced her trust with her husband's judgment.

Fred had never made wrong choices. Fred was always in control of everything. Why did she always doubt him? Jenny felt ashamed and was hesitant to move closer to her husband.

At that moment, Bailey decided he would get involved. Bailey shuffled over to Jenny, and while gently grabbing her wrist in his mouth, coaxed Jenny to stand. Bailey then slowly and carefully pulled Jenny over to Fred's end of the table.

Jenny's crying had subsided slightly and she looked into her husband's eyes, raised her hands, and once again burst into a flood of tears dropping onto Fred's lap.

She put her arms around his shoulders and sobbed out.

"Oh Fred . . . I'm so sorry . . . Please forgive me for thinking the worse before you had a chance to explain. When am I ever going to believe in your philosophy? I love you so much . . . Oh my gosh . . . Look what I'm doing to your suit . . . I'm ruining it with my tears . . . Cause I'm so Stupid!"

Fred patted his wife on the back.

"It's okay sweetheart . . . It's a hard philosophy to live by sometimes . . . But I do know that everything which may happen, happens in a certain way for a reason. I'm not sure what the reason is for this right now . . . But we will see it . . . Eventually."

Fred scratched his head as he appeared to be absent for an understanding for that reason, at that moment.

Fred gave his wife a kiss on her cheek and for a few moments in silence, Fred cradled his wife in his lap and arms.

Five, maybe ten minutes had passed when Jenny sheepishly asked, "Was she prettier than me?"

"Who?"

"Mitchell . . . Was she prettier than me?"

Fred chuckled and answered, "Not a chance . . . Besides, this woman was exaggeratingly flaunting her feminine ways to lure me to the job . . . And you know how I feel about women like that . . . You should know me better than to think like that."

Jenny softly replied, "I do . . . Just checking." And then she giggled.

The two started kissing and as each second passed the embraces and kisses became more intense and passionate. It appeared that the couple was heading for a very romantic interlude. Bailey, realizing that he had completed his task, then moved back to the pantry door of the kitchen, and flopped back down to the floor.

Ah . . . Excuse me . . . Fred and Jenny . . . Hello . . . Remember Dave Baker is here working on the milk truck! Let's not start something that cannot be finished . . . At least right now . . .

Jenny jumped up. "Oh my Gosh, Dave Bakers here working on the milk truck . . . I forgot to tell you."

Fred laughed, "I know . . . I saw his truck out back when I came home. I'll go see him in a few minutes."

Fred pulled his wife back into his lap and tried to start a second round.

"Fred . . . Fred . . . You beast . . ." Jenny jumped up again and continued, "Why don't I start dinner and you go see what Dave is up to . . . Besides . . . It's only two o'clock and maybe . . . Maybe we can have an early night." Jenny winked at her husband as she walked to the refrigerator to see what she could make.

Dave was up to his ears in grease . . .

Dave had the whole top of the engine off and greeted Fred immediately with a smile, "Found the worst of it . . . Maybe . . . The intake manifold is fine but the gasket is gone. Sucking in too much air. If I can't get one, I can make one."

"Good . . . I guess." Fred answered.

Dave wiped some more grease off his hands and looked at Fred, "Sorry about the job Fred."

Fred looked dumbfounded and jerked his head back a little, "Huh . . . How'd you know?"

Dave shamefacedly grinned and said, "Well . . . Went to the door to fetch ya . . . And I couldn't help to overhear a little. You left the door open. I wasn't eavesdropping or nothing like that mind ya. Only heard a little and got right back here to work . . . Ahem."

Dave looked down at the engine again appearing slightly embarrassed.

Fred pursed his lips, "Mmmm . . . I see . . . Well that's okay . . . No harm."

It was all Fred could do to keep from laughing.

"I see you have things under control here Dave so I'm going to get back up to the house and help Jenny with dinner."

Dave smiled and Fred turned to go back to the house but he had only taken two or three steps before he heard Dave ask, "Did she really look like a Super Model?"

Fred didn't want to turn toward Dave as again, Fred was about ready to burst out laughing. 'Didn't hear too much did you Dave' Fred thought to himself.

"Who?" Fred decided to play Dave out and put him on the spot again.

"Ah . . . Ah . . . Mitchell", Dave answered.

Fred turned and grinned at his friend and while nodding his head side to side. "Guess you can't keep anything a secret in this town . . . Can you Dave?"

Dave smiled and gave Fred a big wink while chuckling, "Don't count on it my friend . . . Don't count on it!"

The Day ended up being a fruitful day indeed. Fred flirted with Jenny the whole time she was preparing dinner and Jenny seductively teased him back. And of course the couple retired early for the evening. Well that's enough for now and we don't want to be too nosey . . . So good night.

CHAPTER SIX
FRED'S PHILOSOPHY

Remember, it's only been a couple of weeks since this whole story began and Fred and Jenny definitely have not been lacking any excitement or controversy.

Friday afternoon arrived and Fred and Jenny were so busy that it felt like only a few short hours ago, it was Thursday morning. Fred was jammed as he was trying to close up the final details on illustrations for a cereal box proposal at Fairbanks and Jenny received three more projects to edit with short deadlines.

One of the advantages of working for John Fairbanks was that Fred was allowed to take on Free Lance work as long as it was not in direct competition to Fairbanks Clients. But Fred also had to catch up on those projects as well.

Glad to be home from the city, Fred parked the car and he noticed that the milk truck was not in the shed. He slowly made his way to the kitchen door and his eyes started to survey the length of grass out in the pasture.

Knowing that he was definitely not looking forward to the prospects of jumping on the Kubota that evening, Fred muttered out loud, "Why does grass grow so fast? Maybe I should teach Bailey how to run the tractor. Hah . . . Or maybe buy a hundred goats . . . Mmmm?"

"Fred, who are you talking to?"

Jenny caught Fred by total surprise as she was standing behind the screen door of the kitchen and the late afternoon lighting prevented Fred from noticing her.

"Oh hi sweetheart . . . Caught me talking to myself Hah."

Jenny chuckled, opened the screen door, stepped onto the stoop, and turned to the pasture right behind the house.

"You look tired sweetheart . . . The grass can wait till tomorrow and it would be better if you wait for better light, if you want to give Bailey his first lesson." And with that Jenny laughed in a teasingly manor.

Ushering her husband through the door, Jenny went to the counter and beckoned her husband to be seated, "I'll fix you a cup of coffee." She said sweetly.

"Thanks dear . . . How'd your day go? You must be tired too?" Fred said with empathy in his voice.

"Yeah . . . And don't ask me why, but Pearson flooded me with assignments today. And they all have to be done by next week."

Jenny continued to fix Fred's coffee and continued, "It's nice having the work and all but . . . Too bad this didn't happen before I was pregnant."

Pearson was the Publisher which Jenny had worked for out in Columbus and she was fortunate indeed to be able to continue working part time from her home after the wedding.

Fred all of a sudden realized he was being too self-indulgent because he was tired and his concerns immediately switched to his wife.

"Gosh . . . I'm sorry sweetheart. I shouldn't be complaining. You're the one that's pregnant, not me. How you doing anyway and when's your next Doctors appointment?"

"Next Tuesday and I'm not sure why but I really don't feel any different . . . Except today . . . I'm a little run down but I think it's cause I've been constantly typing today. Do you want to come?"

"Where"

"To the Doctors with me . . . Silly."

"Well . . . Are Husbands supposed to do that or something?" Fred queried while cocking his head slightly to one side.

Jenny smiled, "Yeah . . . Some do, some don't. But I think it's part of the fun if you experience this with me . . . Together. But you don't have to. Don't you want to know all about child birth and what to expect?"

"I guess so . . . I think . . . But I just took a day off this week and . . . ", Fred looked a little unsure at the moment.

Jenny brought the coffee over and placed it in front of her husband and took a seat right next to him rather than at her normal spot at the other end of the table.

"By the way, some mail came in for you today. Might be interesting . . . Didn't get a chance to look it over."

Jenny reached over to the end of the table a slid over a big pile of envelopes for Fred to look at.

Fred gave a double take and started flipping through the pile and began verbally indexing the pile into smaller piles.

"Junk . . . Bill . . . Insurance . . ." He looked up to his wife who was intently watching her husband sort the mail, resting her chin in one of her hands.

Fred continued, "Junk . . . Junk . . . Garbage. I promise I'll come to the next appointment Okay sweetheart."

Jenny patted her husband on the shoulder and got up. "I'm going to start some dinner Fred . . . Pork chops okay?"

"Bill . . . Electricity . . . Yeah that sounds great hon! Bill . . . Bill . . . How come so many bills?"

Jenny laughed and got busy with dinner.

"Junk . . . Bill . . . WHOA WHAT"S THIS?"

"What is it Fred" Jenny exclaimed as she hurried back to her Husband's side.

"It's from Andross Foods . . . Mmmm!"

"Open it . . . Open it . . . Just don't sit there and look at it Fred."

Both Fred and Jenny were excited. Andross was one of Fred's free-lance accounts. Fred had designed some packaging logos about a year ago for some of their snack cakes and he made some pretty good money in the process.

Fred unfolded the letter and Jenny leaned over his shoulder, "What's it say Fred what's it say . . . Darn, I don't have my glasses."

"Hon, I can't read it . . . You keep jiggling my arm!"

Jenny sat back down in the seat next to Fred and tried to patiently wait for Fred to finish reading the letter.

Fred turned to his wife, "This is great news Jenny. They want to talk about a new project. Something about logos, labels, and packaging for a new line of flavored bottle water."

Jenny had a very quizzical look, "Bottled water?"

"Yeah . . . Bottled water . . . It's a big thing now I guess."

Fred looked up to the clock above the kitchen sink, "Well, it's too late to call today so we will just have to remain in suspense till Monday."

"Oh my gosh . . . The pork chops!" Jenny jumped up and ran to the stove, "Sheew . . . I forgot to turn the burner on . . . Good thing . . . Can't burn my husband's dinner."

Jenny flitted around the kitchen busy preparing dinner, "This could be good . . . Unh Fred."

Jenny felt a little relieved, most likely from guilt over her reaction to Fred's recent job interview.

"It most certainly could . . . Most certainly could sweetheart."

Fred stood, pushed the pile of mail to one side of the table and started to set the table for dinner. On one of his passes by Jenny, he swatted his wife across her back side.

"See", he exclaimed, "Everything happens for a reason Doll."

"I know . . . Again, I'm sorry about being so upset the other day about that job Fred. I guess I never had a Dad around to teach me about having faith in anything."

Fred put his arms around his wife and whispered in her Ear, "It's Okay sweetheart . . . I forgive you . . . Now don't burn the chops . . . All of a sudden I'm starving!"

Jenny smiled and then slapped her hand on her cheek, "Oh gosh . . . Did I tell you, Dave and Tony came by and picked up the milk truck . . . Dave said something about giving it a tune up at the shop and tires or something . . . Darn, I forgot what he said! But he did say he will bring it back tomorrow morning."

"Mmmm" was all Fred muttered as he was lost in the possible prospects of what Andross's letter may offer and he didn't appear to hear anything Jenny said.

Dinner was great and the two continued to buzz over the chain of events which had transpired over the last few weeks and Bailey lay content in front of the pantry. When dinner was over, Fred volunteered to do the dishes as Jenny had about another half hours' worth of work to complete on one of her new projects and of course, Bailey accompanied her.

Fred, obviously enthusiastic about a new possible job with Andross, made short work of doing the dishes. While faintly singing and slightly dancing, Fred completed his chore.

Fred Joins Jenny in her office . . .

Jenny looked up above her reading glasses when she noticed Fred standing in the doorway to her office.

"How's it going . . . Am I disturbing the Editor?" Fred whispered quietly.

"Nope . . . Just about done. C'mon in and pull up a chair . . . Here, read this . . . . Does this sound okay to you?" Jenny said.

Fred's face twitched as he started to read the script for the pamphlet Jenny was working on.

"You gotta be kidding me . . . Somebody out there really thinks that it is important to know how to arrange your silverware in a drawer!"

Jenny laughed, "Yep . . . That's very important to people of society you know . . . These are helpful tips for Domestic Home Care Employees."

"Domestic what?" Fred scratched his head.

"Professional Maids, Servants and Butlers," Jenny replied looking at Fred with a smile on her face.

"Ridiculous . . . Well I guess it helps put food on the table?" Fred replied.

Fred handed the draft back to his wife and she placed it back on her desk. Jenny paused a moment and sat back in her chair.

"Let me ask you a question Fred . . . Sooner or later the Doctor is going to take an ultrasound."

"A what?"

"An ultrasound . . . A picture of the baby. But the question is . . . Do you or do we . . . Want to know whether it's a boy or girl?"

"Ah . . . No . . . I mean yeah I guess so . . . I don't know?" Fred confusingly answered.

Jenny found this amusing and watched her husband squirm a little as she knew that Fred really was hoping for a son.

Fred scratched his head and tried to explain how he felt.

"Well . . . I guess it's like this . . . I realize it might be a girl but it would be great if it's a boy . . . And if I find out that it's not a boy, too soon . . . I guess I can't hope for a boy! I don't know . . . Something like that I guess."

Jenny Laughed, "That's okay . . . We don't have to decide tonight."

Fred looked into his wife's eyes from his chair and said, "Honey, you look tired. Maybe you should think about getting to bed. I'll let Bailey out, close up, and join you."

Jenny put her hand to her forehead. "I'm exhausted, Good idea and . . ."

Bailey all of a sudden jumped up and moved to the edge of the desk where the phone was. Jenny pointed, "Look Fred . . . Bet the phone is goin . . ."

But before Jenny could finish, that is in fact what happened. The phone started ringing. Fred's eye brows rose and Fred pointed to the phone beckoning Jenny to answer it.

"Hello . . . Ah just a minute."

Jenny paused a second. Then cupping the mouthpiece with her hand, she leaned and whispered to Fred, "Its Ben Shiff, He would like to talk with you."

Fred shrugged his shoulders and took the phone from Jenny.

"Hello, Ben . . . How you doing . . . Haven't heard from you since . . . I don't know when. What can I do for you?"

Jenny sat back down in her chair and listened to her husband's side of the conversation and of course, quite curious to figure out what Ben Shiff may be up to. Jenny knew that Ben and Fred never really got along that good. Although Ben's Dad, Howard, was thought well of by Fred's Aunt Ruthie and Uncle Harry, they never cared too much for his son. But Jenny really couldn't figure anything out because it appeared to be a one sided conversation which was filled with a lot of I See's, Unh unh's, Mmmm's, and interesting's.

After about two minutes, Fred said, "Let me see if that's okay with Jenny."

Now Fred cupping the phone, looked to his wife.

"Ben and his wife Darcy would like to stop by tomorrow, early afternoon . . . He wants to talk about some business and would like to have you meet his wife."

Fred shrugged his shoulders like he was confused but also in an accepting sort of way and Jenny nodded a hesitant approval.

"Sure Ben . . . About one o'clock will be fine . . . See you tomorrow." Fred placed the phone down.

"What's that all about Fred? From what you told me about that Darcy women . . . Doesn't sound like I would like her too much."

"Not too many people do sweetheart. But Ben sounded kind of different from what I remember and the thing that caught my attention was that he mentioned something about leasing the front barn! More money for us."

Fred had grown up and gone to school with Ben and Darcy but Ben was a bully. He always picked on Roger and most everybody else. Aunt Ruthie always referred to Ben as the Gentleman Farmer's spoiled brat.

Darcy was a drama queen and she alone, thought herself to be the most popular girl in high school and probably to this day, was still unaware that she hadn't been!

Ben had taken over most of the business end of the large neighboring Shiff Farm from his father about a year before Uncle Harry passed away. And Ben, being sort of the con artist that he was, tried to woo Aunt Ruthie out of a lot of the Goodman equipment after Harry died.

Aunt Ruthie, a shrewd business women herself, would have no part of Ben's insulting offers. According to the local gossip, Ruthie gave Ben Shiff a lecture he would not forget and Ben never set foot on the Goodman farm again.

Jenny stood and placed one hand on her hip.

"Guess it can't do any harm in hearing him out . . . But I'm not looking forward to meeting her . . . That's for sure."

"Well . . . We will just have to see what happens I guess?" sighed Fred.

Fred was certainly surprised by the call and of course he was very skeptical. And Fred never really had much of a reason to talk with Ben, as long as the checks for the leased land showed up every month.

From time to time, Fred would bump into Howard Shiff down in town and Howard being the gentleman he was, would always lead the conversation in a cordial and caring manor.

It was getting late so Jenny switched off the computer and the desk light. Fred took Jenny by her arm and showed his wife to the door. But suddenly Jenny stopped and without much warning. Fred nearly tripped over his wife.

"Fred . . . See I told you . . . And you didn't want to believe me. Bailey knows when the phone is going to ring . . . Did you see that!"

"Mmmm!" was all Fred mustered up at that moment, switching off the light in Jenny's office as they entered the hall way.

Although Fred had noticed Bailey's unusual reaction seconds before the phone rang, he never could resist the opportunity to tease his wife.

"Probably just a coincidence Jenny, if Bailey would just turn the coffee maker on for me in the morning, before I get up, so I don't have to wait for my first cup of coffee . . . Now that would be something."

"Hardy Har Har . . ." Jenny chuckled.

"Wise decisions may come from unexpected circumstances." Fred muttered seemingly out of the clear blue.

"What's that supposed to mean Fred?" Jenny asked.

Fred lifted his eyes up to the ceiling and said, "Just came to mind. Uncle Harry use to say that a lot . . . Not sure what it means?"

Things really seem to change quickly around the Goodman Farm, don't they?

CHAPTER SEVEN
AN UNLIKELY PROPHET

"Are you absolutely sure about this Bailey?" Fred bent over and roughed up the top of Bailey's head.

"You know Jenny is going to be real disappointed if she gets up and you're not there to greet her."

But Bailey wouldn't budge away from the rear kitchen door. He just kept walking around in a tight circle while he persistently made small lunges at the closed door. He wanted to go out with Fred. As Fred took the final sip of his second cup of coffee for the morning and placed it in the sink, Bailey continued his little practice of first sitting, then standing, and then motioning toward the door.

"Okay . . . Okay . . . Okay . . . Let's get going Bailey; we have a lot of field to cut this morning."

Fred headed to the Barn with Bailey right alongside. Flipping on the light switch in the front barn, Fred continued his conversation with his canine companion.

"What on earth am I doing Bailey? It's not even 6am . . . It's not even light enough to mow yet. I must be out of my mind but I guess this is what you have to do on a farm . . . Unh, boy?"

Fred gave the tractor a quick once over, checked the gas and the play on the belts, and then opened up the rear door. He stood for a moment looking out to the rear acreages.

"Mmmm . . . Guess I better work on the service roads today."

This usually took quite a bit of time, especially for the first time of the season. Fred normally would have to go slower so as not to run over any hidden sticks or branches. Many times, Fred would have to stop and move a stone which may have fallen off one of the stone walls which lined much of the service roads. To top it all off, there were about three miles of road to go over on this farm. Some of them were wide enough so that Fred would have to make two or three passes to cut the entire width of the road area. Besides, Fred didn't want to wake Jenny too early and he certainly would if he mowed the rear pasture and around the house.

Turning quickly back toward the tractor, Fred stopped in his tracks, "What the hey?" Fred said out loud.

Bailey was standing on his hind legs with his front paws placed upon the seat of the Kubota. Bailey softly whimpered as he looked at Fred.

Fred laughed and never would pass up the opportunity to tease, even if it was his dog.

"I was just kidding Bailey . . . When I said I'd teach you how to drive. Besides, your too young . . . You don't even have a license! And the seat won't hold the both of us."

Fred nudged Bailey away from the tractor and climbed on to the seat. But Bailey kept pacing and whining and wasn't going to take no for an answer. He wanted to go for a ride!

Fred placed one hand under his chin thinking about Bailey's request for a moment or two.

"I've got it." Fred waved his arm to his new farm hand and said, "Follow me Bailey, I have an idea!"

With that, Fred started the tractor and went to the next barn where he backed the tractor up to the front doors. Leaving the engine running, Fred struggled to slide one of the huge doors off to one side and pulled out a good sized yard trailer and hooked it to the back of the Kubota.

"How's this my friend?" Fred exclaimed as he motioned for Bailey to climb aboard.

And that is exactly what Bailey did. He didn't even have to be coaxed or asked a second time.

Fred laughed and took his seat on the tractor and turning back to Bailey he said, "Hang on Bailey . . . Let's go get some work done."

Now Fred wouldn't be able to use the trailer if he was mowing the grass or the field around the house because the trailer wouldn't be able to make the tighter turns required to do the job. But it wouldn't bother Fred while doing the service roads.

This particular trailer did not come with the Kubota. It was an older trailer which was used behind one of the much older John Deere's which long since, had died. Rube had modified the hitch and it worked fine behind the Kubota.

The morning sun was starting to beam revealing light patchy streams of mist off the ground from the colder night before. Fred and Bailey slowly headed up the road which led to the pump station and the cemetery, spewing shrouds of fresh cut grass and weeds.

The old Grandfather clock in the Parlor just sounded his report that it was now 9am, and Jenny was just starting to stir . . .

Jenny slowly sat up on the edge of the bed rubbing her eyes hoping to see the daylight.

"My gosh . . . Its 9:20 already . . . I don't even feel like I slept an hour. Why am I so tired?"

"Don't be silly Jenny." she said to herself. "Your pregnant . . . That's why you're tired."

Standing up while holding one hand to her hip as she stood, Jenny suddenly realized that her side kick was among the missing.

"Bailey . . . Where are you . . . My faithful dog?"

Jenny threw on her robe and somewhat perplexed over the absence of her new friend, sluggishly made her way to the kitchen but Bailey was not there to greet her or in his newly accustomed residency on the floor in front of the pantry.

"Mmmm" Jenny said as she poured a cup of coffee. She went out to the rear porch to look out into the pasture to see if Bailey might be enjoying an early summer's morning.

She stood holding her cup in both hands and just as she was about to return to the kitchen, Jenny heard the faint sound of the Kubota slowly making its way back down the service road toward the house.

She intently watched and listened as the clicking, clacking, and the drone noise of the tractor gradually grew stronger. Occasionally the large mower would catch an occasional small stone and spit it out startling Jenny with the loud snap of the blades meeting the granite obstacle.

For just a moment, the Kubota disappeared into a small valley hidden by the rise of the gentle sloping back acreage but when it re-appeared, Jenny could not believe her eyes.

"Oh my word . . . I don't believe this."

Jenny couldn't help but smile as she saw Fred approach the barns absorbedly talking and waving his arms as if he was having quite the conversation with his passenger.

Bailey was bobbing up and down and side to side, struggling to keep his balance in his chauffeured limo. He too focused on Fred, listening attentively to Fred's banter.

"I just have to see this up close for myself." Jenny muttered and scurried down the porch stairs and out to the driveway between the house and the barn just as Fred pulled to a stop.

Bailey bounded out of the trailer toward Jenny and ran to her side.

Jenny was beaming as she looked at her husband and said, "Well . . . Well . . . What on earth prompted you to think of that Fred Goodman?"

"It wasn't my idea . . . It was Bailey's. He insisted on going." Fred answered with a smug look upon his face.

"I see . . . Did he turn the coffee on for you this morning Fred?"

Fred just smiled and climbed off the tractor and went to his wife and gave her a hug and a kiss.

"What are you doing up so early sweetheart . . . We didn't wake you did we?"

"Early . . . Are you crazy . . . It's almost 10 o'clock Fred. Why did you let me sleep so late. I still have some more work to do before your friend and what's her name show up."

"I let you sleep because you're tired and . . . And it's Ben and Darcy . . . And I love you . . . That's why."

"Do you have time for a coffee and pastry before you two head out again?"

"Of course . . . I still have to get the lower roads down to the river. Should only take a few more hours. I should be back in plenty of time."

The trio made their way back into the kitchen and Fred groaned as he seated himself at the kitchen table.

"That tractor is a little rough on the back I'll say."

Jenny smiled and said, "Fred, are you a little curious as to what Ben wants?"

"A little . . . But don't be nervous or anything. We'll just listen to what they have to say . . . Be good neighbors and good hosts. Have a cup of coffee and send them on their way. Fairly simple really."

"Mmmm . . . I see . . . Everything is really pretty simple for you to handle Fred Goodman. Nothing appears to bother you too much. But that's only . . . Let's see . . . Reason Number 312 as to why I love you so much. You take everything with so much grace and ease."

"No sense being concerned about something until it is actually something to be concerned about. Everything will be fine dear."

Well, Fred and Bailey got right back to work after Fred slurped down a cup of coffee and gobbled up a cheese Danish. Jenny disappeared into her office to work on her projects, and of course Bailey partook in munching on a few Dog treats before he and Fred left to mow the lower roads . . .

Almost three hours had past when Fred cut across the Pasture Road and up the driveway back to the barn. The first thing that jumped into his vision when he cleared the rise was the sight of the old Divco Milk truck.

"Whoa, look at that!" Fred said out loud as he shut down the Kubota and jumped off the seat.

The truck was glistening in the morning sunlight. Dave and Tony must have washed, waxed, and buffed the old truck and Fred had never seen it look so good.

"Like it?" Dave said as he and Tony hobbled off the rear porch. Jenny must have served them some coffee and pastry as there was a whole plate of them sitting on the porch table.

"It looks terrific Dave . . . Hi Tony. You guys didn't have to do all this. I would of washed and waxed it before the parade."

Tony piped in quickly, "Well, since it was down in the shop anyway . . . We decided to clean her up.

After all, we have all the paraphernalia to do it the right way. The Misses was nice to serve us some donuts and coffee . . . She said you would be back in soon."

Dave stood with his hands on his hips taking the time every once in a while to pick a fleck of something off the shiny new surface of the Divco.

"Dave what do I owe you . . . I'll go in and get a check." Fred was always was prompt to pay his bills.

"Ahem . . . Your wife already offered but me and Tony decided that . . . Well . . . This one is on us . . . In memory of your Uncle and Ruthie. Sorta something like that . . . Right Tony."

Tony shook his head in agreement to Dave Baker's offer.

"I can't let you do that Dave . . . I insist."

Before Fred could finish, Dave with a strong tone of power in his voice said, "I'll hear no more about it Fred Goodman. And we have to get going now. I have to pick up my wife at the hairdressers and Tony has a Birthday Party to get to."

Both Dave and Tony jumped into Tony's Pick up and didn't give Fred another chance to argue his case, and Tony's truck threw up a shield of dust as it sped down the drive.

Just as the truck disappeared behind the leafy boughs of the large Maples which lined the drive, Jenny had quietly arrived at her husband's side and while she placed her hand on Fred's shoulder she said, "It sure looks nice Fred . . . Looks like a new truck . . . Almost!"

"Yeah . . . Sure does but I'm a little upset they wouldn't take any money."

"I know . . . I tried too. But Dave wouldn't listen to me either. Guess sometimes people feel good when they help others . . . I guess."

Fred turned his wrist to look at the time, "Let me park the tractor . . . I'll be right back."

And that's what Fred did. He dropped off the trailer in front of the large barn and backed the Kubota into its berth in the equipment barn. Jenny waited in the driveway for her husband and as he walked toward her, he glanced once more at his watch.

"Maybe I'll have enough time to clean up a little before Ben and Darcy get here . . . But . . . Maybe not?"

Both Fred and Jenny turned toward the drive to see a blue Ford pickup just turning into the long drive which led to the house.

"Well I'll go and make a fresh pot of coffee." Jenny said as she started to dart toward the kitchen door.

Fred could sense Jenny's apprehension toward this meeting with these two strangers. Jenny had never met either one of these people and only heard a lot of town gossip about them. It wasn't that Fred didn't care about Jenny's feelings, it's just that he knew Jenny always had to be coaxed away from her shyness when encountering new situations.

Fred quickly grabbed Jenny's hand and pulled her gently back to his side.

"Now wait a minute here . . . I need you by my side. Don't you think I'm a little nervous too? Need your support Darling . . . Ha!"

"Yeah right Fred." Jenny sighed as the Ford drew up to the barn and stopped.

Ben Shiff pulled up and stopped in front of the equipment barn, some distance away from where Fred and Jenny stood. As Fred focused on his guests, it was all Fred could do from breaking down into total laughter.

Jenny squeezed Fred's arm and whispered, "What's so funny Fred?"

Ben and Darcy got out of the truck and started walking toward Fred and Jenny. Fred nudged Jenny quietly saying while he smiled, "Shush!" I'll tell you later dear . . . Hi Ben . . . How you doing . . . Haven't seen you guys in a long time."

Fred extended his hand in friendship toward his old High School nemesis, still with a big smile upon his face.

Even as Fred exchanged the normal cordial formalities with Ben Shiff, he still had to suppress an out load laughter. What was so funny to Fred was that here in front of him stood Ben Shiff, the big school Bully – wearing glasses!

Fred wore glasses. He did his whole life, well at least till he switched to contacts, and Fred never could forget how Ben always teased and tormented him over his deficit with vision.

And Fred wasn't the only target of Ben's attack on the four eyes, as Ben referred to them. Ben always had a whole repertoire of other unkind adjectives to use for people who wore glasses.

As a matter of fact, one time at a birthday for Adam Michael's, another neighbor in the area at the time, Ben had knocked Fred's glasses off his face which broke in half. Fred remembered his Mom marching over to Howard Shiff's farm insisting Howard pay for a new pair of glasses which his malicious son had damaged, and Howard Shiff did.

Roger was always a favorite target for Ben, and not just about wearing glasses. Ben un-mercifully picked on Roger for everything and Fred always had to come to Roger's rescue which usually ended up with Fred getting the innards beat out of him.

Another time, the ruthless Ben Shiff ripped the glasses right off little Tommy Moran's face, put them in a paper bag and then proceeded to smash them to bits with a hammer.

Fred imagined that old man Shiff must have had to pay for a lot of new glasses when his son was in his prime bullying years!

Fred had switched to contacts when he went to college and so did Roger and Tommy. Now Fred was standing with the only grasshopper eyes left in the graduating class of 1994. Hilarious Fred thought!

Anyway, Fred decided to return to the moment and turned to Darcy Smithfield, of course now Darcy Shiff. Her statue had remained so very thin and lanky, as she was in High School. Referred to as the Queen of Anorexia, outside her circle of her friends, she sure could hold claims to that title even to this day.

Darcy extended her hand out to Fred, "Hi Fred . . . Why you haven't changed too much. Nice to see you."

Fred returned the greeting but he couldn't help but notice how sweet and soft her voice had transformed into.

Darcy always had a loud and foul mouth and Aunt Ruthie use to always say . . . 'With a mouth like that, That girl should be up on the four lane drivin a semi!'

Ben kept the cordialities going, "And this must be your wife Jenny . . . We have heard all sorts of good things about you."

Jenny shook the hands with the couple and chimed, "Well . . . Let's not just stand around out here. C'mon in . . . I'll get a fresh pot of coffee brewing and we can get this . . . ."

Jenny paused. She wanted to say 'get this thing over' but she quickly changed it to, "Get started with what's ever on you mind . . . I bet Ben and Fred have a lot of stories to share . . . Huh!"

Jenny showed the couple into the kitchen and Fred followed behind. Ben and Darcy took seats at one end of the table. Jenny put some pastry out and started the coffee pot and Fred sat down at the side of the table right next to Ben.

Darcy stood momentarily before she actually sat down and looked all around at the old farmhouse kitchen.

"Wow . . . This is really like what everybody in town has said it is. This is beautiful Jenny . . . Is this the way it was just like a hundred years ago?"

Jenny turned and smiled but Fred answered, "Pretty much . . . That's not the original cast iron stove but Harry and Ruthie said it was from around 1910."

"Do you still use it?" Darcy asked.

"Occasionally . . . Mostly for heat . . . When I feel more like Fred Flintstone rather than Fred Goodman!"

That little bit of humor brought a chuckle from both Ben and Darcy.

"We use it for keeping food warm sometimes, but we use the range over there for most of the cooking."

Fred used his fingers to guide Darcy through the kitchen. She seemed genuinely interested in the architecture, especially the old glass pantry cabinets, the bread oven built into one side of the stone chimney, and Bailey.

Bailey appeared to take a liking to Darcy because he kept nudging his head onto her hand looking for some attention.

Fred went on to explain that his Uncle Harry abandoned the use of the old cooking hearth and fireplace in 1950, but let it stand at one end of the kitchen for sentimental and historical reasons. Fred was enjoying himself because he could never resist the opportunity to boast about the old Goodman homestead.

Jenny brought over the coffee and looked over to Darcy while she sat and said, "Well, maybe when were done talking . . . I can show you around the rest of the house? It's really quite interesting and unique."

Fred was somewhat surprised at his wife's offer. He thought Jenny just wanted to get this thing over and done with but he also knew that Jenny was also very proud of this old house.

Darcy responded with a big smile and said, "I would love to!"

Bailey who was patiently waiting for everybody to be seated finally decided to take his spot in front of the pantry.

The four of them sipped on their coffee for a few moments and exchanged some small talk tidbits and pleasantries but Ben finally took the initiative and decided to get down to business.

"I guess I owe you a few apologies Fred."

Ben placed his hands together on the table and the tone in his voice reflected sincerity which did catch Fred and Jenny's undivided attention.

Ben went on. "I guess I'm not quite the man my father is but I finally have realized that there is a much better way to act to your friends and neighbors, than I ever have! Let's face it Fred . . . I was a real shmuck to you and a lot of others here in town. Especially when we were kids . . . And I even tried to scam your Aunt Ruthie into selling me a lot of the equipment on this farm when Harry died . . . For . . . Let's say less than fair value!"

Fred interrupted, "Yeah . . . I heard all about that."

"I bet you did, but give her credit. Your Aunt gave me a chewing out that day . . . That's for sure! To tell you the truth Fred, When I left here, I was really embarrassed over the way I acted and the things I had said. I don't think I ever felt embarrassed before, until that day. So I started to think how my Dad use to do things."

"How is your Dad and Mom by the way? . . . I see them in town every once in a while."

"Their doing fine . . . Mom, well she still likes to cook and Dad . . . He really doesn't want to be too involved with the business end of things anymore. He just likes to go out and ride the tractors . . . working the fields."

"I see", Fred said and continued, "So what can I help you with Ben . . . You mentioned something over the phone about another business deal or something?"

"Well, the co-ops are dropping the prices on the milk their buying. The economy and inflation and all. And their increasing their quantity demands on many of the farmers so I was going to add more cows to bring up the production. You know things are changing drastically in this crazy business of ours!"

Fred interjected, "Yeah, I heard Bill Aristotle is thinking of retiring."

"Heard that too . . . Wonder what he's going to do with his land . . . Did you hear that the Peterson farm got sold over in Sullivan?"

"No I didn't." Fred shook his head while he answered.

"Yep . . . Some developer is going to build a Mall on the other side of the interstate and somebody said someone is going to be putting up condos or something on this side of the highway . . . Mmmm."

"So again. . . What's on your mind Ben?"

"Peterson has a pretty good price for 100 head of his Guernsey's. But my problem is that I don't have the space for all of them and it's really expensive to think about building a new barn. You have that beautiful barn right in your front yard . . . Which unless I'm mistaken . . . You're not using it. Since we have a lease going on the pastures near it . . . Would you consider letting us lease out your front barn?"

Fred pushed his seat back from the table slightly, turned, and raised his eyebrows at Jenny. Ben was right. The front Barn was the newest barn built on the Goodman farm and was designed for the Milking Business. It wasn't being used for anything and wasn't that far outdated that it couldn't be updated for Bens needs, but at whose cost? Jenny only smiled letting Fred know that it was okay with her to hear the whole deal out.

Fred decided he should be up front with a few things. "I'm not sure I have the capital to make any necessary upgrades you might need."

Ben Shiff broke right in and would not let Fred finish his thoughts.

"I'll take care of all the modifications and it would only be fair to leave them intact if and when we terminated. Also, obviously . . . I will pay for the electricity directly. We can have a separate service and meter installed. Only thing is the water. . . We can work something out on that."

"Water shouldn't be a problem. That Spring up there hasn't run low in . . . In . . . I guess never." And Fred was correct.

This farm was blessed with a large spring fed pond tucked up in the back woods. Uncle Harry had rebuilt the pump house which was only needed for the back fields and restored the damn. Because the spring was up high on the hill, the elevation made it so water pressure to the barns and house, was never a problem.

"Of course Ben . . . You might have to service the reservoir and filter system down at the barn? Not sure when the last time it was done?"

"No problem Fred. Listen, I'm not sure how you want to handle the financial details of this but why don't I have my Attorney draw up the lease . . . Saves you a little expense . . . And send it over to your Attorney."

"Sounds fine Ben." Fred answered firmly.

Fred knew it would be best to refrain bartering over any of the legal issues and leave it up to Morris Rothberg who had been Harry and Ruth's Attorney for years.

"Fred glanced to his wife, "Does that sound okay to you dear?"

Fred would never leave Jenny out of any decision which had to be made and Jenny enthusiastically shook her head in approval.

Ben and Fred discussed a few more minor details about Ben's proposal and just when it looked like the meeting had run dry of business and small talk, Ben threw a little surprise twist into the discussion . . .

"So Fred . . . When are you going to start planting the fields again?"

"Well, I'm not so sure I know enough about farming to do that Ben?"

All of a sudden the room became so very still and quiet. It seemed like for minutes. Then Ben slid his chair back and at first started to chuckle. It wasn't long before the muffled chuckle spurred into a hearty humorous laughter. Fred looked somewhat dumbfounded over Ben's reaction and tried not to show any expression at all.

Up until now, Darcy had remained fairly quiet with her chin resting on one hand, elbow on the table, and twirling a lock of her hair in her other hand. But the more Ben laughed, the more a large smile spread across her face. And then she too burst into laughter. It was a warm infectious laughter and not too much longer, Jenny could not help herself to join in.

Fred sat there mystified and maybe a little embarrassed. He couldn't understand what was so funny to everyone seated at the kitchen table.

Even Bailey stood up and started shifting his weight from one front paw to the other while energetically wagging his tail. He didn't want to be left out of the gaiety which permeated the old kitchen, which was normally a peaceful solitude for him.

Finally, Fred smiled a little, shrugged his shoulders and said, "What the heck is so darn funny to you all?"

Ben paused slightly in between his chuckles and while pointing his finger at Fred he blurted out, "You Fred . . . That's what's funny . . . Don't know much about farming . . . That's a killer Fred!!"

Recovering from an uncontrollable laughter Ben went on.

"Fred you were driving the tractors around this farm since you were twelve . . . You've ripped and cultivated the fields since you were 14 and worked the Combine almost every year since you were 16! Don't know anything about farming Unh . . . Why remember you're second year in college . . . You left school early to help plant the fields when Harry was sick with the flue. Gosh Fred . . You're a riot . . . Don't know anything about farming."

Ben was right and Fred knew it but Ben had a few more things to throw in.

"I don't like to admit this Fred . . . But when you're Aunt Ruthie gave me the chewing out of my life . . . And I made the mistake of mentioning you're name, Ruthie said and I'll never forget it . . . She said, Don't you dare put yourself in the same category with Fred Goodman! A better man in this valley right now, exceptin maybe you're Dad, doesn't exist. I ain't sellin anything on this farm cause Fred will come back and he will know the right thing to do! So take your Daddy's checkbook with you and leave."

Jenny smiled a warm admiration type of smile. Aunt Ruthie was right. Fred Goodman was indeed a great guy. The two couples sat silent for a minute and Fred, while scratching his head turned toward Jenny.

"Gosh, I don't know . . . I do have a full time job and everything."

Ben cut Fred off again.

"Listen Fred, you have the richest farmland in the county if not in the whole State. This farm has produced the best table corn for years and you have fields laying fallow that are ready for planting. Look, You don't have to jump into it all at once. Why if you didn't have all the equipment, well maybe you wouldn't be able to pull it off but you do have all the stuff . . . You've seen what's in those barns."

"Yeah but I don't know if it all still runs?" Fred answered.

"Jeez . . . Rube kept all that machinery in A-1 condition . . . You know that Fred . . . Why do you think I wanted to buy it."

Jenny was just looking to Fred for his reaction to all of this, but placed her hand on Fred's arm and Fred just kept rolling his eyes and shaking his head.

Ben stood and placed his hand on Fred's shoulder.

"Fred, maybe I can help . . . If you would let me. Why don't we check the equipment out. Now would be a good time to turn the fields, a few of them anyway. In the fall I'll have my guy come up and test them so they can be ready for next spring. Don't worry about the manure, I have plenty and I'll truck it up to the fields for ya . . . I won't charge ya anything either."

Fred looked up to this long time bully and he could feel the sincerity in Ben's voice.

"How about it Fred? Maybe it's time for us to work together . . . Like my Dad and Harry use to in this valley. Maybe it's time you let me off the hook for being the big jerk I have always been. How about it? I'll buy the feed from you and help you get back into the co-op and do what I can to help out. I'm sure we can make it work . . . Even if you have that full time job."

Fred stood and placed his hands on Jenny's shoulders.

"Guess I always knew I would have to come to some decision about this. Let me talk it over with Jenny and I'll let you know . . . Besides . . . Jenny and I have to consider our new family.

With that, Darcy jumped to her feet, "That's right, Oh my gosh . . . How could I forget . . . Congratulations guys . . . How far along are you Jenny?"

"About 7 weeks or so." Jenny answered softly

Ben piped in with the excitement. "That's great! Now you'll have a son to help you out Fred.

Darcy moved closer to Jenny and bent down slightly and placed her hands on Jenny's knee.

"That's terrific. You know whether it's a boy or girl already . . . Wow!"

Jenny gave Fred a subtle glare and while shaking her head spoke, "You guys . . . We don't know yet. Darcy, I think these two guys are just optimistic, wishful thinkers!"

Jenny stood, placed her arms around her husband and with a playful wink said, "Hope you guys won't be too disappointed . . . And what would be wrong with a daughter helping you out around the farm . . . Unh!"

Fred and Ben cocked their heads a little to one side, and both while shoving their hands in their front pockets, swaying from side to side, sheepishly muttered at almost the same time things like this, "Mmmm . . . I guess nothing . . . Nothing wrong with that at all . . . I guess."

Well, what perhaps started off to be a tense or awkward gathering for this foursome, certainly transpired into a warmer cordial atmosphere?

Fred and Jenny gave Ben and Darcy a guided tour through the old farmhouse and Fred was able to give his guests quite a history of the Goodman Farm; something he didn't always have an opportunity to perform but was greatly encouraged by their genuine enthusiasm.

Darcy was truly taken back by the artifacts and history of this old house and at the conclusion of the tour, Darcy turned to Jenny and said, "Wow guys . . . This would make a great Museum!"

Both Jenny and Fred instantly looked to each other and their eyes widen as this wasn't the first time the word Museum had surfaced!

As a huge surprise to Fred, Jenny and Darcy hit it off great, and Bailey tagged along switching his loyalty back and forth from Darcy to Jenny, never passing up the good fortune to be patted on the head so many times.

What could we possibly expect next?

CHAPTER EIGHT
A REVELATION

It was Sunday morning and Fred was conscious of the fact that neither he nor Jenny had attended Church lately.

He could extend some sympathy toward his wife's reluctance to go to Church since she had not been feeling her best. Fred also surmised that Jenny probably wasn't too keen on possibly bumping into Claire or Helen Crenshaw, whom Jenny absolutely loathed.

Jenny had been fairly active with the Church Activities in the past but not so recently. Jenny was also extremely exhausted shortly after Ben and Darcy had left the afternoon before, so he and his wife really didn't get much of a chance to even discuss the visit by the couple. As a matter of fact, after the couple left, Jenny barely ate a chicken salad sandwich which she had made for herself and Fred, and then slipped off to bed supposedly to take just a short nap. She never awoke and Fred didn't have the heart to wake her. She slept right through the night and Bailey was reluctant to leave her side as Fred had to coax the dog several times to take his evening walk.

Fred was surprised when he turned from the door after letting Bailey out for the Morning ritual.

"Morning sweetheart" Jenny said standing at the entrance to the kitchen.

"Well, Sleeping Beauty has awoken!"

"I'm sorry Fred . . . I don't know what got into me? Gosh, I was sooo tired."

"That's okay Darling . . . Here sit . . . I'll get you a cup of coffee."

Fred held the chair for his wife. "Something I wanna ask you."

"What?"

"Do you think I could talk you into going to Church with me today?"

Jenny frowned, as Fred knew she would. "Do we have to Fred . . . I'm really not up to seeing Claire or that . . . That Witch!"

"I know sweetheart . . . But I think that it might be important, especially after our meeting with Ben and Darcy . . . And the thing coming up with the Andross proposal . . . Remember? Well, it didn't go too bad yesterday with Ben and Darcy, did it?"

"No, I guess not. Darcy didn't seem at all like you described her to me Fred."

"Yeah . . . I saw that too. I guess people can change!"

"You can say that again." Jenny shook her head and frowned, "Look at Claire and Roger . . . Well, Claire anyway . . . Roger's always been a meathead if you ask me."

Fred chuckled, "Now, now Dear . . . Let's be nice."

But Fred did know what she meant about Roger.

"Fred, Is that a good deal about leasing out the barn . . . How much do you think we can get?"

"Not sure? Morris would have a better insight to that than I would. I'll call him in the morning and tip him off that Ben's Attorney will be contacting him. Better to let them work it out. Morris will let us know. All I can tell you is . . . That Barn is just standing empty. Not doing anybody any good. Might as well let it work to our advantage . . . Don't ya think?"

"Of course . . . Hey, wouldn't it be funny if you and Ben became good friends?"

Fred just laughed and nodded. He also knew that Jenny had not mentioned anything at all about Ben's idea to start up the farm again and Fred decided to postpone any discussions in that direction. At least until Fred could muse it over a trifle himself.

Now, it took a little doing but Fred was finally able to convince Jenny to go with him to Church . . .

Arriving about 10 minutes early for service, Fred and Jenny sat in an unoccupied pew, as most of them were. Attendance was very light this Sunday. Jenny immediately folded her hands and looked down and pretended to be reading the Church bulletin. She did everything but dare to look around.

Fred knew what she was avoiding and at one point whispered into Jenny's ear, "What are you doing?"

"Praying." Jenny quietly answered.

Fred smiled and said, "I think your prayers have been answered . . . I don't see a sign of the Crenshaws or Claire."

Jenny smiled but quickly put back on the serious look. "Makes no difference . . . I'm not here to see them." And that inspired a chuckle from Fred.

The service was fairly short as Pastor Smith knew how to speed things up a little when attendance was low.

Fred, intentionally, wanted to be the last out of the Church if possible, and so when they reached the front steps, Pastor Smith was beaming a tremendous smile.

"Fred, Jenny . . . How nice to see you."

Jenny extended her hand in greeting but before she could say anything the good Pastor went on. Pastor

Smith had been the Reverend at this Church since Fred was just five years old. Very animated with his gestures and his movements, the man could not stand still for even one second, and his head always moved up and down continuously. Jenny once told Fred that Pastor Smith reminded her of a Bobble Head Doll, and he did!

"Dear Jenny . . . I was just about to call you last week and ask you if you would like to chair the Women's Christmas Bazaar but then I heard the tremendously good news. Congratulations you two! Oh my word . . . It isn't even June yet and listen to me babbling on about the Bazaar!"

The Pastor looked now at Fred and heartily grabbed his hand and shook it vigorously. Fred thought for a second his arm was going to be ripped off by the over exuberant Pastor!

"This must be so exciting for you Fred . . . Just imagine, another Goodman son ready to help with the farm."

"Excuse me." Jenny tried to interrupt the Pastor but she was not successful.

"Why this is the best news . . . Wonderful . . . Just wonderful . . . Is he going to be named Fred Junior?", the Pastor asked.

"Excuse me, Pastor." Jenny tried again.

Pastor Smith finally slowed down. He needed to take a breath anyway as that man usually spoke a mile a minute.

"Who told you it was going to be a boy?" Jenny blurted out.

The Pastor looked confused for a moment, "Ah . . . Everyone . . . That's what I heard anyway."

Jenny was smiling and Fred could tell she wasn't really perturbed but rather she wanted to set the record straight and possibly at the same time, have a little fun!

"Now what could possibly be wrong with a Goodman Woman . . . Running the Farm?" Jenny quipped.

"Ah . . . Ah . . . Ahem . . . Nothing at all, nothing at all . . . It's just that . . ."

"Just what?" Jenny queried. While raising her eyes quite high and cocking her head to one side, as she sported that very feminine 'Gotcha now Mister' look!

Pastor Smith realizing he had been trapped quickly found a polite way to dodge the bullet, "Ah . . . Mrs. Macyntire . . . How good to see you."

An older woman shuffled up just behind Fred and Jenny and the sly Pastor found his escape.

"Excuse me Fred and Jenny . . . How nice to see you again." The pastor leaned over and quietly whispered and finished his thoughts, "I must see how this dear old woman is doing . . . She's been terribly sick you know."

The Pastor moved away quickly to greet the women and Fred and Jenny proceeded down the steps toward the parking area with Fred slightly snickering.

Jenny looked up at her husband. "What . . . What are you finding so amusing Fred Goodman?"

"You're merciless sometimes Jenny. You had the old Pastor cornered and you knew it . . . And may I dare say . . . You looked like you enjoyed it!"

Jenny smiled a spry smile and Fred continued to chuckle as he opened the door of the car and helped his wife in.

Arriving back at the farm . . .

As Fred and Jenny headed toward the kitchen door, Fred stopped suddenly and commanded what seemed to be an order instead of a request.

"Why don't we go in and change into some jeans. I want to do something with you."

"What would that be Fred?"

"Oh hush . . . Would you just humor me and do what I asked."

"Okay . . . Okay." Jenny replied.

Fred looked like he was in a hurry and the two had no sooner changed into some older clothes when he was ushering Jenny out the door.

"C'mon Bailey . . . You can join us too."

Jenny became very curious as to what her husband might be up to. Fred opened up the rear of the equipment barn and wiped off the passenger seat of the antique 1944 Willys Jeep. Harry had bought it from a surplus dealer over in Sullivan and it apparently served our country well over in Europe.

"Ah C'mon Fred. . . Where are we going?"

Motioning for Bailey to hop in the back, Fred answered, "To find some answers. . . Maybe . . . And enjoy the day!"

Fred drove up the rear service road, way up behind the pump house and then maneuvered the jeep up a steep crest to reach the highest point of the farm.

This section of the farm was still clear and not overgrown. They approached a small plateau which had five gigantic stones stacked together with one precariously perched upon the other four. Fred turned the jeep around so it was overlooking the farm and parked.

Jenny looked over at Fred, "You never took me up here before . . . Wow, what a view of the farm and valley."

"Almost forgot about this part of the farm." Fred said as he stared out at the horizon.

"Fred, what are these big rocks here for?"

"They have always been here. Maybe forever . . . Just rearranged. Uncle Harry discovered an old foundation here. He said the stones were the base for the chimney. He had some Historical people up here and they said the old foundation dated back to about the Revolutionary War. I guess they did some digging up here and found a whole bunch of artifacts including an old flint lock rifle. Harry just piled the stones on top of one another and was going to plant something up here . . . Never got to it I guess."

"Where's the gun now?" Jenny asked.

"Down at the Town Hall . . . Someone refurbished it and it's hanging up on the wall in the Mayor's office."

The view was magnificent and the warm afternoon sun felt good. It was so quiet and peaceful. Jenny was amazed and just kept staring out at the horizon.

The couple sat quietly for a while and then Jenny said, "Listen . . . Do you hear that?"

Fred leaned forward to barely hear the faint drone of a tractor somewhere off in the distance.

"Sounds like somebody is turning a field" Fred quipped.

"Are they planting something?"

"I don't know . . . Maybe or just getting ready for next year I guess . . . Just like Ben said we should be doing"

Jenny sat up a little as if she was trying to get a better view over some of the trees.

"Fred . . . How much land do we own?"

"Gosh . . . A lot . . . Look way past those silos. Do you see the line of pine trees?"

Jenny squinted and answered, "Yes I see them."

"Well just beyond those pines is the Shuntook River. We own down to there and if you look to the left you can see Rte. 16 climbing up the hill. Our property borders Rte. 16. Now you can't see too much to the right because of all the wooded areas but we have four large fields nestled in there as well."

Fred was standing in the jeep holding one hand on the wind screen and directing Jenny's tour with the other. Jenny did appear to be in awe of the expanse of the farm.

Fred continued, "Now behind us . . . Our land goes all the way up to the base of North Mountain but much of it is still wooded or overgrown. Uncle Harry told me some those fields hadn't been worked since maybe the 1930's."

"Wow!" Jenny exclaimed as Fred sat back down and sighed himself.

Now neither Fred nor Jenny had noticed that Bailey had jumped out of the back of the jeep and was keeping busy doing something in the field on the other side of the rocks. He was scratching and clawing at something. He looked as if he was enjoying himself. Fred got out of the jeep and leaned up against the front fender. Jenny joined him and held his hand.

"You know Fred . . . Maybe there is something to what Ben was talking about yesterday?"

"What's that?"

Jenny had a big warm smile on her face. "You're Uncle and Aunt didn't leave you all of this . . . To just have you stand here and look at it for the next fifty years!"

Fred grinned and said to Jenny, "I was wondering when that subject would come up . . . I guess I was looking for some sort of a sign or something . . . And of course your support."

Just then, Bailey came bounding over to his Masters dragging some type of long dead looking weed with him . . .

"What is it Fred?"

"Hmm . . . Some sort of vine . . . Looks like a pumpkin vine or something? Bailey, show me where you found this."

Jenny and Fred followed Bailey back into the open field whence he dragged his prize from. It was early enough in the season that the thick grass and underbrush did not make it impossible to rumble through. Bailey poked his nose down in the brush and Fred knelt down beside him.

"Whoa!" Fred exclaimed as his hands slowly moved away some of the grass.

Fred plucked a small green stem from the ground and held it up for Jenny to see.

"Okay . . . What is it?"

"A young pumpkin vine."

"Are you sure Fred?"

"Yep! . . . And look over here."

Fred pointed down to the remains of a fairly big pumpkin most likely from the year before and pulled up a remnant of a mature vine.

"How'd it get up here . . . Did your Uncle and Ruthie have pumpkins?"

Jenny removed the green stem from Fred's hand and started to examine it.

Fred was scratching his head, "Not that I know of. Ruthie did sell a few pumpkins at the stand but she bought them at the co-op. She just wanted to have them there for the fall season."

"Well didn't somebody have to plant these Fred . . . They just didn't show up by themselves . . . Could they?"

"Not exactly" Fred answered. "But maybe Harry dumped the old ones that didn't sell at the stand, up here. Then maybe they seeded themselves for all these years."

Jenny obviously did not know too much about the country life when she asked, "Can they do that . . . I mean plant themselves?"

"Ah . . . Yes . . . Mother Nature Hon . . . Mother Nature! This piece up here gets a lot of sun. Pumpkins need a lot of sunlight. I imagine most got smothered out by all this brush but obviously some have survived."

"Is there a market for pumpkins?"

"Oh yeah . . . Kids at Halloween, seeds . . . How about Pumpkin Pie . . . I guess I never thought about pumpkins. Always thought about corn. I'll run it by Ben. Only problem with pumpkins is . . . They have to harvested by hand. It's lot of back breaking work. Some pumpkins can get a little heavy!"

Fred laughed and softly poked Jenny in the arm, "A strong son would help out with that problem! . . . Ha!"

Jenny just lovingly smirked at her husband and laughed. "Is this your sign Fred?"

"Maybe perhaps part of it!"

The couple walked back to the jeep and Jenny held the small green stem in her hand. She brushed the stem across her cheek and nose, as if it were a fragrant flower. Fred leaned one hand on the hood of the old Gallant WWII veteran vehicle and placed his other hand on Jenny's shoulder.

"If you think about it Jenny . . . Standing here looking out at this farm . . . How can you not wonder? How many footsteps of others have we crossed or walked along side of . . . Only a hundred or perhaps two hundred years later. Were there children here in this very field playing and hoping for their future? How many other husbands and wife's stood here or elsewhere on this farm laughing with their joys or . . . Or lamenting in their tragedies. So many lives and dreams started here and ended here as well. This rich farmland remains eternally fertile, so it seems, through the passage of time. And the only difference this land may experience is the people who set foot on it. Amazing and truly staggering!"

Jenny was intrigued with her husband's compassion and the sentiment of the moment. She placed her arms around his waist and gave him a tender kiss.

"You are something else Fred Goodman . . . Maybe you should try your hand at writing . . . Ha!"

Fred took his wife's hand and sighed, "Naw . . . I think I have enough to do. . . Don't you think?"

Whistling for Bailey, the couple climbed back into the jeep and made their way slowly back to the house. Furthermore, it would be realized that the lives and dreams of this couple indeed were to make an impression on this old farm, leaving yet another set of footprints upon its soil.

CHAPTER NINE
FRED HOLDS THE LINE

If you're wondering what's going on with Roger and Claire; you will now find out a little more.

Fred couldn't help himself from feeling anxious so he decided to leave work early that afternoon. Even though it was Monday, he just wanted to get home, fill Jenny in with all the details about his phone call to Andross Foods, and straighten up his studio so he could start working on the new project.

But as he was driving home, Roger crossed his mind. Feeling a little guilty as he flew by Doc Olsen's street, Fred quickly turned into the empty parking lot which use to be the grain and feed store and brought his car to a halt.

"Damn . . . I don't really have time for this but . . ."

Fred grumbled out loud as he turned his car around and headed back to Roger's apartment. Fred really just wanted to get home but his better consciousness, or should we say his unwarranted burden of guilt, which Roger was so good at making Fred feel, got the best of Fred.

Fred was in luck. Roger's car was parked on one side of Doc's Barn and Roger was stuffing something into the trunk. When Roger turned and saw Fred getting out the car, Roger closed the trunk quickly and started walking briskly toward the stairs which led up to Roger's apartment. Roger kept his head focused to the ground avoiding Fred until Fred hollered out.

"ROGER . . . What the heck Roger . . . Why are you avoiding me?"

Roger stopped instantly and with a persistent surly and sarcastic attitude decided to acknowledge Fred's appearance.

"Well, well, well . . . If it isn't my old friend Fred WORSEMAM."

And with that Roger let out a much exaggerated phony laugh.

"How's your new JOB Fred . . . Must be nice to be SOOO POPULAR!"

"Rogg, Knock it off . . . Will ya", Fred responded.

Just as Fred answered his noticeably upset friend, Doc Olsen stepped out of the side door to the Barn. Realizing he may have interrupted something, Doc tried to go back into the Barn but the door had closed and locked. Roger couldn't see Doc from where he was standing but Fred noticed Doc out of the corner of his eye. Doc held one finger up to his lips and waved his hand indicating to Fred that Doc preferred not to be seen, if possible.

"Hate to tell ya Rogg . . . But I turned the job down. Not interested in it."

At first, Roger didn't respond. He just kept starring at the ground but after a few seconds, Roger decided he wasn't going to let his friend off the hook.

"Well, well . . . That is a surprise Fred and I'm sure you will be just fine working at Fairbanks. Least YOU still have a job . . . Eh Fred . . . No need to worry about anyone ELSE . . . Eh Fred."

Fred shook his head. He felt sorry for Roger but he knew he had to help his friend see his own folly.

"You know Rogg . . . I have been you're friend for a long time . . . I still am . . . But the only way I have let you down, maybe, is to not to tell you this . . . Something I should of said years ago. I'm pretty fed up with you trying to make everybody feel sorry for you. We all, that is . . . Everybody in town knows what you went through. We have shown you the compassion you needed. But we totally let you hogtie our emotions with this crapola about 'feel sorry for me'."

Roger was shocked. He was so shocked by what Fred was starting to dish out that he didn't even think to block his ears or walk away. Fred continued to seize the moment.

"You lost your job Roger cause you screwed up! If you really think that you can goof off from work 16 days since the new year . . . And then call in sick for a whole week . . . Then actually think it's somebody else's fault . . . Well I can't help you. You're a smart man Roger. You got that job because of it. But you lost it because you didn't own up to the responsibility that comes along with a job like that."

Fred glanced quickly over to where Doc was hiding and Doc Olsen winked at Fred and gave Fred the thumbs up.

Roger just stood there, lost somewhere between maybe understanding, and embarrassment, or maybe Roger was just frustrated. Fred couldn't tell but Roger still didn't want to let anything that Fred was saying sink in. At least not yet.

"Well hotshot . . . What am I supposed to do now? You who knows so much . . . Unh hotshot?" Roger hollered.

Fred tried to smile but wasn't quite sure it was coming across the way Fred intended.

"Not sure Roger? I do know that good old Doc isn't going to let you stay her for nothing . . . Guess ya gotta get a job!"

"Sure, Sure and where, pray tell Mr. Wisdom?" Roger answered in a gruff tone.

"Dunno Roger . . . You have a lot to think about Roger besides a job, but a job seems like the first place to start."

"Oh you're a big help!" Roger stood there smirking a smirk which couldn't be beat.

And Fred decided to throw one more zinger of thought into Rogers's brain before leaving.

"Why don't you try Ben Shiff. Heard he might be expanding . . . Maybe he needs some extra help!"

Doc Olsen cocked his head and smiled while he bounced up and down a few times as if he was saying to Fred, 'That's a Good One.'

Roger started to roar with sarcastic laughter.

"Oh Woowww . . . You're a riot today Fred . . . A real riot. Maybe you should have your own comedy show. Ben Shiff . . . Wow . . . Just when you think you know somebody . . . SLICE . . . They stab ya right in the back!"

With that Roger flayed his arms at Fred a few times and stormed up the stairs and went inside, slamming the door behind him.

Doc Olsen still didn't want to be seen but nodded his head several times. He apparently approved of Fred's performance.

Fred pursed his lips, swayed his head a few times, and strode back to his car looking once back up to Roger's door, and then he left for home. Not being sure he had done all the right things, Fred slowly made his way back to the farm.

Jenny listened patiently while Fred explained all about Roger, and Doc Olsen getting cornered on the side of the barn.

With excitement in his voice, Fred explained all the good news about the new Andross project which Fred couldn't wait to get started on.

Fred almost forgot to tell Jenny about the phone call to his Attorney. Mr. Morris was very enthusiastic for Fred and Jenny over Ben's proposal for expanding a lease.

"Hey Hon . . . Would you mind too much if I started straightening up my studio while you're getting supper? Gosh . . . Don't think I've set foot up there in about a month?"

Jenny put her arms around her husband, "Not at all. I'm really excited about this new project and the offer they made is . . . Is . . . Unbelievable!"

Fred laughed, "Let's not get too carried away. They first have to like my proposed design . . . Then they would draw up the contract . . . Stuff like that."

"Are you going to start it tonight?"

"No . . . I think I better wait till they send me their design perspective which they said will be in the mail today."

Jenny looked puzzled, "Design what?"

"They will be sending stuff like their ideas for advertising . . . Stuff like slogans, tags, marketing ideas and targets . . . Stuff like that. They don't want to sacrifice their ideas with only my insight." Fred smiled as he finished.

Jenny, still not exactly sure what her husband meant, just said, "I see . . . You know more about that than me . . . I'll give you a five minute warning for dinner . . . How's that?"

"Perfect . . . See ya later!" and Fred disappeared into the narrow stair well which led to his studio above the kitchen.

About 45 minutes later . . .

Fred heard the old stairs creaking with each footstep Jenny made as she climbed the steep narrow staircase and soon her head appeared above the top stair tread. Fred was waiting for her to float up into view and she just smiled.

"Guess someone couldn't sneak up on you here . . . Could they? Can't you do something about that, like oil the stairs or something?"

Fred laughed, "Nope"

Bailey surfaced just after Jenny and hugged close to Jenny's side.

Fred noticed that the color in Jenny's face was quite flushed. He stopped what he was doing and went over to his wife who was slightly leaning over to her left side and holding her hand on the top of Fred's computer. Bailey put his weight gently up against Jenny as if he was trying to support her.

Fred cradled his hands on Jenny's cheeks and looked into her eyes.

"Are you feeling okay sweetheart?"

"Okay I guess . . . Just got a little dizzy coming up the stairs just now . . . I guess?"

Fred was concerned about his wife, "Have you been feeling alright today . . . Have you gotten dizzy before now, at all?"

"No . . . No . . . I did a little work in the office . . . Got a little tired so I took a nap. But other than that I felt fine. Besides . . . My Doctors appointment is for tomorrow, remember!"

"That's right . . . Make sure you tell him about this. Maybe I should take you?"

Jenny gently touched his cheek and said, "Stop, I'll be fine . . . Besides I'm feeling back to normal now. I'm not a baby Fred, I'm having one."

"Well I guess?" Fred didn't want to baby his wife but he was kind of concerned.

"Mmmm . . . We'll see . . . Is dinner Ready?"

"Yeah, that's why I came up . . . To get you. I'm feeling better now so come see what I have prepared for you! . . . Something special!"

Fred was so caught up in the Roger thing and wanting to get started cleaning up the studio, he didn't even notice what Jenny was fixing in the kitchen. He took his wife by the arm and walked with her down to the kitchen, this time using the front staircase which was wider and didn't make a much noise! Bailey insisted on remaining close to Jenny's side and took a position on the other side of Jenny.

Although Lasagna ranked on the top of Fred's favorite list, BBQ Spare ribs held the #2 position and that's what was for dinner. Sounds good . . .

And Fred thought so too as he devoured about 10 of them. Jenny was unusually quiet during dinner and Fred became very aware of Bailey's constant attention to Jenny. Bailey didn't sprawl in front of the pantry as he normally might have, but instead hovered close to Jenny. If Jenny got up from the table, so did Bailey. Fred didn't want to point it out to Jenny but his curiosity was certainly aroused by the dog's sudden concentration to his wife. And Fred also thought back to the fact that only about 3 weeks ago, Bailey was always trying to sneak up on Jenny and scare the daylights out of her. Why the sudden change of behavior by the canine?

Fred volunteered to clean the dishes and insisted that his wife just sit and relax after preparing such a fabulous feast for him. She became more talkative while Fred maneuvered through the chore.

"I'm really proud of you Fred . . . About Roger I mean. You handled it very well. Do you think he will straighten up a little?"

"Hmm . . . I don't know . . . Maybe . . . Only time will tell. Which reminds me, how's the situation doing with Claire?"

"Anh . . . I haven't heard a word from her."

"I know that . . . You would have mentioned that. What I mean is . . . Are you going to try and get a hold of her?" Fred clarified.

"Not sure . . . Don't think I have to, I've tried calling umpteen times . . . Left about 10 messages and spoke to her sister, Sally . . . Not sure what else I can do?"

"Hmm!" was all Fred could say.

He knew Jenny was still upset and hurt about the situation but he also knew that time would heal the problem and who knows; maybe Claire would miss the companionship, and make contact with Jenny?

It was becoming more and more obvious that Bailey was staying as close to Jenny as he possibly could. Bailey again, did not choose his normal laze in front of the pantry and took a position right alongside of Jenny's chair. It didn't seem to bother Bailey to have to move every time Jenny decided to get up from her seated position. Jenny made no mention of it rather than to ask Bailey once, to move over when she went to grab the salt shaker. But Fred noticed and was somewhat perplexed; what could this mean? He did not want to over worry but he was remaining very alert to Bailey's behavior.

The very next morning, Jenny felt pretty good. Although Fred wanted to take Jenny to the Doctor's, she would not hear of it . . .

Bailey appeared apprehensive as well. Jenny had to squeeze her way out the door, closing it behind her while pushing Bailey's snout away with her hand.

Feeling a little guilty Jenny said, through the closed door, "I'm sorry Bailey. . . If I let you come, I would look like a Wooly Mammoth by the time I got to the Hospital . . . All covered in your Dog hair. Sorry pal."

She left, but she felt bad for her new companion and by the sounds of his muffled whimpers, Bailey appeared to be heart broken.

County Hospital was about 45 minutes away located in Claremont, a much larger town than Oak grove, absent of any of the farms, fields and pastures.

"Wow what a difference in scenery" Jenny said out loud as she traveled through the busy streets of the city. "Not like Oak Grove . . . That's for sure."

Maybe for the first time, she noticed a difference; a difference which perhaps she had not taken the time to notice before.

Jenny arrived at the Doctors office . . .

"Good morning Jenny . . . And how are we feeling today Mom!" The Doctor greeted her as he stepped into the examining room where Jenny was waiting.

"Actually pretty good today but . . ."

Jenny smiled and went on to explain her small dizzy spell, the day before. Doctor Chapman listened intently. The Doctor went on to explain his plans for this visit with quite a bit of detail and explanation.

Doctor Chapman was a real well renowned OBGYN. He had been practicing here at County Hospital for almost 35 years and certainly was dedicated to his field. But he was not the only Chapman practicing here. His Brothers John and Frank were surgeons at County Hospital. They found their calling here in Claremont. Maybe not so unusual given that both the parents had been Physicians as well!

When the Nurses had finished up, Doctor Chapman returned to the room, charts in hand and took a seat.

"Well, so far Jenny . . . Everything looks fine. Feeling sick or even sometimes dizzy isn't that abnormal during pregnancy but we'll wait for the lab to give us the blood test results. We'll see if anything surfaces? But I would keep taking those vitamins you've been taking . . . And let's see?"

The Doctor glanced down at his papers a second or two.

"Ah yes . . . Next visit maybe we will do an ultra-sound. We should be able to let you know if it's a boy or girl."

Jenny looked quizzical when the Doctor mentioned the ultrasound and he couldn't help but notice as he peered up over the top of his reading glasses, at that very moment.

"Mmmm . . . Most Mothers can't wait for the first chance to see their baby."

Jenny chuckled, "Oh I am Doctor but I'm not so sure Fred is?"

Jenny went on to explain Fred's desire to hopefully have a son. Jenny also explained that she knew Fred would be okay with it being a girl, but with everything which had been going on at the farm; Jenny thought maybe it should wait a bit.

"We can keep it a secret for a while Jenny . . . You don't have to tell him right away."

"That's true . . . Oh I want to have the ultrasound and all but I don't want to have to lie to my husband. Will I be able to tell?"

"Hmm . . . Maybe not the first time . . . Mmmm . . . We'll see."

The Doctor laughed and assured Jenny once again that at least for the present, everything looked normal. Of course like all good Doctors, he gave her those last minute reminders and instructions like, don't drink alcohol, don't smoke, get plenty of rest, and whole list of basic pregnancy helpful care tips.

Jenny still felt great when she left the Hospital, and decided to stop at the Pharmacy in Oak grove to pick up some more vitamins, and a few other needs . . .

She turned off of Route 16 onto Main Street and slowly made her way down into the center of town. Oak Grove was a pretty little town, with older

Victorian Homes on both sides for a stretch. It eventually transformed into a small but quaint business district, but only on one side. The other side was mostly open land looking over the River Valley which meandered through the heart of Oak Grove.

There was a small Picnic and Fairground right across from the Town Hall which hosted all sorts of events from fairs, craft shows to band concerts, and boasted an old wooden Bandstand. This is where the Mayor would normally give his Annual Memorial Day Speech and Memorial Day was approaching this coming weekend. Jenny could see some of the town workers making preparations for the Holiday celebration. Red and white Banners were being strung across the old Bandstand and Flags were being hung on the street light poles which lined both sides of the street.

Jenny, being raised in the inner City of Columbus, never really experienced life in a small town like Oak Grove. She in fact never spent much time in a rural country setting.

She did go to Camp once somewhere in Minnesota when she was a child, and hated every minute of it. And although she had lived here with Fred for two years, she never up until now had started to recognize Oak Grove's splendor or the significance of its history.

The main street had angled parking on both sides, she noticed a spot directly in front of the Drug Store and she pulled in. When she got out and looked out into the valley, she suddenly was surprised at what she saw. Straight in front of her, she could see the rising hills of the Shiff and Goodman Farms. "Oh my Gosh" she exclaimed out loud.

Jenny had never noticed this before. Jenny could actually see the spot where she and Fred were perched the day before and the tops of the silos not 100 feet from her house. The trees and new foliage of the summer hid the house and barns but she could see the silos and cows grazing over in one of the pastures. Jenny stood a moment gazing over the horizon while she thought to herself, why haven't I ever noticed this before? She had been here several times before?

Once inside the Drug Store, Jenny was again stricken with the vision of the soda counter. It looked as if it was straight from a rendering of a Norman Rockwell's Picture of a vintage downtown America, complete with its Red vinyl swiveling stools and the old Ice Cream freezers.

She knew it to be this way, as she had seen it before but apparently Jenny had never noticed it in the manner as she did today. Fred had told her that this old Drug Store with the Soda Fountain and all, may in fact be one of the last ones still operating in the Country. Jenny scratched her head over her newly found appreciation of this old store.

She shuffled through the isles picking up some shaving cream and a few other things for Fred. When she turned the corner to the shelves which displayed the vitamins, she saw Sally, Claire's sister.

Sally looked up with a friendly smile. "Hi Jen . . . How are you doing dear."

Sally's voice was sincere and Jenny knew that it was not Sally she should be upset with.

"Fine Sally . . . And you?"

"Okay I guess but I'm getting older that's for sure." And then she laughed.

Sally was a rotund woman, about fifty now, and she was always easy to recognize anywhere because she always wore her long green apron. The one she wore at the diner which had 'The Best Cookin in Town' printed on it.

Fred said he even saw her wearing it in Church one Sunday. Jenny liked Sally and wouldn't press her on the Claire thing but Sally offered up the subject.

"Hey listen . . . About Claire . . . You know she's a little stubborn sometimes but somethin else is goin on with her . . . Dear Lordy!"

"Like what . . . Is she okay?"

"Oh yeah, she's fine . . . Like I said . . . A little headstrong!"

Jenny didn't want to pry so she waited for Sally to further explain.

"Guess about two months ago she met some guy over in Shuntook . . . Bowling or something? Anyway, a week ago she comes home and says she is going to stay over there for a few days and she would be back. Well, we didn't hear from her for about a week. Jim and I were getting a smidge worried and just when we thought we should call the Police or something . . . Guess who walks in . . . Claire. Then she tells us she is going to pick up a few things and asks if we could do without her for a while at the diner. Well, I gave her a piece of my mind . . . You know . . . Living with some guy . . . Not being married and all. But that girl wouldn't listen. Don't know what's gotten into her I tell ya!"

"That's strange Sally . . . Claire never mentioned anything about meeting some guy?"

"Didn't mention it to us either."

Sally looked upset and just kept shaking her head, "Dear Lordy!" Sally repeated several times.

Sally and her husband Jim had run the diner for years and had taken it over from Sally's parents who started it back in the forties. Claire tried going to college but ended up flunking out of one school, tried another, but didn't seem to see the value in a college education.

Sally and Jim let Claire stay with them while she worked at the diner to give Jim and Sally a break now and then. But she didn't seem like the type at all, who would just take off with some guy without really knowing him?

"I'm sorry to hear that Sally . . . I truly am." Jenny sympathetically answered.

"Well . . . We just worry about her and as for that little spat you and she had . . . I told her it was up to her to make things right. She does have a big mouth sometimes and she knew she did wrong. But she doesn't like to admit it that's for sure."

"Don't worry about me . . . I'm more concerned for you. Must be hard at the diner without her help?" Jenny sympathized.

"To tell you the truth . . . Business isn't like it used to be. Not since they put that new rest facility up on the interstate. We use to get a lot of business from travelers to truckers . . . But not anymore. And the local trade, well . . . This town is changing . . . You can see that. The farmers are leaving . . . The Grain and feed left . . . The small shops are going out cause of the new mall over in Sullivan . . . Lordy. No Jim and I will get by . . . I should get back to the diner, it was so nice to see you Jenny and give my best to Fred for us will ya."

"Of course . . . And you take care as well Sally."

Jenny smiled as Sally disappeared around the corner of the isle which they had met in.

Jenny opened up the door to her car but before she got in, she turned once more to look across the valley to the Goodman Farm, her farm. And then she looked back again to the Drugstore which dated back to a different era than the present. This store, this town, and the people who lived here, were they like the last tree of a once lush forest; in line to be felled by a premonition about the future?

A few miles from town, Jenny passed what was once the Willouby Farm, the first casualty of the ominous future for this community. Completely deserted now, Jenny could see the remains of rusted old farm equipment. The house stood back from the road a ways but Jenny could see the broken panes of glass in the second story windows. The Barn was leaning to one side and didn't appear that it would stand much longer.

Jenny remembered Fred telling her the story how Arnold Willouby no longer could operate his farm successfully and took a job as a hired hand on the Petersen Farm. Both Arnold and his wife June, passed away in the late seventies leaving the farm to their only son, Arnold Junior.

Young Arnold had no interest in farming and was a successful business man somewhere in Florida. The property was on the market for a few years and no one knows for sure what Arnold Jr. plans are for the dilapidated farm other than, he keeps the property taxes current. It loomed out as a ghostly reminder to all, what may lie in store for them.

Jenny also recollected the story of old Howard Shiff's prophecy for the farming community. He tried to organize all the farmers and suggested that they band together and possibly form their own co-op and deal directly with major distributors as a whole. But no one could see the future, including Fred's Uncle Harry.

Howard, adhering to his own advice, modernized his farm. His gloomy visions for the future were not unfounded as the Shiff Farm today remains the only productive farm in the county, and one of only a handful remaining in the entire State.

But the thing which bewildered Jenny the most was; why was all this becoming sensitive to her now? All she kept thinking about was that this town was doomed to be extinct, consumed by the greedy appetite of land developers. Unless, she thought, something could be done to slow down the inevitable. But what she wondered? What could be done before this once proud farm land was strewn with malls, condos, and subdivisions, and its heritage lost forever?

Jenny drove up the drive to her farm and as she approached the house, she could see Bailey, paws propped on the window sill, diligently looking out of one of the kitchen windows, anxiously waiting for her return.

CHAPTER TEN
MOMS, DADS, LAWYERS AND DOGS

Jenny Returns from the Drugstore.

"I'm coming Bailey . . . I'm hurrying as fast as I can." Jenny called out to Bailey as she was fumbling for her keys and juggled the packages from the Drug Store. Bailey was whimpering and crying on the other side of the door delighted that Jenny had finally returned home.

"Gosh Bailey . . . Don't tear the door down . . . Hang on Dog!"

Jenny finally pushed her way through the door as Bailey could hardly refrain from jumping all over her, but he did. With his tail wagging a mile a minute, Jenny greeted the beast with a round of affection, by rubbing his head and caressing his floppy ears.

"Hi Bailey . . . . Did you miss me Sweetie Pie? Looks like it . . . Why I remember the time you would hide from me . . . But look at you now! I love you . . . You over grown lap dog. Why the change Sweetie Pie?"

Jenny continued to shower Bailey with loving and petting for a few more moments.

"C'mon Sweetie . . . Let me call Fred. I'm sure he is patiently waiting for me to call . . . To hear how I made out at the Doctor's!"

Jenny filled Fred in about everything that happened and everything the Doctor had said during her visit. Fred was not satisfied until all the details of her exam had been relayed to him in its entirety . . .

"Well . . . I guess the Doctor knows what's up but I'm still worried about you sweetheart." Fred mentioned.

"Then you will just have to come along the next time Fred Goodman . . . And you can ask him yourself!"

"I'll just have to do that. Listen, is it Okay if we have dinner a little earlier than normal?"

"Sure, what's up?"

"Morris Rothenberg called . . . Said the lease papers are already to look at and he would like to stop by early this evening because he will be going out of town for a few days."

"Boy he and Ben work quickly don't they . . . Maybe a little too quickly!"

"Not really Jen . . . Summers coming and Ben wants to move on that deal with Petersen and as long as the papers are sound, I don't see any reason to hold off. By the way I should warn you . . . This guy Morris is a great Attorney but maybe a little on the . . . Let's say . . . Eccentric side!"

"Hmmm . . . I see." Jenny answered kind of brushing Fred's comment off.

"Okay Doll . . . I'll be home about an hour early and Morris said he should be there about 5:30 . . . See ya."

Fred arrived home to find Jenny just finishing up in the preparation of the evening fare with Bailey glued to her side. Yum, Chicken Cordon Blue. That Jenny's quite the cook isn't she! . . .

The table was all set when Fred seated himself. Jenny placed a plate of one of her many specialties in front of her husband. The couple had no sooner finished their dinner and the cleaning of the last dish when Morris announced his arrival with a series of loud knocks, which was even loud enough to startle Bailey.

Jenny was just about to offer the aging Attorney a seat but before she could, Morris plunked his briefcase down on the table and commenced pulling out all sorts of documents placing them into three piles. One set of documents for Fred, one for Jenny, and of course one for himself. Jenny had never met Morris Rothenberg, the longtime Goodman Farm Attorney.

The speedy manor in which the lawyer conducted business did not allow Fred the time to exchange the formality of introducing his wife. Morris had been the attorney for the Goodman Farm for many years and he obviously had done business in this kitchen before. Just as Jenny was about to ask the gentlemen if he would like a drink or a coffee or something, Morris walked over to the cabinets and grabbed a glass filling it with water from the sink.

"Morris this is my wife . . . Jenny." Fred blurted.

The lawyer poked his eyes up for a split second to look toward Jenny.

"You've got great water here Fred . . . Nice to meet you Jenny."

Jenny just smiled and rolled her head to Fred. She tried to extend her hand to Rothenberg but Morris didn't even notice. He took a seat at the table motioning Fred and Jenny to do the same.

Slightly on the portly side, he was a neatly manicured man and dressed in a very modest gray suit. Balding on one side of his head, he did that silly vanity kind of a thing which Jenny always found so amusing with older men; grow it long where they can and comb it over to the other side hoping to hide his obvious loss of hair. It didn't.

"These came to my office yesterday Fred . . . I looked them over and it looks like a clean deal Fred. Didn't see a need for any changes. I'll let you two look it over."

Morris sat back in the chair, crossed one leg over the other and proceeded to roll his pen robustly between the palms of his hands. He looked as if he had set a timer for their perusal.

Jenny was finding this fellow quite interesting. She started reviewing all the legal gobbledy gook, the best she could. It took Fred about five minutes and when he finished he turned to his wife.

"What do you think Hon?"

"Looks great Fred but do you . . ."

Jenny couldn't finish before Morris was glaring up as if he was saying, 'What, a question, How could you possibly have a question?'

Fred nodded, letting Jenny finish her thought.

"Is Three thousand a year fair Fred?"

And Fred was just about to speak when Morris fielded the question but directed the answer to Fred rather than Jenny. How rude, Jenny was thinking to herself but Fred patted her arm hoping she would let it slide.

"Well, you probably could get a little more but if you consider the fact that the barn is idle at the moment. Time will have a way of changing the asset to a liability with increased expenditures for maintenance. I wouldn't advise squeezing young Ben for more, even though he could afford it . . . You might want to look over the list of improvements which will remain the property of the owner rather than the tenant. Also, He is paying a small percentage on the dollar for every gallon of milk yielded from this arrangement along with a statement of accounting and payment on a quarterly basis. Actually I think he has been more than fair."

Fred had a little experience with the other lease deals so he turned to Jenny for the final approval.

"I think it's fine Dear." And Jenny nodded her assent to the deal.

Fred signed the lease in triplicate and before the pen left the paper, Morris Rothenberg scooped up the copies.

"As you can see, Ben has already signed. Keep this one for your records Fred and I'll have a copy of the final Docs delivered to you tomorrow."

As abruptly as the Attorney had arrived, so was his departure.

Fred walked the Lawyer to the door and Jenny moved to the kitchen window and when she saw Attorney Rothenberg's car rolling down the drive . . .

She started roaring with laughter.

"You have got to be kidding me Fred . . . That's your Attorney?"

"I told you he was a little . . . Eccentric!"

"Oh he's eccentric alright but you ought to add in Rude and Snotty."

Fred chuckled a little as well. "Yeah but he knows the Farm Business and stuff. Don't think I'd use him for anything else!"

"How's he know the Farm Business anyway?", Jenny asked as she stood with her arms folded.

"Guess most of his clients are Farmers and besides, He grew up on a farm!"

"He doesn't look like the farmer type . . . Where's his Farm . . . And how come he's a lawyer?" Jenny snipped.

"His Mom and Dad had a three hundred acre spread over in Fulton but he sold it after they died."

"Is it still a farm?"

"Nope . . . Guess he subdivided it and sold it off. What once was his farm, is now a McDonalds, two Gas Stations with Convenience Stores, and a small shopping area . . . Made a bundle I heard."

Jenny smiled and said, "Not such a True Blue Farmer is he Fred"

"Well don't forget . . . He's also an Attorney!" Fred answered with a sarcastic laugh.

"Mmmm . . . I see, but in a way that angers me a little."

"How's that sweetheart?", Fred inquired.

Jenny proceeded to share her thoughts which she mused over earlier that afternoon on her way to and from town and Fred listen with great interest. Jenny's concern grew more heated with intensity, the more she explained . . .

"And it's ruthless greedy men like Morris which lead to the demise of a heritage such as Oak Grove."

Fred was thoroughly surprised with his wife's sudden concern over the plight of this small farming community.

"I didn't know you felt that way Hon . . . What brought this on?"

"I'm not sure . . . I guess it just hit me all of a sudden." Jenny let out a sigh.

Fred could see that Jenny's joyful ranking on Morris Rothenberg had now changed to a genuine serious concern over what she was feeling.

Fred went over to his wife and gave her a long loving hug burying his head into her soft blonde hair. Jenny had unusual features. Although she was a natural blonde, her complexion was more on the darker side. Fred assumed it was a mix from her Mother's Danish heritage and her Father's Slavic ancestry.

"You're just full of surprises." He said as he placed his hands on her shoulders.

"I've seen a lot of changes in this small town Jenny. I've watched siblings of dedicated farmers turn their backs on their Father's and Grandfather's livelihood. My own Father and Brothers included. Yes and unfortunately, unscrupulous land raiders have taken advantage of aging Farmers who without a son or daughter, had no choice but to sell . . . And . . . There have been some children who ran far away from their farms, only to return to collect their inheritance by selling off the Farm with the hopes of capitalizing off those greedy men as you referred to them. Jenny do you have any suggestions on how we might be able to stave off the world of progress and preserve a piece of our history?"

Fred softly rubbed his wife's shoulders as she somberly remained in deep thought.

"I don't know Sweetheart . . . I just don't know . . . But something just occurred to me."

"What's that Jen?"

"You and Ben have the only large Farms left in the County!" And Fred put his arms around Jenny again, and while looking up to the ceiling and taking a deep breath, Fred let out long soft sigh.

At that moment, the couple may not have disclosed to each other what their individual private moment of visions were, but time would reveal their mutual revelations to each other. Jenny went to straighten up her office a little, while Fred went upstairs to get back to task of preparing his studio for his next Andross project . . .

Fred heard the squeaking and moaning of the old wood plank floor with every step Jenny had made as she approached the studio, this time from the main hallway.

Jenny swung the old door open and it made the sound similar to someone scratching a chalkboard with their finger nails.

"Oooh . . . Guess Bailey and I can't sneak up here this way either . . . Can we?"

"Nope . . . Heard you coming with the very first step you guys took on the stairway down near the Parlor!"

Jenny looked down at her belly.

"Not much yet but soon I'll probably weigh as much as Bailey! No offense Sweetie . . . But you are quite a large load!" Jenny said as she playfully slapped Bailey on his backside and laughed.

Bailey made a slight gruff as if he might have been insulted or something.

Fred smiled while shaking his head and waited for his wife to continue.

"Hmmm . . . Well . . . Would you mind too much or would I be bothering you if I made a few calls up here? Thought I should call my Mom . . . About the news."

"Not at all . . . I enjoy your company and maybe when you're done . . . I should call my Dad. I'm just clearing out some stuff on the computer."

"Are you all set to go with the new project?" Jenny asked

"Yep . . . Pretty much." Fred answered quickly.

Fred continued focusing on his monitor and Jenny curled up on the large sofa which Fred had brought in from one of the spare rooms on the second floor. It was an old Victorian piece and had seen a lot of use and it was so worn that you actually would fall into the sofa rather than, sit on it! Fred insisted that the couch was for 'think tanking' as he called it; for meditating over ideas for his projects but Jenny had found him sound asleep a few times when he was busy working on his projects, but she understood.

Fred kept a full platter in front of him most of the time with his full time job, the farm, his freelance ventures, and of course, a wife. She never could understand where all of his energy and drive came from but she sure was glad she had found a man like that. As she tucked her legs up onto the sofa she warmly looked over to her husband who was busy at his computer.

Fred happened to glance up and see his wife smiling and staring in his direction.

"What's so funny . . . What are you smiling at dear? Did I do something wrong or something?"

"You haven't done a thing wrong Fred. I just love you Fred . . . You're a terrific guy . . . . Have I told you that lately?"

"Ah . . . no" Fred shook his head a little with a humorous quizzical look upon his face and then went right back to work on his computer passing off his wife's womanly sentiment.

Jenny had a pleasant conversation with her Mother. Her Dad was out of town on a job, as usual, but Fred could tell Jenny was very excited and enjoyed the call with her Mother. The days to follow would be filled with many calls from her sisters, Aunts and Cousins, all ready to give Jenny a whole bunch of free advice on child rearing and offers to help out in any way they could . . .

Fred stopped what he was doing and went over to the sofa and plumped down next to his wife and placed his hand on her lap.

"Well that went very well didn't it sweetheart?"

Jenny, still smiling answered, "Yeah . . . Mom really never has anything negative to say and she always has been pretty supportive but I'm sure I'll get an earful from Mr. Bachman!"

From what Fred knew of Jenny's Dad, and some of the stories she had told, he was sure that would be the case.

Jenny never had much love or respect for her Dad which was sad indeed. He was never home very much for his wife or children and when he was, he was nothing more to them than a lecture filled tense time. He was the type of self-righteous man who was always criticizing or belittling all of them. Although Jenny was always sweet and cordial to her Father, to his face, she continually referred to him as Mr. Bachman otherwise, as if he were a complete stranger. Fred assumed that the man was exactly that to his daughters, a total stranger. He didn't even make it to their wedding. Jenny's Uncle John did the honors of giving the bride away and of course Jenny's Dad did not approve of her choice in a husband but that really didn't bother Fred.

Jenny appeared to be content however and Fred took the phone from her hand, sat back on the couch and started to dial. "My turn." He said with a smile on his face.

"Hello . . . Dad . . . How you doing?"

"Just fine son." Fred's Dad answered normally like he does but continued on with a slight bit of sarcasm.

"Hear you doing pretty good yourself Fred . . . Made a new deal with Shiff I hear and . . . Going to start a new family I hear. When do you think you were going to get around to letting your Mom know Fred? You know how women are about things like that . . . They like to be the first told you know."

Fred was flabbergasted and slightly caught off guard. Jenny sat up a little and gave Fred a concerned type of look.

"Ah . . . Sorry Dad, we just found out last week and we were waiting for Jenny's next appointment, which was yesterday . . . To be sure . . . You can understand that? We weren't leaving anybody out."

"Oh I understand son but your Mother . . . Well that might be a different story."

"How did you find out already Dad?"

Fred's Dad laughed, "C'mon Fred . . . You live in Oak Grove . . . You can't keep anything a secret . . . For more than five minutes anyway."

The elder Goodman continued to chuckle, "You also forget Fred that even though you're Mother and I moved to Florida . . . We still have friends in Oak Grove."

"Oh yeah . . . Guess I forgot about that Dad. Is Mom there?"

"Nope . . . She is over at a friends but don't worry, I'll smooth things over for ya. Call her tomorrow."

With a more cordial tone in his voice, Mr. Goodman went on, "So did you get the corn planted this year Fred."

"Ah . . . No . . . But your about the fifth person who has asked me that . . . Didn't think it would matter much to you Dad."

"Look Son . . . Even though I detested the farming life . . . Doesn't mean I'm against anybody who happens to like it. You always had a passion for it. That's why I never kept it from you. Your Uncle Harry would be rolling over in his grave if he found out you are letting another year go by without the Goodman corn."

"Ah yeah . . . Actually I'm going to be turning over some fields this summer for next year."

"Well . . . Get to it boy . . . Your Uncle Harry and Aunt Ruthie didn't leave you that place to be just raising kids on it."

Fred was slightly surprised with his Father's words. He and Fred never really discussed much about the farm but Fred felt somewhat honored and inspired by his Father's support. Fred always felt as if his Dad was harboring other misgivings about the Farm, sort of like he was hiding something from Fred. Fred never really had the gumption to ask his Father for his true feelings.

They closed off the conversation with a run down about Fred's brothers, the latest in Oak Grove, and a few political discussions. Fred felt assured his Mom would understand. After Fred got off the phone, he turned his attention back to Jenny.

Letting out a deep sigh Fred turned to his wife and said, "Guess we took care of that little detail . . . I think it's time to get some sleep."

Fred started to lean forward on the sofa to get up enough momentum to stand but Jenny gently pulled him back. She tenderly and quietly said, "I'm sorry Fred."

He looked a trifle confused. "Sorry about what?"

"Well . . . If I had just kept my big trap shut and didn't blab my mouth off to Claire . . . Well . . . You wouldn't have had to be so much on the defensive with your Dad and most likely your Mom."

"Ah . . . Don't be silly Jenny. Dad didn't seem that upset and besides . . . That's history and it's all forgotten about."

Fred once again leaned forward and made his second attempt to get up but once again Jenny pulled him back into the worn seat of the sofa however this time, with a playful manor.

"Now what?"

Jenny slightly giggled, "Remember that night we had that . . . That little argument about Roger and Claire spoiling our little secret?"

"Yeah . . . So?"

"Remember I asked you about when we should tell the folks and you said, with big mouths like Claire and Roger . . . You wouldn't be surprised that in a few days that the whole darn world would know!"

"Yeah?" Fred said in a kind of manor which sort of implied, 'But what's the big deal about that?'

Jenny chirped, "Guess you were right!"

Fred gave Jenny a weird kind of look and while shaking his head said, "Your silly . . . You know that don't you . . . I love you anyway . . . Now can we get to bed?"

Jenny laughed, "Yes . . . Now we can go to Bed my tired husband . . . But be careful when you get . . ."

Fred didn't let Jenny finish and as he lurched up out of the sofa. Fred did not realize that Bailey had lain down in front of Jenny on the floor, wedged between the sofa and the coffee table. Fred proceeded to step on Bailey's head. Bailey let out a wail that was deafening and bounded up so quickly that he knocked Fred over the coffee table and on to the floor on the other side. Fred lay on his back with his arms spread out.

"AGHHHHH . . . You stupid dog!"

Jenny got up and rushed to her husband's side showing some concern but at the same time barely holding back some laughter as it was quite a humorous site to see.

"Are you okay Fred?" She murmured as she stroked her husband's forehead.

Fred picked up his head and looked at Jenny.

"What's with that beast anyway . . . He's stuck to you like glue lately!"

"Fred, I tried to warn you but you didn't let me finish when you so abruptly stood up."

To make matters worse Bailey moved over to Fred, showing his concern for his master and started licking Fred's face.

"Oh stop it will ya . . . You king-sized lap dog you. Jenny, when did he sneak in front of us?"

"When you were talking to your Dad and I wouldn't think that a one hundred and fifty pound dog could actually sneak into that space without you seeing him."

"Oh sure . . . Now you defend him . . . About a month ago you were ready to send him to the pound, when he was sneaking up on you!"

Jenny with a very indignant tone in her voice answered, "Fred Goodman . . . Things have changed between Bailey and I . . . That's history and all is forgotten . . . Just like you just said . . . I would have never sent this sweet adorable puppy to the pound! How could you say such a thing?"

Jenny started rubbing Bailey's ears and he whimpered with delight over her affection.

Fred groaned, "Jeez, Sweet adorable puppy my _____! Will you help me up so we can finally get some sleep . . . Jeez!"

Well, the threesome made their way down the front stair case and Jenny waited with Fred in the kitchen while Bailey took his evening ramble out in the pasture. Fred really wasn't very mad at Bailey about the circus act in which Bailey aided Fred in performing up in the studio. As a matter of fact, Fred had been feeling a little uneasy and at the same time, intrigued by Bailey's sudden guardianship over Jenny. What did Bailey perhaps know that Fred didn't?

But both Jenny and Fred would eventually find true meaning in that old adage, 'Man's best friend'!

Chapter Eleven
The Parade Passes By

The rest of the week was basically uneventful and Jenny appeared to be in good spirits.

Fred and Dave Baker scurried that Friday evening to install the passenger seat in the Divco Milk Truck. This was so Rube could make his appearance as a passenger in the Town's Memorial Day Festivities which was scheduled for the next Morning.

Fred had to look high and low for the spare seat which came with the Divco. The extra seat had been removed to allow the delivery driver to simply step out of the truck without the seat getting in the way. Fred knew it was around somewhere because he had seen it nearby, but couldn't quite remember where it was kept. Fred finally uncovered its hiding place, way up in the loft of the old corn barn. He marveled at what great shape it was in. Rube and Harry certainly were meticulous about any and all of the Farms equipment.

Both Fred and Jenny arose early that Saturday Morning. Fred had just let Bailey in from his morning saunter when Jenny shuffled into the kitchen, dressed and ready to go for the day.

"Fred . . . What time is Jeremy and Rube showing up to get the truck?"

"Jeremy said they would get here about 9:30." Fred said while pouring himself and Jenny a cup of coffee.

"Why so early?" Jenny inquired.

Fred smiled and took a seat at the table, "Oh . . . Maybe Rube wants to look the Farm over and see if I'm doing all the right things!"

Jenny smiled but got up quickly from the table, "Be right back . . . Don't want to forget!" And with that Jenny disappeared into the parlor.

Fred was curious but sat back in his chair and gazed out the kitchen window, impressed with the morning view of the lower acreage and noticing the slight whispers of steam hovering over the Shuntook River.

Jenny returned cradling a pile of picture frames and loose photos. She placed them down on the table and started to spread them out for Fred to see.

"Look what I found the other day Fred."

"Where did you find these Jenny?" Fred mused as he started to peruse the old photographs of the Farm, Uncle Harry and Aunt Ruthie, and of course Rube.

"Well some of these were on the wall in the parlor and the other day, I was in the room we are going to turn into the nursery, and I found a ton of these photos in a box in the corner. Thought Rube might get a kick out of them!"

Fred smiled and exclaimed, "Wow . . . Some of these are real old . . . Look at this one of Rube dressed in his Milkman's uniform, hat, tie and all!"

"That has to go back to the fifties Huh Fred . . . And look at this one!"

Jenny held up a wedding picture of Uncle Harry and Ruthie!

"Whoa . . . These are something else!" Fred looked up to Jenny who was standing by his side as they meandered through the pile of memories.

"That was very thoughtful of you Jenny . . . What made you think to do this?"

Jenny smiled, "It's funny how many times we pass through that old parlor and don't always see what's really there . . . There must be over a hundred framed photos hanging on the walls or propped on tables. When you called Jeremy Thursday evening, I decided to see if there was something we could show Rube when he came to get the truck. Since they are arriving early . . . Maybe he can take some time to look them over!"

An hour passed while Fred reminisced about his experiences on the farm and the history of the old Goodman Estate.

Rube finally arrives . . .

Jenny noticed Jeremy's car driving slowly up the driveway and she and Fred both stepped out on to the rear stoop to greet them.

Jeremy got out of the car quickly and walked to the passenger side to help Rube out of the car. Rube was dressed in black pants and had on a light blue shirt, sporting a bright red tie.

As Rube stood, having to use a cane to support himself and get his bearings, he slowly moved his eyes over the farm.

After a moment or two, he quickly moved his head in Fred and Jenny's direction, "Where's the truck Fred? I don't see the darn truck!"

Fred smiled, "It's in the barn Rube . . . I'll pull it around in a minute. Since you're a little early, why don't you and Jeremy come in side for a cup of coffee or tea!"

Rube who was starting to feel the symptoms of Dementia, stood for a moment looking confused.

"Jeremy . . . Jeremy who . . . Oh yeah . . . My Nephew!" And Rube started to walk around the car toward the kitchen stoop.

Jeremy went to help Rube support his walk and Rube quickly responded, "Oh Bolder Dash . . . I don't need your help . . . I can still walk without your help!"

Jeremy smiled and backed off a little bit as both Fred and Jenny walked over to Rube to greet him.

Jenny gave Rube a big Hug, "Hi Rube . . . Good to see you . . . Nice day for the parade . . . Why don't you come inside . . . I have something to show you."

"Huh." Is all Rube said as he slowly walked toward Fred and the Farm House?

Fred beamed a big smile, shook Rubes hand and gave him a gentle sort of bear hug, "Nice to have you back on the Farm Rube . . . We have missed you!"

Rube stopped and quickly looked around again, "Where's the corn . . . I don't see no corn Fred?"

"Ah . . . Next year Rube . . . Next year I promise." Fred answered not really knowing how Rube would respond."

"Bolder Dash . . . Next Year . . . Next year . . . It's always next year with you young whipper snappers!" Rube shook his head and continued on to the kitchen stoop.

Fred exchange a quick hello and hand shake with Jeremy and Jenny held Rubes arm as they maneuvered up the steps to the stoop.

Fred leaned over to Jeremy and whispered, "How's he doing?"

"Not so good Fred . . . He's failing fast. I wasn't quite sure he was going to make it today. One minute he's with it and the next . . . He's in another world."

"Hmmm . . . It's sad to see." And Fred continued, "There was a time that man could have picked you up under one arm and me under the other and then thrown us on the roof. Now look at him!" Fred uttered.

"Yeah . . . Sad indeed . . . I just hope he goes peacefully when it's his time. I'm afraid that's not too much longer from now." Jeremy Lamented.

Both Fred and Jeremy watched as Jenny held the screen door open for Rube. But just before he stepped in the foyer, Rube stopped, then backed off and started to kick off his shoes.

"You don't have to do that Rube." Jenny insisted.

He answered, "Don't want to catch the dickens from Ruthie . . . Big trouble if you track Doo Doo on her clean kitchen floor."

Jenny didn't quite know what to say. She remembered Fred telling her the story of how Ruthie insisted Harry and Rube, remove their boots before they entered the house after working the fields. Jenny helped Rube take his shoes off, and then turned and smiled at Fred and Jeremy. It was obvious Rube was living in two different dimensions, one of yesterday and one of today. You really didn't know for sure when it would switch on him.

Once inside, Jenny helped Rube to a kitchen chair and started to show Rube and Jeremy the photos she had uncovered.

Rube looked over the photos with intensity but without saying too much. Occasionally you would see him smile but suddenly he turned to Jenny, "You didn't by any chance, find the picture of me and the Governor?"

Jenny paused a moment, "I don't think so . . . Wait a minute . . . I'll be right back."

Jenny scurried out of the kitchen and shortly returned holding a large portrait.

"Is this the one you meant Rube?" She held the portrait down so Rube could see it.

"Yep . . . That's Governor . . . What's his name . . ."

Rube paused, "Gull dang it . . . Can't remember his name . . . Anyway . . . See me shaking his hand? Got an award for . . ."

Rube paused again, "Holy tarnation's . . . Can't remember what I got an award for either . . . But anyway . . . That's me shaking his hand."

Jenny held the picture up for Fred to see and he shrugged his shoulders. No one in the room knew the name of the Governor Rube was shaking hands with or what award he received. Only Rube knew, and he forgot.

Poor Rube, for some reason or another, that portrait had some sort of significance to the old timer. After all, he asked about it but he couldn't connect its importance at the time. But Jenny and Fred would uncover the secret of that portrait in later years!

It was time for the Parade . . .

Jeremy and Jenny helped Rube out to the driveway while Fred went and got the Milk truck out. When Fred pulled up to the kitchen door, all stood smiling in wonder. The Truck looked terrific.

But Rube stood there, totally stricken with the site. And not remembering Fred telling him a few short weeks ago about the trucks need for repairs, exclaimed with glee, like that of a young child at Christmas time, "Oh Gosh by Golly . . . It's a beaut Fred . . . You kept it up just like you promised!"

Fred felt a little sheepish as he knew he kind of had neglected the old Divco this past year. Fred got out and walked over to Rube and took him by the hand to help him into the truck.

Rube turned to Fred and as he did he could see a few small tears running down Rubes face. Fred reached around to Rube's back pocket and pulled the handkerchief out. Rube always carried one with him. A bright white handkerchief, neatly folded with one corner protruding out of his pocket. Fred handed it to Rube and he slowly wiped his eyes.

Fred helped Rube into the passenger seat while Jeremy made sure Rube was fastened in securely as the sliding door, would be open for the Parade.

Fred flipped Jeremy the keys and Jeremy jumped into the driver's seat. "Drive careful now." Fred stated and Jeremy gave Fred the thumbs up.

Fred put the window down on Rubes side and slid the door closed issuing instructions to Rube, "Now don't slide this door open till you're actually in the Parade."

Rube was still speechless. Fred patted the top of Rubes hand which he had rested on the bottom of the window opening and Rube suddenly grabbed Fred's hand with his other. Rube and Fred stood there, motionless for quite a few seconds, looking right into each other's eyes.

Jeremy started the old Divco and put it in drive. Fred was choked up, and so was Rube. Somehow they both knew. Just before Jeremy slowly started moving forward, Rube choked out his final spoken words before he left for the Parade.

"Watch over this Farm Fred . . . Harry, Ruthie and I are counting on you." And with that, the truck slowly moved down the Drive.

Fred stood there for a minute as the Divco finally disappeared behind the trees. Fred turned to his wife. Jenny too had tears streaming out of her eyes. Fred went over to his wife and wrapped his arms around her.

Fred was a strong man, but Fred new this was the end of a legend.

The Parade went off like a charm . . .

Fred and Jenny went to the festivities, their eyes were filled with joy as the Old Milk Truck and Rube crawled down Maine Street right behind the National Guard Marching Band, who was playing their version of John Philip Souza's, Stars and Stripes Forever.

But it was only a few days later . . .

The Town of Oak Grove gathered again. This time, the community joined together to commemorate the passing of a Town Patriarch and a vestige of an era about to disappear.

Rube Gildman passed away, in his sleep, two days after his last appearance with his old friend, the Goodman Farm Divco Milk Delivery Truck.

Chapter Twelve
The Summer Flies By

The summer was over before you knew it!

Ben Shiff made good on all his promises to help Fred get the fields ready. He even sent his mechanics over to help Fred start up and check out all the equipment making preparations for the re-debut of the Goodman Farm.

Fred turned over about 300 acres for the next season and even managed to build a small service road up to the top acreage. This is where he and Jenny sat after Church one day early in the summer admiring the view of the valley and contemplating the Farms history and its future! On a whim, Fred turned over about 2 acres for a special project, pumpkins!

Darcy and Jenny, believe it or not, hit it off very well and were starting to become real good friends. Just as well because Jenny's relationship with Claire never re-emerged. Claire was still among the missing.

Oh yes, sixty new Holsteins took up residency in the front Goodman barn. Bailey spent a lot of his time, when he wasn't glued to Jenny's side, investigating and hanging out with the lady cows!

If anyone is wondering what ever happened to poor Roger, he finally faced some reality and asked Ben Shiff for a job. Amazingly enough, Roger was doing fairly well. Besides running some of the equipment and being an all- around farm hand, Roger helped Ben design and install some new software programs on the Shiff computers to help with inventory and tally spread sheets. Ben was very impressed and was getting along fine with Roger. Who would have guessed, but Roger still avoided Fred's calls. Fred could only hope that time would heal Roger's resentment toward Fred.

Of course the summer was marred by the passing of Rube Gildman. The Town of Oak Grove dedicated the Fourth of July ceremonies to this icon of the small farming community. Fred took Rube's death with dignity and turned his grieving into a renewed inspiration and drive to the re-birthing of this once proud Goodman Farm; in honor of this dedicated farmer and of course Fred's Uncle Harry and Aunt Ruthie.

The Andross project turned out to be a success and quite lucrative for Fred. He also signed two more special jobs with Andross. Jenny and Fred were ecstatic over these ventures as Jenny's work load had dropped off considerably, perhaps just as well as the pregnancy had set in hard and Jenny appeared to be having a tough time of it.

But not all was to be a rosy outlook for the Goodman's. Come late September the prospects for continued good news for the young couple, came to an abrupt rude awakening . . .

It was once again a Friday and Fred loved the end of the week. He always looked forward to getting back to the farm and working on all his projects over the weekends. With a renewed interest in the farming life, Fred's latest attentions turned to the Farm Stand. He had recently found the time to repair the roof and make plans for the grand re-opening next summer of his Aunt Ruthie's favorite passion.

But this indeed was to be an unusual Friday. John Fairbanks announced an important mandatory meeting earlier in the week which was to be held today at 9:00 AM. Everybody in the firm was expected to show up promptly. Rumors had been flying around the office like wildfire for the last three weeks; John Fairbanks had been in many closed door meetings with several unknown executive looking gentlemen.

Some were concerned about a close down and others wondered if a 'buy out' was in the offing. For some reason, Fred really didn't seem to be concerned one way or another. He was probably too wrapped up in all his thoughts about the farm, Jenny, and his new family.

*Well, all doubt was removed in the first two minutes
of the meeting . . .*

John Fairbanks, who was known for getting to the
point very quickly, but with emotion and regret,
announced the sale of the firm to three investors
from New York City.

The new company would be moving but John
Fairbanks who had always watched out for his
employees, secured generous provisions for his staff.

Fred along with two other graphic designers, were
given the exclusive rights, if so desired, to continue
independently with two selected accounts each.
Fairbanks took care of all the fees and legalities and
each also received a small severance. The clerical
and the remainder of the staff received a generous
bonus and quite a substantial severance. So despite
the closing in just one month, nobody felt concerned
about their future.

Still, even after hearing this climatic news, Fred
had no negative reaction to any of this. Perhaps
because of his developing relationship with Andross
Foods, along with the acquiring of two more
profitable free-lance accounts, and the opportunity
to work at home. Fred appeared to be almost
nonchalant about the turn of events. Some of the
employees showed concern and sadness, yet others
like Fred were very reserved about their feelings.

Fairbanks closed out the meeting with an invitation
to an informal lunch to be held the following week.
Fairbanks also prepared written out instructions for

the staff regarding the closing down operations, and announced an early release for all the employees this Friday. With that, John Fairbanks left the office with the three execs from New York.

Fred seized the opportunity and left the office as soon as he could despite the insistence by others to linger at the office and kibitz or discuss the events this morning had ushered in.

While driving home, about 4 hours earlier than normal, he decided to wait until he got back to the farm to tell Jenny the good, or the not so good news. Fred couldn't decide which it was but he did know that something of urgency was insisting that he drive a little faster than normal.

Fred felt somewhat puzzled over his emotions and his present lack of un-decidedness as to what he should be feeling over this new development in his life. Should he be worried or be happy and excited? He didn't know, but Fred was always a firm believer that all things happen for a reason. We just don't always know what that reason is, at the beginning of those changes in our lives.

Occupying his mind the whole commute back to the farm with mundane trivia, Fred just shrugged his shoulders as he drove up the drive to the house. As he passed the front barn he saw the cows being led out to the pasture, and he smiled.

Fred noticed Darcy's car parked near the house. That in itself was not abnormal because Darcy had been spending quite a bit of time at the farm lately. But Fred did start feeling very apprehensive as he walked to the back door and saw that the screen was completely ripped out from the outside door. He paused slightly but then bolted into the kitchen. Fred threw his briefcase on the table and briskly walked toward the front hallway door. He was just about to holler out for Jenny when Darcy bolted into the kitchen, and was startled by Fred's presence.

"Oh Fred . . . We tried to call you . . . First at work and they said you left and then on the cell!" Darcy exclaimed while she held her hand to her chest.

Fred took his cell phone out and saw that the battery was dead, "Darn . . . I gotta make sure this doesn't happen again . . . Darn!"

Fred refocused to the situation, "Is everything okay, and is Jenny okay?" Fred spurted out in a concerned tone.

"Yes . . . I mean no . . . Let me explain. She's fine now but I guess she fell in the back hallway. She said she got dizzy and she also said Bailey tried to hold her up. But when I got here she was still on the floor. Anyway . . . Jenny's seems okay now . . . She's just resting in bed but she appears okay."

Darcy was talking a mile a minute so Fred interrupted her, "Did you call the Doctor?"

"No . . . She wouldn't let me . . . But . . ."

Fred interrupted again, "Were you here when she fell?"

"Yes . . . No not exactly."

"What do you mean not exactly Darcy?" Fred's impatience was beginning to show.

"Well I was down at the barn picking up some paperwork for Ben and just as I was getting into the car, Bailey came barging down the drive barking his head off and motioning back and forth to the house, so I drove up here. I saw the door screen ripped apart and followed Bailey right to Jenny."

Fred paused a moment and then said, "That dog! Mmmm . . . Darcy, can you stay a while? Let me go see Jenny and see what's going on with her? Maybe I might need your help for something . . . Or something?"

"Sure Fred . . . I was just coming in here to make her some tea. Of course I'll wait . . . Go . . . Go see Jenny."

With that Darcy lightly pushed on Fred's shoulder motioning him toward the door.

Swiftly walking down the back hallway, Fred hesitated for a brief moment before entering the master bedroom. He first peeked in so as not to disturb Jenny if she was sleeping. He was surprised to see her propped up against the head boards with all the pillows as a cushion, reading . . . A Farm Equipment Catalog. . . Huh?

Jenny looked up as Fred came to her side of the bed, of course Fred had to coax Bailey out of the way slightly, and then Fred sat on the edge of the bed.

"Hi sweetheart." Jenny responded to Fred's appearance acting as if nothing had happened.

Fred took one finger and pulled away the catalog so he could peer down and see what she was so engrossed in or pretending to be engrossed in.

"Mmmm . . . Planning on buying a new tractor Jenny?" Fred said in a soft funny tone.

Jenny with a smug look set upon her lips answered, "Maybe . . . But they don't seem to have the color I want."

Fred could tell Jenny was going to try to make light of what had just happened and she appeared to be her normal self, maybe just a touch pale, but in good spirits.

"And what color would that be dear?"

"Pink . . . All they seem to have is stupid red or green . . . Do they make pink tractors Fred?"

Fred chuckled, "Ah . . . No . . . I don't think so but maybe I could special order you one. Now let's stop this nonsense. What happened today Sweetheart? How ya feeling?" Fred took the magazine from her hands and tossed it to the foot of the bed.

"I'm fine . . . Just felt a little dizzy . . . That's all. It's happened a few times, you know that."

"Yeah but this time you fell. You could of seriously hurt yourself." Fred exclaimed as he rubbed his hands through Jenny's hair, probably looking for some bumps or bruises.

"Fred don't be silly, I'm fine . . . Besides Bailey was here and helped me to the floor."

Fred looked down to Bailey and stroked the top of his head.

"Hmmm . . . Good job Bailey . . . Glad you were around boy. Well I think we should call the Doctor, I'll do that in a minute. Darcy's making you some tea."

"Fred, don't be silly . . . I'm fine . . . Besides I just saw the Doctor a week ago. I'm not going to the Doctors. It's bad enough Darcy called you away from work."

That's right, Fred thought to himself. Jenny thinks he was home early because Darcy called him? Now would not be a good time to tell her about the Fairbanks situation. Fred decided to wait till later.

"I'll go see what's keeping Darcy with your tea. And I'm going to at least call the Doctor and let him know what happened."

"Fred . . ." Jenny rebutted in a disapproving note.

Fred ignored Jenny and hurried back to the kitchen to find Darcy sipping a cup of tea and she motioned to Fred that a hot cup of coffee was sitting on the table awaiting his return . . .

"Thanks Darcy . . . How'd you know I like coffee?"

"Ah Fred . . . How many times in the last few months have I been here when you came home from work. Jenny always gets you a cup of coffee! . . . How's Jenny?"

"She seems okay . . . Looks a little pale. She doesn't want me to but, I'm going to call the Doctor. To at least let him know what happened."

Darcy stood up and grabbed another cup of tea which was sitting on the counter, "Good idea Fred. I'll bring this to Jenny."

With that, Darcy disappeared through the door and Fred grabbed the phone from the wall and sat back down at the table.

Fred trusted in Doctor Chapman and had even gone to several of Jenny's appointments with her in the recent months.

After listening to Fred's story about the events of the day, the Doctor did not appear to be too alarmed over the incident but also suggested that he should bring Jenny in for an exam early Monday morning. Jenny was having appointments now every two weeks as her pregnancy was well into the second trimester but the Doc thought it best to see her sooner. Trying not to alarm Fred, the Doctor did instruct Fred to watch her closely and if something else similar was to occur, bring her immediately to the hospital. Fred was concerned despite the Doctors reassurance.

Fred sat at the table and cupped his hands to his face.

"Wow" he said to himself out loud, "What a bunch of stuff to work out!"

Just as he said that, Darcy came back into the kitchen and saw Fred mumbling to himself.

"Fred, are you okay . . . What did the Doctor say?"

Fred waved his hand up slightly.

"Well, he said he wasn't too concerned but at the same time, he wants to see Jenny first thing Monday morning! Jeez . . . Doctors . . . Sometimes you have to read between the lines with those guys . . . Jeez! Don't worry but make sure you come in first thing Monday he says! Don't worry . . . Hah! . . . And with everything else that happened today!"

With that, Fred stopped. I guess he didn't want to make the same mistake he made before with Roger and, speak out of turn so to say. Better that he wait and tell Jenny first about the Fairbanks closing.

Darcy was quick to pick up on Fred's last comment and said, "Something else wrong Fred?"

Fred waived his hand up again, "Ahh . . . You'll find out about it tomorrow I'm sure."

Darcy and Jenny always went grocery shopping together on Saturday mornings and Fred was going to have to tell Jenny today about Fairbanks, whether he wanted to or not.

"Fred . . . Well I have to go now unless you need me for anything else?"

Fred stood up, "Naw, You've done enough today and thanks . . . Thanks for being here for Jenny."

Darcy smiled, "Glad I could help but it was Bailey who was the hero today. I was just fortunate to be down at the barn. That dog is something else I'll say. Call if you need anything Fred."

"Yeah. . . Bailey is something else that's for sure! Thanks again for all your help Darcy."

Fred walked Darcy to the door and looked down at the screen door which Bailey had destroyed on his mission to alert someone about Jenny's fall.

"Another job on the list I guess?" Fred smirked.

Darcy left and Fred slowly walked back into the kitchen and to his surprise, Jenny was standing near the table, dressed in her clothes but wearing her wooly long bed robe. And without surprise, Bailey was right by her side.

Fred motioned for Jenny to sit and as they sat at the kitchen table, Fred not only told her about the conversation with Doctor Chapman and the upcoming appointment, but he filled her in about why in fact he was home so early.

Fred left nothing out of all the details regarding the Fairbanks crisis earlier that day. Expecting concern and some disappointment from Jenny, Fred was surprised once again, to see just the opposite type of reaction from his wife!

"Gosh Fred . . . That's kinda good news don't you think? You always dreamed of getting your own freelance interests going. You know . . . Working at home . . . Starting up the farm again. Wow. What a great set of circumstances for us Fred. And two more great projects with Andross . . . I think it's all terrific."

Fred didn't quite seem as enthused as Jenny.

"Yeah, I guess."

"Why Fred Goodman . . . What on earth is wrong with you? . . . Are you forgetting about your own philosophies you have been trying to convince me of?"

Jenny stood up. In an animated type of voice which sounded as if she was trying to imitate her husband, Jenny said, "You always have to look below the surface at things Jenny. Everything happens for a reason dear. Look for the silver lining . . . Ha . . . Remember Fred?"

Bailey even stood and joined in the lecture by wagging his tail and ruffed now and then while Jenny preached Fred's theories back to him.

Fred chuckled and said, "Do I really sound like that Jenny?" Fred leaned over and stroked Bailey's head.

"Sometimes Fred . . . You always speak with a great deal of confidence, you know." Jenny laughed.

Fred smiled and gently encouraged his wife to sit on his lap, which she did.

"Guess I'm worried about you sweetheart?"

"Fred . . . There's nothing to worry about. You'll see when we go to the doctors Monday. Oh my Gosh . . . What about your work Fred?"

"It's all set. I called Fairbanks right after I talked to the Doctor. No problem he said . . . Very understanding as a matter of fact. But I do have to be there next Wednesday. John has the attorneys coming in with the contracts for MY two new accounts and I guess he arranged a phone conference with Allied Packaging and Commodities LTD."

Jenny leaned over and gave her husband a kiss on the forehead, "Those are two of the best accounts aren't they Fred?"

"Well . . . There steady accounts. Fairbanks has had them for years. Won't make a fortune I suppose but it will be a stable income that's for sure."

Fred paused a moment, and sighed. Then with a burst of anxiety blurted out, "Pink Tractor . . . Jenny, do you know something I don't"

"Like what Fred?" Jenny had a smirk upon her face.

"About the baby . . . PINK tractor??"

"Ah C'mon Fred I was just teasing. We agreed, remember . . . We would BOTH wait to see if he baby was a boy or a . . . A girl!"

Jenny smiled and rubbed her hand across Fred's face, "I wouldn't go back on my word sweetheart."

And that was true. About the beginning of July, both Jenny and Fred decided it would be better to wait to find out which gender the new Goodman Farm 'Person' would be.

Fred just looked up at his wife with somewhat of a doubtful look, "Hmmm!"

The three Goodman's, Jenny, Fred, and Bailey, lingered in the kitchen for the remainder of the day. Fred insisted on making dinner for Jenny and prepared a great meal of spaghetti and meatballs! Fred was not without culinary talent himself and he also made a delicious double fudge mousse for dessert!

Chapter Thirteen
Good Things and Bad Things

Monday Morning at Jenny's Doctor Appointment.

Fred tried to sit as quietly and as patiently as he could. Several times he even muttered out his frustrations, quietly of course.

"These are the most uncomfortable chairs I have ever sat in! You would think that a hospital like this could afford better chairs . . . Jeez . . . What's taking so long? Doesn't matter what time you go to the Doctors I guess, you always have to wait! You wouldn't think that a Doctor could get that far behind at 10 o'clock in the morning . . . Jeez!"

Just as Fred stood and decided to look at the pictures on the wall, as he did three times already, a frumpy old nurse barged through the door next to the receptionist's window, "Goodman, Mr. Fred Goodman?"

She peered around the waiting room impatiently awaiting a response from the Mr. Fred Goodman, even though Fred was the only one in the darn waiting room!

Fred shrugged his shoulders and responded with a good deal of sarcasm, "That would be me!" and then he followed her through the hallway.

Fred followed the waddling nurse until she stopped, opened a door and with a waving hand said, "The Doctor will be with you two shortly."

Jenny was sitting in a chair and she smiled at her husband and patted the chair next to her, "Hi Hon, Come sit."

The nurse shut the door with a slight slam and Fred looked down at the chair. It was the same as the ones out in the waiting room.

"No way . . . I'll stand . . . Besides, those aren't chairs, they're torture racks!" Fred was still in a sarcastic mood apparently.

Jenny smiled, "I'm sorry it took so long . . . They did a lot of blood work and tests and things."

"That's okay . . . What did the Doctor say?"

"Not much . . . Said he would come in and talk to both of us in here."

Jenny could tell Fred was noticeably concerned as he slowly started pacing from one end of the room to the other gazing up at the pictures and health posters on the wall so as not to appear to be nervous.

Knocking lightly on the door, Doctor Chapman came into the room, shook Fred's hand, smiled, and sat down at the small desk in the corner of the room. He spread out some files and turned toward the couple leaning forward with his arms on his legs and his hands folded.

"Well, here's where I think we are at folks. The fetus looks great and everything appears to be normal and right on schedule . . . The ultra sound looks good as well."

Doctor Chapman paused when he saw Fred look over to Jenny with a curious look and quickly continued and beamed a big smile.

"Ah . . . Don't worry Fred. We only showed Jenny what she needed to see . . . The secret is still safe."

He then chuckled and went on, "Only the nurse and I know . . . And we are not telling!"

Fred seemed relieved. He still was hoping for a boy but he really didn't want to make a big deal out of it so he changed the subject slightly, "Is there anything to be concerned about Doctor?"

"Ah well . . . Let me finish . . . We did some blood work and took a urine sample. We'll wait to see how the results turn out but here is what I want to be cautious about. Jenny has always had a slightly higher than normal blood pressure. And it is even a little bit elevated since last week so we are going to check for protein in the urine."

Jenny spoke up. "What would that mean?"

"Well Jenny, seeing as this is your first pregnancy, it's my job to cover all the bases so I'll tell you this, not to alarm you, but to let you know. We want to make sure that everything goes smoothly. This way we can make sure we give you and the baby the best possible care that we can!"

Both Jenny and Fred sat back in their chairs bracing for some possible bad news.

Doc Chapman who really had a great bedside manner and an excellent demeanor in dealing with new parents again smiled.

"Oh don't look so gloom folks . . . What I'm going to be looking for here, is the possibility of high protein count in the urine. I do have concerns about your high blood pressure, these dizzy spells and the headaches you're having Jenny. If the tests come back with a high protein count I may ask Jenny to come in for a few days so we can test the urine through a 24 hour period. But we haven't gotten there yet so . . ."

Jenny interrupted, "Could you be a little clearer Doctor?"

The Doctor cleared his throat and continued, "I want to rule out any possible problems with Preeclampsia."

"Pre . . . What?" Fred anxiously asked.

"Preeclampsia Fred . . . It's not real common but about 10% of all first time Mom's may have problems with it. Sometimes it only effects the mother. Sometimes just the baby or both."

"Is it serious Doctor?" Fred asked as he looked over to Jenny who was patiently waiting for some more information.

"It can be Fred . . . If it leads to a full Eclampsia and what we have to do together is look out for all the symptoms. Jenny has only a few symptoms right at the moment . . . Dizziness, headaches and high blood pressure. We'll see about the urine sample when it comes back . . . So don't get too carried away with your worries. These symptoms are normal for a pregnancy but here's what we want to look out for, increased frequency and severity of the headaches, dizzy spells, extreme fatigue, twitching, and fainting. Symptoms like that, and Jenny you could be a big help if you kept a brief log of all these symptoms."

The Doctor shifted his focus directly to Fred, "Fred, it's going to be your job to make sure Jenny sticks to the diet I prescribed for her and make sure she gets some rest and do not hesitate to call me if you feel uncomfortable with . . . Anything."

Leaning forward Jenny fired a robust round of questions at the Doctor and he tried to answer them in the order she listed them in.

When the Doctor was done Fred had to ask, "Doctor, you said something about Eclampsia and that could be bad. How would we know . . . I mean what would I do?"

The Doctor waved his hand, "Whoa Fred . . . Slow down, we are a long way from that BUT . . . Since you asked . . . Fred . . . Jenny . . . If you ever experience convulsions or seizures . . . Even if their mild . . . Don't wait to call me. Just get Jenny here to the hospital immediately."

Fred stood and with his eyes wide open and had to also ask, "How bad would that be . . . I mean what could happen?"

"If it ever got to that point Fred . . . It could be a life threatening situation for both Jenny and the baby. The farther along Jenny gets in the pregnancy without this complication . . . The more likely we have of undergoing a normal delivery."

Now Jenny stood, "What could be done Doctor Chapman?" Jenny now looked a little frightened.

"Well we would simply induce labor and or do a cesarean. That's why I say the later in the pregnancy the better. But at this juncture folks . . . Let's not be too hasty with concern. I would not be doing my job if I didn't make you aware of all of this and it's better that you know what to look for. One more thing Jenny. Until we get a handle on this, I don't think it would be wise to drive or go out too much without company. After all you did faint Friday and we don't want to take any chances."

With that the Doctor nodded his head and smiled. "Now go home folks and enjoy the rest of the day and I'll call you the minute I get the test results back."

Obviously both Fred and Jenny had hundreds of thoughts rolling through their mind as they quietly and slowly made their way back to the farm. Jenny reached out and held Fred's hand for most of the trip. The best way to describe the atmosphere would be tender, not tense. Neither one of them said too much until they arrived back at the farm.

Bailey was excited to see Fred and Jenny but even Bailey was gentle, not being too rough on Jenny upon the greeting. He too must have sensed a solemn mood on the part of his masters.

Jenny fixed coffee and a sandwich for the both of them and Jenny finally addressed the subject dealing with the Doctor's appointment.

"Fred, I'm worried about you . . . You've been so quiet . . . It's not like you not to find something positive to say?"

"Wow, don't worry about me . . . It's you . . . It's you and the baby we should be concerned about."

Fred stood and moved behind Jenny's chair and started rubbing her shoulders.

"No Fred I'm serious. With all you have to do and think about like the farm, the new accounts, Andross Foods . . . Now you have to worry about me. And I know you Fred. You're going to be a nervous wreck and feel like you have to be tied right inside this house, or something bad is going to happen! You're not going to be able to concentrate on what you have to be concerned about."

Well, Jenny was perhaps right about that. Fred already was wondering how he could finish up at Fairbanks in the city, or even work out on the farm without feeling like he should be closer to Jenny, in case the worst would occur. And Jenny knew it. Fred sat again and placed his hand on his chin. He knew that the best thing he could do for his wife through all of this was to in fact be, strong and positive.

"Of course your right sweetheart. Besides the Doctor said that a lot of women get dizzy and have headaches. And I'm sure that if need be . . . That is, if we needed a little extra help or something . . . My Mom . . . Or even your Mom could come for a while."

Jenny nodded her head, "See . . . That's the Fred Goodman I know . . . My Mom already volunteered, remember?"

Now Jenny even appeared to perk up a little now that Fred underwent a small attitude adjustment.

The early afternoon flew by and about 3 o'clock Darcy called to see how things went earlier that day. Both Ben and Darcy were down at the barn so Jenny invited them both up for a cup of coffee . . .

Jenny told Darcy the news as Fred and Ben went out to the fields which Fred was preparing for next summer. Ben was enthusiastic about Fred's venture with pumpkins and offered to bring up a few loads of gravel to firm up the road for next season.

The Shiff's were fortunate to have a small sand and gravel pit on the northwest side of their farm and they basically just used it for their own needs.

Darcy also was wrought with concern for Jenny and she too offered to help Jenny in any way she could. She offered to do things like run errands, grocery shopping, cleaning up around the house and so on.

Darcy was genuinely frightened with the experience of last Friday after being summoned by Bailey and of course finding Jenny lying on the floor. Darcy insisted on stopping in more often and Jenny promised to leave the door unlocked if she was home alone.

Fred and Ben returned from their jaunt in the fields and the two couples sat in the kitchen for about an hour sipping coffee and nibbling on cookies. It was near the end however when Ben produced a considerable surprise for Fred . . .

"Listen . . . Forgot to mention that I have one of my guys coming over with quite a few loads of manure for ya . . . If it's okay . . . I told him to see you and dump them in the fields where you want."

Fred asked, "Do you think I'll have to spread it this fall?"

"The soil testing guy is going to be here in a couple of weeks and if you don't need all the manure, you can always save it for next year."

The girls were half paying attention to Ben, but Jenny over heard enough to ask, "Isn't that going to smell Fred . . . Ooo . . . Stinky." Jenny smiled and jokingly held her nose

Chuckling, Fred answered, "Ah, we do live on a farm Dear!"

"Whatever Sweetheart, just don't put it too close to my bedroom window . . . Ha! . . . Just teasing. Actually I kind of like the smell of manure!"

Ben slid his chair back a little and raised his hands in the air and with a good deal of enthusiasm exclaimed, "YEESSS! . . . The Goodman farm is back in business!"

Everyone looked strangely at Ben and he explained his exuberance.

"When the women on the farm like the smell of manure . . . You know you're gonna have a good farm life. . . I think?"

Continuing to look strangely at Ben, the other three just broke into simultaneous laughter.

Now Ben didn't have his little surprised planned quite this precisely but as Ben and Darcy stood to leave, the distinct sound of a tractor rumbling up the drive could be heard.

Fred poked his head out the window and then with a jerk, glared back at Ben, "Its Roger . . . With the manure."

Ben shrugged his shoulders and Fred rushed to the kitchen door and hurriedly went to the edge of the drive. The others followed to peek at this uncertain reunion between Fred and Roger, yet keeping a fair distance, so as not to interfere.

With his hands on his hips, Fred waited to see if Roger was going to stop and of course Roger could see Fred standing there.

Roger throttled the tractor down and came to a slow stop. With it still running, Roger leaned forward and placed one arm completely over the steering wheel and with his left hand turned off the ignition.

Only seconds passed but to the others watching, it felt much longer. They were anxiously waiting to see who would speak first.

Fred smiled, "Hi Rogg . . . How ya doing!"

Fred knew that things would go pretty decent when Roger replied with, "Well Fredster. . . Things are doing fine . . . You?"

"Well . . . Not so bad . . . Heard you were working with Ben . . . How do you like being a farmhand?"

"Well Fredster . . . You got it wrong my friend. I'm not a farmhand."

Oh oh, Fred cringed a little. Did Fred say the wrong thing? . . .

"Nope . . . No Sir . . . I'm not at all a farmhand."

Ben, Jenny and Darcy mouths dropped down expecting something bad rather than good to transpire over this long awaited reunion between the two but Fred obviously sensed something the others couldn't.

Fred tucked one hand in his pocket and looked to the ground first and then back up to Roger who really didn't have any type of emotion going on, for the others to judge.

"So . . . If you're not a Farmhand Rogg . . . What are you doing for gainful employment lately then?"

You could tell by the expressions of the other three watching on, that they were expecting a disaster.

"Well if it should be known Fredster . . . I'm what you call an Agricultural Development Engineer! Yep. That's what I am . . . Proud of it too!"

Fred stood somberly for a moment and suddenly a large grin overtook his face.

"You know something Rogg . . . Your still a bonehead . . . You know that don't ya Rogg . . . A real Bonehead!"

Roger's face lit up with a large smile and a laugh. He jumped off the tractor and went over to Fred and gave him a large bear hug lifting the much smaller Fred right off the ground. He dropped Fred and backed off and raised his arms and said something Fred had heard a hundred times before.

"Yeah but I'm your Bonehead friend Fredster . . . Remember?"

"Do you want to come in for some coffee and sit a while Rogg?"

Roger nodded toward Ben Shiff, "Can't . . . That slave driver over there has too many things for me to do!" Roger was pointing his finger at Ben.

Ben shuffled his feet and sprang out a hearty laugh and Fred continued.

"Well how about dinner tomorrow night?" Fred turned toward Jenny very quickly and she smiled and nodded her head in approval.

"Sure . . . Under one condition however!" Roger shook his finger.

"Name it." Fred answered quickly.

"Only if Jenny does the cooking . . . Your cooking Fred . . . Well . . ." Roger rocked his hand back and forth in the air a few times.

Of course that drew a round of laughter from everyone and with that Roger started the old John Deere and headed up to the back pasture, where one of the fields were awaiting for the hopeful bounty of next season.

It had turned out to be a good day after all despite the concerning news of Jenny's appointment. It was good that Ben and Darcy had come by and Roger's reunion with Fred couldn't have come at a better time. Both Jenny and Fred felt much more optimistic when the evening closed and went to sleep with only positive thoughts of the future.

Chapter Fourteen
The Last Peaceful Days for Awhile

Fred was running behind this Tuesday morning as he scampered to get himself ready for work. Jenny was still asleep and Fred didn't have the heart to wake her. Just as Fred picked up his briefcase to head out the door, the phone rang.

It was Doctor Chapman and Fred answered with a noticeable impatient manor. Who would be calling this early he wondered?

"Ah . . . Hello"

"Hi Fred . . . Doctor Chapman . . . Sorry to disturb you this early. I got the test results in late yesterday but I had a few emergencies to tend to . . . Hope this isn't inconvenient?"

"Ah . . . No but Jenny is still sleeping."

The Doctor butted in quickly before Fred could go on any farther, "Please don't disturb her . . . I can relay this to you and if she has any questions, she certainly can give me a ring later."

Fred shuffled over to the table and sat down, "Okay, What's going on Doctor . . . Anything to worry about?"

"Well . . . Any pregnancy can have its complications and like I said yesterday . . . I want to ensure that everything goes smoothly. Jenny does have high protein in her urine. That and along with the high blood pressure has me a little concerned. I would like to have her come in for a few days so we can monitor the protein level over a 24 hour period. Now I have taken the liberty to book her in for first thing Thursday morning . . . You can have her back sometime Friday afternoon . . . In time for the weekend."

The Doctor was speaking quickly and Fred could hear the Doctor's pager going off several times. Doc Chapman continued but in a hurried pace.

"If that's a problem . . . Well, just call me later this morning and leave a message. We'll figure something else out. If I don't hear from you, I'll expect you here at 8:00am on Thursday . . . Okay?"

"Ah . . . No problem Doctor . . . That should work out fine . . . I'll see to it she is there?"

The Doctor closed out the conversation quickly and hung up before Fred could finish with a, 'I Think?'

Fred sat down at the table and murmured to himself out loud "Hmm . . . Thursday is okay I guess. Fairbanks should understand? Wednesday is the big contract signing day with my new accounts. Wonder how Jenny is going to take this? Guess I'll give Fairbanks a call at 8:00."

Fred looked up at the clock and it was 7:30 so he grabbed another cup of coffee and decided to hang out in the kitchen till Jenny got up. John Fairbanks, no matter what, was always promptly in his office at 8am every day. Fred couldn't even recollect one day that he wasn't.

Fred waited until 8:01 and called Mr. Fairbanks. John Fairbanks was more than understanding as he even let Fred off the hook from not just coming to work this day but also working out the remainder of the month to assist in the close down. Expecting to see Fred on Wednesday, John offered his best wishes to Jenny and offered Fred another, hearty thanks of appreciation for all of Fred's hard work at the ad agency.

Nervously sipping coffee and tapping his fingers on the table Fred patiently waited for Jenny to awake. At just about 9:15 Fred could hear the slow click, click, clicking of Bailey's nails on the old hardwood floor as no doubt, Jenny and Bailey were approaching the kitchen. Fred thought to himself, thank goodness. If he had to drink one more cup of coffee, he would probably be flying around the kitchen.

Fred didn't want to scare his wife so he sat quietly but as soon as Bailey and Jenny appeared in the doorway, she jumped with a jerk and held her hand up to her chest.

"My Gosh Fred . . . What are you trying to do? . . . Scare me to death? What are you doing here? Why aren't you at work?"

Jumping up to settle his wife, Fred gave her a big hug, "I'm sorry Sweetheart . . . Come sit . . . I'll explain it all. Let me get you a coffee."

Jenny sat down but waved her hand. "Oh . . . No coffee now . . . I'm a little queasy, but thanks. What's going on?" Jenny mumbled as she rubbed her hands up to her cheeks as if she was trying to wake herself up.

Looking down at Bailey who seated himself right up against Jenny's chair, Fred rubbed the top of Bailey's head, "You take your duty seriously boy . . . Don't you."

That was for sure. Bailey would get up with Fred for his morning meal and his run out in the pasture but Bailey faithfully returned to the bedroom to maintain his closeness with Jenny. As a matter of fact, Bailey never left Jenny's side except for his normal 'business appointments' as Fred called them.

Explaining the phone call from the Doctor, Jenny's expected arrival at the hospital, and John Fairbanks accepting and thoughtful considerations, Fred somewhat expected Jenny to be upset about something. But she wasn't.

"Sounds GOOD, Mr. Goodman . . . I will love your company and it will be nice to have you work from home. It will give you more time for the farm." Jenny smiled and patted Fred's hand, "Sit dear and have a cup of coffee."

"No way . . . I've had about 5 cups already . . . But can I get you something to eat."

Jenny laughed, "Don't spoil me Fred. I could get use to this . . . Some cereal would be fine. So what are you going to do today Fred . . . With this extra time you got today?"

Fred grabbed a bowl and a box of cereal and placed them on the table in front of his wife.

"Ah . . . Well let's see . . . Hmmm?" he said as he went to the fridge, grabbed a bottle of milk and on his swing back to the table, Fred pulled a spoon out of the silverware drawer and set it in front of Jenny.

"It's a good day . . . Think I'll go and fix the door at the farm stand. Shouldn't take me too long . . . I want to get it done before winter."

"So you think we can sell something down there next year . . . Is it ready to go?" Jenny inquired as she spooned a big mouthful of Cheerios into her mouth.

"Well I have to get the water on, but I might as well wait till the spring for that because I would just have to shut it off for the winter. So tell me what are you going to do today my lovely wife?"

"Mmmm?" Jenny gurgled as she held her finger up in courtesy waiting to answer until she munched down another spoon of her breakfast.

"Pearson has been a little slow lately . . . Just as well I guess so I'm going to straighten up my office and then clean up in here a little before our dinner guest arrives."

Fred almost had forgotten, "That's right . . . Roger's coming over for dinner!"

"That's correct sir . . . Remember . . . You invited him!"

"Guess I had temporary amnesia or something. You know I can call him and cancel if you want. If you're not feeling up to it?"

Jenny didn't let Fred finish, "Don't be silly Fred. I'm feeling fine this morning."

"Yeah, maybe this morning . . . But the day is young . . . And . . . What are we going to serve him tonight anyway?"

Again Jenny interrupted her husband, "Listen . . . I know the Doctor is doing his job and all but I don't think there is anything really to worry about. I'll go and take his silly tests but I think he is overreacting a little. And I'm going to roast a chicken, with mashed potatoes and gravy. That's one of Roger's favorites . . . Remember?"

Fred answered with just a simple yes, because his mind was lost in another direction for the moment. Fred couldn't figure out whether Jenny really wasn't too concerned or just putting up a front. Fred looked down to Bailey who had not even budged an inch as he leaned up against Jenny's legs. Fred couldn't help but to think about what this dog knows or senses about the future. Was Bailey trying to let them be aware of something? Bailey's continued companionship with Jenny was puzzling to say the least and it made Fred feel uneasy.

Fred just shrugged his shoulders as he stood.

"Mmmm . . . Well I'm going to change and get started. Call me on the cell if . . . If you need me or something."

Fred wasn't going to abandon his cautiousness, and neither was Bailey.

Jenny grabbed his arm and smiled, "Oh I'll call you alright Fred . . . When it's time for lunch! Now go and do what you need to do . . . I'll be fine."

Jenny chuckled and with that Fred left to do his repairman thing for the day.

The day was productive and calm, except for when Fred cut his hand while repairing the door but it was easily remedied with a Farmers Bandage as a roll of duct tape happened to be handy for the first aid procedures. Jenny appeared to be okay and in good spirits and later Fred found her humming while she scurried around the kitchen preparing for Roger's arrival.

Roger arrives for dinner . . .

"Knock, Knock, Knock!"

Roger stood at the screen door not really knocking on the door, but verbalizing his arrival as he always did. It was a beautiful late September day so Jenny had left the kitchen door open allowing the early fall breeze to cool off the kitchen.

Fred was still changing so Jenny hollered out as her hands were full with basting the chicken, "Right on time Roger . . . Let yourself in!"

"Okie Dokie", Roger replied in his kooky type of voice which was a trademark of Roger's. With animated gestures, Roger sort of slid across the floor rather than walk in, just as Fred entered the kitchen.

"Hey Rogg . . . Right on time."

Fred greeted his long lost friend with a warm smile.

"Well you know me Fredster . . . You can call me anything you want except . . . Late for dinner . . . Ha!"

Roger was always a grandstander and made the colorful entrances even though he was the most insecure person Jenny had ever met. With a brown paper bag in one hand, probably a bottle of wine and a small bouquet of flowers in the other, Roger raised both his hands in the air and smiled at Jenny like he was looking for a hug.

"Jenny, Jenny, Jenny . . . Long time no see . . . And these are for you Mrs. Fredster."

Roger graciously bowed and handed the bouquet to Jenny.

"Why thank you Roger . . . And they're so pretty! How sweet of you." With that Jenny gave Roger a big hug.

"And this is for Mr. Fredster." Roger handed Fred the bag.

Expecting the bag to reveal a bottle of cheap wine, Fred pulled out a green bottle of . . . Of . . . Seven-up?

Fred laughed but still managed to thank Roger.

"Ah . . . I remembered you guys don't drink. And I thought it appropriate to bring something . . . And besides . . . It's my favorite!"

"That's fine Rogg . . . You didn't have to bring anything. It's enough to have you here again."

Fred continued grinning, "Have a seat Rogg."

Bailey was no stranger to Roger so he too joined in the greeting as Roger tussled with the dog in a playful manor and then Roger plunked himself down on a kitchen chair. But when the greeting wore out, Bailey immediately sat next to Jenny who now had seated herself at the kitchen table.

"You have a new friend I hear Jenny?" Roger pondered as he pointed to Bailey and continued.

"Heard all about his daring rescue of the Damsel in distress . . . Good thing he was here!"

Both Fred and Jenny agreed and the three sat and talked for about a half hour as they waited for dinner and dinner turned out to be delicious. Roger scoffed down the meal as if he hadn't eaten in a week but Roger always did have a big appetite. The conversation was limited to farming topics and Roger really appeared to love his new career working for his old nemesis, Ben Shiff.

As a gracious guest, Roger even volunteered to wash the dishes explaining there was no need for a dishwasher when a Rogo-Matic 500 was at hand. Jenny accepted the offer as she was beginning to look tired and remained at her seat quietly as Fred and Roger did the cleanup.

The evening came to a close. Fred walked back into the kitchen after he and Roger made their final wise cracks and come backs to each other, as they always had in the past.

Jenny immediately remarked, "It's like nothing ever happened between you two guys! He acted like his normal obnoxious self." Jenny threw in a giggle or two at the end of her comment.

"Yeah . . . Roger never could carry on a serious conversation for long." Fred reasoned.

"I'm surprised he didn't say anything though?" Jenny snickered.

"Like what? Fred replied.

Jenny jeered, "Like an apology or something?"

"Naw . . . That's not Roger . . . He avoids confrontation and any type of uncomfortable issues. That's just the way he is. You should know that Dear?"

"Yeah . . . But a real man would have enough of a back bone to apologize when he's wrong Fred."

"That's true Sweetheart but we can't expect Roger to change completely I guess . . . I guess it's enough that he showed up. Which I suppose is Roger's way of saying he is sorry." Fred speculated.

"Maybe you're right Fred . . . I just don't want to see you get sucked up into that 'Pity Me' thing again, which Roger is so good at perpetrating on his friends?"

"Don't worry . . . I believe I am cured of that Sweetheart but holler out if you see me slipping!" Fred smiled at his wife.

"Now don't you worry . . . I will." Jenny affirmatively shot back.

Fred with concern gazed over to his wife, "You look a little pale and really tired."

"Yes I am . . . Tired anyway . . . Can't see how I look!" Jenny humored and stood up with a groan.

Jenny wobbled a little and Bailey nudged close to her side providing a stable handrail for Jenny as she rose from her seat. "Guess I'll get ready for bed Fred?"

She looked down at Bailey and spurted, "I'll send this canine paramedic back for his evening walk when he has safely escorted me to my quarters." Jenny laughed as she and Bailey shuffled off to the bedroom.

Fred stared at the two as they exited the kitchen and politely answered, "Okay . . . I'll be along as soon as I put these last few dishes away and close up shop for the night."

A little uneasiness befell Fred as he also piped in, "Gee . . . I hope you're alright Sweetheart?"

Jenny yawned and waved her free hand. The other rested on Bailey's head, "I'll be fine . . . I'm just a little tired."

It was only a few moments after they had left for the bedroom when Fred was frightened with the loud shrill barking from Bailey . . .

Fred was so startled by Bailey's alarm, he dropped the plate he was trying to put in a cabinet. He had never heard such a sound from this dog and Fred rushed through the parlor to find Jenny, on the floor, resting up against the hallway wall.

Sliding about five feet on his knees over the slippery wood floor Fred cradled his wife's head as it appeared she was having a tough time keeping it up.

"Honey . . . Are you okay . . . Sweetheart . . . Talk to me . . ." Fred gently wiped Jenny's cheeks.

"Oh stop with the melodrama Fred . . . I just got a little dizzy again . . . I'll be fine in a second."

"Riigghhtt" Fred sneered as he picked up his wife in his arms and carried her into the bedroom and laid her down onto the bed.

Fred pointed to Bailey with stern orders, "See that she stays here Bailey, I'm going to call the Doctor."

Bailey gave a quick report of a bark indicating he understood the command and would fulfill its intent. Jenny looked as she wanted to raise an objection but Fred held up one hand letting her know that she had no choice.

Fred moved to the other side of the bedroom where there was a small alcove. This was where Jenny and Fred had arranged a small desk, a chair, and a phone.

It took about an hour before Doctor Chapman returned Fred's call and in the meantime Fred put some cold compresses with a wet face cloth on Jenny's forehead. She did return to her full senses after about twenty minutes but Fred would not let her get up.

The Doctor was concerned and was very inquisitive to know whether there were any signs of twitching, shaking, or convulsions. Upon feeling comfortable that there weren't, he confirmed the hospital visit on Thursday.

Understanding the importance of Fred's last day at Fairbanks when Fred explained it to him, the Doctor also recommended that someone might drop in on Jenny a few times during the next day. Considering the Doctors advice, Fred immediately phoned Darcy and she was more than willing to stop in about 8:00 AM and stay until Fred's return.

"No way Fred . . . I'm not a baby . . . There no need for Darcy to screw up her day to . . . To BABY SIT ME!" Jenny snorted.

"Well I can't miss tomorrow . . . And . . . You have no say in it Mrs. Goodman. You better start realizing that this is for your own good . . . And the Babies! Now not another word."

Fred had never spoken to his wife with that kind of authority or dictatorship but Fred was not going to let his wife's silly pride cause her any problems.

Fred looked down to Bailey who was standing at Jenny's side of the bed with his head on her waist.

"Bailey . . . Why don't you explain it to Jenny." Fred ordered.

To the surprise of both Fred and Jenny, Bailey propped his two front paws on the edge of the bed and proceeded with his version of Fred's sentiments on this matter, "Rah, Rah, Rah . . . Rah, Rah . . . Rah, Rah, RAH . . ." And so on and so on!

Fred went to close up the house for the evening, pick up the broken plate he had dropped when Jenny fainted for the second time in four days and Bailey; well he continued his lecture to Jenny until she finally pleaded for him to stop.

Chapter Fifteen
Autumn on the Farm

Jenny's visit to the hospital that Thursday and Friday in late September brought with it an eerie feeling to the couple as Doctor Chapman now was very concerned about the possible presence of Preeclampsia.

He lined up an in home visit with a Medical Device Firm which specialized in medical alert systems so Jenny would have access to instant assistance and if need be, immediate transportation to the hospital. To add insult to injury, Doctor Chapman thought it would be a good idea if the Medical supply firm would also drop off a wheelchair for Jenny to move back and forth in the expanse of the large sprawling farmhouse. The Doctor also prescribed a special diet for Jenny to follow and of course Jenny was not thrilled about any of these developments. Yet she turned out to be a very cooperative patient.

As late October drew closer, not only did it bring abnormal cooler temperatures but Jenny's headaches and dizzy spells increased in frequency and severity.

Fred struggled so as not to be so besieged with not only his concerns for Jenny, but the additional work load which was increasing.

Roger stayed in contact with Fred but didn't make too much of a pest of himself.

Toward the end of the month, Fred was finding himself preparing all of the meals, doing all the laundry, house cleaning, and not to mention keeping up with a modest work load from his freelance clients.

It was time to close up portions of the house as the threat of an early winter was predicted. Fred still had to spread some manure but where would he find the time?

Jenny's strength was rapidly failing and on many days it was a chore just for her to get dressed. Fred moved a large reclining chair into the kitchen. He insisted that if she was comfortable, she might as well just stay in her robe and pajamas on those days.

And that is just what she did this day. Later that day Fred sat at the kitchen table sorting out and looking over three days of mail which he procrastinated in taking care of. He had ordered a pizza and a salad from the new Pizzarama which opened up in the new strip mall on the south side of town. Up until recently, there was no such thing as delivered Pizza in this old farm town but times were changing.

Jenny had dozed off on the lounger but Fred suddenly heard her whispered voice, "Hi Sweetheart. How long have I been sleeping?"

Fred glanced up a smiled at his wife, "Not long . . . You fell asleep just after I ordered the Pizza. How ya feeling?"

"Not too bad . . . Did the Pizza come yet?"

"Not yet . . . I'll say that I can't get use to that idea of Pizza Delivery anyway!"

Jenny grinned, "I guess your old country town is changing. Probably cause of all those condos and sub developments they are building now over in Sullivan. Guess there is a market for those types of fast food restaurants which are springing up. I feel sorry for people like Sally, I'm sure she's going to feel the crunch of all these modern changes . . . With her Diner and all!"

Fred sighed, "Yep, Oak Grove is not quite the way it was when I was a kid . . . That's for sure."

Jenny sat up in her chair and Bailey had to move quickly from getting clobbered with the foot rest as it banged close.

"Sorry Bailey . . . Fred maybe you could slide this down again so Bailey has some more room?"

Fred chuckled, "I already did . . . Remember?"

Fred looked at the other end of the kitchen where he had already slid the table down as close to the pantry door as he could. He had to, so he didn't have to jump over the sprawling Bailey, just to get out of the kitchen.

Jenny looked warmly over to her husband and said, "I'm sorry Fred."

"Sorry for what?"

"For you having to work this hard . . . Taking care of me, your work, and the Farm. You look so tired Fred."

"Yeah . . . You think so . . . I'm fine."

Naturally Fred Goodman would never complain of being overburdened. He was one of these guys who wanted to think he could handle anything and everything. And most of the time he could but Jenny knew Fred was getting weary. She just kept looking at her husband as he was pouring over the mail, wishing that life could just maybe lighten up for him.

Fred paused while looking at an envelope for a brief second and said, "This is for you . . . It's from Pearson." Fred half stood and leaned over to hand Jenny the mail.

Jenny grabbed it, "Probably a check."

Fred continued to wade through the pile of mail and didn't notice that Jenny was intently reading something her employer had sent to her until she exclaimed in a very disturbing tone, "Great . . . This is just great!"

Fred looked up, "What . . . No check?"

"No . . . . There's a check here but they want me to edit a set of medical study guides . . . Ah . . . . I hate those things. I have to look up almost every one of those disease and medical terms. Gosh, even when I'm feeling well I hate working on those things!"

Jenny slid the letter over to Fred and he picked it up and briefly reviewed it.

Looking up to Jenny out of the corner of one eye he replied, "It says here you got a week to let them know."

"Yeah, yeah, yeah . . . A week, two weeks . . . What difference does it make? If I decline . . . They may not use me a lot . . . If I accept and screw it up??"

Fred sat back in his chair and paused for a moment. Then he folded his arms and with a Fred Goodman type of a look, which Jenny knew a philosophy lesson was coming, he answered.

"Jenny . . . Haven't you seen already that . . ."

"Yes I know Fred . . . Everything happens for a reason . . . That doesn't help us Fred. You know we need the money . . . Not to mention the insurance I get with Pearson!"

Fred stopped a moment and looked over to the wheelchair which was sitting in the corner of the kitchen. Jenny's insurance was covering all the expenses for Jenny's condition. Fred quickly looked back down to the table hoping Jenny didn't notice that Fred was concerned about the Pearson dilemma.

"Yeah . . . That too Jenny but I think we should think it over a few days. You never know what may surface to be a . . ."

Jenny cut Fred off again, "I don't mean to be sarcastic Fred but . . . You never know what solution may arise . . . That's what you were going to say . . . Right?"

Fred realizing that Jenny was upset, "Jenny, You and the baby come first. If you decline that's fine. If Pearson says that's it . . . Oh well . . . We're not doing that badly Jenny."

Fred picked up the check and looked at it and faintly whistled, "That's pretty good . . . Do you realize that with this and the two checks I have upstairs . . . It amounts to almost Eight Thousand Dollars Jenny."

Jenny sighed, "I'm sorry Fred . . . I can't handle the pressure like you can. Can we can discuss this again in a few days? . . . Who knows what may come up?"

Fred quickly replied, "Probably nothing. But who knows, maybe they would be understanding like John Fairbanks was and possibly grant you sort of a maternity leave? You won't know till you ask . . . But I do know that it's not wise to make a decision of any kind when we are upset or something. Think things out first!"

Fred knew that loosing Pearson's Insurance would be disastrous but he didn't want to let Jenny know that!

Jenny started smiling with a renewed optimistic vigor, "Yeah . . . A Maternity leave . . . You're a genius Fred Goodman."

Fred smirked, "Hold on though . . . Just because I think it's a good idea . . . Doesn't mean Pearson will?"

"I know . . . I know . . . Fred that's great about the money Fred, Huh . . . How much is in the farm fund anyway?"

Besides the trust account for the farm which they never had touched, Fred and Jenny had a joint checking and savings. But with an optimistic dream that someday the farm would actually be a farm again, they also started up a checking account called the farm fund. Hopefully they could build it up to a sizable nest egg to cover supplies, seed, equipment repair and possibly some labor to help out. A large portion of Fred's severance from Fairbanks had recently uplifted the farm fund.

Although Fred had gone over the accounts with Jenny just recently, he decided to remind her of their success.

"Right now . . . Before we deposit these checks, we have about seven thousand in the savings and about three thousand in the checking. And the farm fund, thanks to John Fairbanks is standing at about fifteen thousand. I'll go to the bank tomorrow . . . So how do you want to divi this up Mrs. Goodman?"

"Wow!" Was all Jenny could say and the two got a pen a paper and worked out the details for the deposits.

Just as the couple finished with their financial discussion a faint knock sounded from the rear kitchen door . . .

"It's about time . . . I'm starving." Fred grunted.

Fred stood and started fumbling for his wallet out of his back pocket as he hurried toward the door to pay the Pizza guy.

Jenny could not see the door from her chair but she heard Fred say, "Well . . . Well, well . . . Are you delivering pizza now for a living?"

"Hi Fred . . . Are you expecting pizza?"

It was Darcy and she walked right past Fred and into the kitchen and with a chuckle said, "Hi Jenny. Won't stay long. Just wanted to see how well Mr. Goodman is taking care of you today?"

Jenny smiled, "Just fine . . . He's a Sweetheart and you are too!" She pointed at Darcy, "Thanks for doing the shopping today . . . And you didn't have to put everything away."

"Well you were snoozing away in the maternity chair when I got back . . . Didn't wanna wake you. Hope I got everything in the right place."

Fred quickly sniped, "Ah . . . That explains why the sugar was in the refrigerator?"

Darcy pointed her finger to her chest, "Me . . . Put sugar in the refrigerator . . . Not me . . . Your crazy Fred!" and then she let out a friendly cynical laugh.

Darcy took Fred's seat at the table and she chatted for a few moments while Fred impatiently paced the floor continually looking out the kitchen window.

"What's taking so long . . . . Where the heck is my pizza?"

Interrupting the girls conversation Fred asked Darcy, "Did you and Ben ever order pizza from these guys?"

"Naw . . . We still like to go over to Sally's a few times a week . . . Feel sorry for her. We've been doing that for years and it would be kind of sad if that old Diner wasn't there! Remember Fred . . . Everybody use to go there after the basketball games. Why Ben took me there on our first date."

Fred was too hungry to take a trip down memory lane so he just grunted and stared out the window scouting for his dinner.

"Hey Fred . . . That's a great idea . . . Maybe we should start going to Sally's more?" Jenny interjected with enthusiasm.

"Hmmm . . . Maybe when you're feeling better."

Jenny turned back to Darcy and while laughing stated, "Doctor Goodman over here has to lighten up a little I think?"

Darcy laughed, moved forward on the edge of her seat and crossed her feet over one another as Jenny sang the praises for her husband, about how helpful he was and how he hadn't had the time to finish turning the fields, and on and on. Jenny even showed her the letter from Pearson and explained to Darcy the dilemma she was in.

Darcy listened absorbedly and out of the clear blue, scratched her index finger on her temple, jumped from her seat and blurted, "Well, I got a great idea!"

She instantly paused with her thought and went on, "I mean I gotta a lot of things to do." Darcy leaned over and gave Jenny a hug, "See ya tomorrow . . . Bya!"

Darcy waved at Fred and scampered out the door.

Fred shrugged his shoulders and held his hands up, "What got into her?"

Jenny put a grin on her face, "I don't know . . . Maybe she forgot to get something at the store for Ben or something."

Jenny chuckled at Fred's lack of understanding about the fickleness of women but she wasn't going to try and explain it to her husband right at that moment.

"Where the HECK is my pizza."

Of course the pizza Guy eventually delivered Fred's dinner and despite its late arrival, Fred thought it was the best Pizza he had tasted in a long time. The next day was Friday and it arrived quickly. Jenny was surprisingly up early . . .

But Fred wasn't quite aware of Jenny's early awakening yet. Fred always felt uncomfortable if he had to leave the farm or drift too far from the house. Even though he knew Bailey was on the job, he tremendously feared that something might happen to Jenny and help might not arrive in time.

Sheepishly, he even found himself explaining to Bailey where exactly he was going on the farm, in case Bailey needed to find him. Feeling a little embarrassed about it he tried not to let Jenny hear him reviewing his itinerary to the Newfoundland. So Fred would take advantage of the fact that his wife usually slept later in the morning and he would take care of some of the farming duties without worrying too much.

Slowly driving the large tractor out of the back barn, so as not to wake his wife, Fred maneuvered over to the equipment lean-to and hooked up the spreader. It was amazing that this old equipment was in the shape it was. Even Ben's mechanics marveled over the equipment that was on the farm.

He figured he would bring the Deere and spreader down to the lower fields where Ben had dumped some manure. Unfortunately, Fred knew he would have to walk back to get the loader. Fred muttered to himself as this was one of the distinct disadvantages of working the farm by himself.

Chugging back up the drive to the house on foot, Fred only paused once to look into the large barn where Ben had moved yet another 20 cows into their new housing. That made a total of eighty with room enough for another twenty if Ben wanted to.

The lights in the barn cast a warm glow upon the mist still rising from the warm ground as the autumn daylight struggled to appear. It sounded as if the milking was just about to finish up as the muffled whining of the milking machines were dissipating gradually. Sticking his hands in his pockets Fred smiled. This is how he remembered the farm when he was just a kid. Gosh, this was good to see again, he thought to himself.

Contented for the moment, Fred continued up the driveway and pulled the sleeve of his jacket up so he could glance at his wrist watch. It was a little chilly for this time of year as the temperatures were dropping down into the forties at night and barely making into the fifties during the day. A jacket was definitely required. He couldn't delay finishing the prep for the fields much longer so figuring he had just enough time before Jenny would wake up, he decided to bring the front end loader down from the back barn and park it near the house.

Fred would use the loader to drive back to the fields, load the spreader and cast the manure. He also thought that he could use the loader as a means of transportation back and forth to the barn, until he finished the job.

Now this old loader was one of Fred's favorites. Uncle Harry taught Fred how to operate this same loader back when Fred was only twelve. It was a 1962 Trojan and was in tip top condition. Of course it sat idle for quite a few years but Ben's boys refurbished the hydraulics and seals and got the old work horse charging like it used to back in the sixties.

Being aware that Jenny may still be sleeping, Fred maintained the machine at an idle as he crept down the drive and parked the loader right near the kitchen door, just as Uncle Harry did so many times before he went in for breakfast. Tilting the bucket down so as to catch the edge of the turf, Fred climbed down and threw a chock in front of one rear wheels.

Again reminiscing about the past, Fred started to chortle out loud. He couldn't help but to remember when he and his Aunt Ruthie were returning from the chicken coop with the eggs for breakfast one day, were horrified to see the unmanned loader careening down the drive. Weaving and bouncing the loader managed to miss the front barn but demolished about two hundred feet of fencing and one of Aunt Ruthie's Maple saplings and finally lunged to a stop in the muddy fields across the street. What a sight!

Fred thought for sure that Rube and his Uncle were going to get into a brawl over this incident as each of them accused the other of being the last one to be on the loader, and forgetting to chock the wheels. Ruthie settled the squabble with explicit instructions on how to park the Trojan. She even climbed on board and demonstrated to the red faced gentlemen how to accurately drop the bucket at the precise angle into the grass on the edge of the drive and chock the wheels properly. Both Rube and Harry didn't say a word at breakfast that morning.

Still sporting a large grin, Fred was slightly lost in the past when he walked into the kitchen . . .

"What's so funny Sweetheart?" Jenny stood with a baking pan in one hand a cup of tea in the other.

Taken back with what he was seeing Fred blurted, "Jenny . . . What on earth are you doing up."

"What . . . Am I supposed to lay in bed all day or something?" Jenny smirked.

"Umm . . . Yes . . . I mean no . . . It's just you normally have been sleeping till ten!"

Jenny stood there in a pair of sweats and a maternity top which barely covered her protruding belly.

"You remember what the Doctor said . . . Eat when you're hungry . . . Sleep when you're tired . . . And don't let your husband give you a hard time!"

"Ha . . . Ha . . . Ha," was Fred's response as he sat down at the table.

"If you must know Mr. Goodman . . . I'm preparing my husband's favorite dinner . . . Lasagna! And being the good husband that he is, when he goes to the bank this morning, he can swing by the bakery and pick up some fresh Italian rolls!" Jenny proclaimed.

"Mmmm . . . I guess?"

Fred was somewhat flabbergasted. He was getting terribly confused about how and what to worry about with his wife. On Wednesday Jenny suffered miserably with migraines. She couldn't even get out of bed. Yesterday, she was just plain exhausted and today she was up and about like nothing bothered her.

Fred calmly said, "Well . . . Just don't overdo it Hon."

"Don't worry, I won't . . . I'm sure I'll get tired and conk off in the chair. I see you're getting ready to turn the fields . . . Did I get the terminology right Darling? Want to make sure I meet all the standards for a good farmer's wife."

Chuckling slightly she continued, "Now why don't you go to the bank and then do your farmer boy thing and play with your manure . . . Or whatever you have to do with that yucky stuff!"

Fred laughed, stood and gave his wife a big hug, grabbed the checks and the deposit slips which he filled out that morning, and left for the bank.

As he climbed into the car his concern for his wife totally consumed his thoughts. He sat in the seat for five minutes hashing over his various anxieties.

Jenny was in such a good mood and she seemed fairly stable. Fred reasoned to himself that she would be alright by herself, for a little while anyway.

Besides, Bailey was there and he had already proven twice, that he knew how to handle a crisis. She had the medical alert bracelet but Fred didn't really want to trust the system that worked on a wireless patch to the telephone. Heck, Fred rationalized, out here in the country; you could hardly get a good radio station without a lot of static, so how could this device be dependable? Nope, he wasn't going to trust in it completely.

Fred continued to ponder; but why was Jenny doing so well today? For weeks Jenny had been feeling terrible so why today did she seem so much better? Maybe it was a good sign? Fred was only pessimistically hopeful but still very apprehensive.

Well, Friday was to turn out to be a long day and it wasn't quite over but I guess we will just have to see how the remainder of the day goes . . . In the next Chapter.

Chapter Sixteen
A Long Friday with a Big Surprise

Yes, it's still Friday . . . For the moment anyway so let's see how the day progressed.

Even though Jenny was in a fairly happy mood, Fred hurried with his errands to the bank and bakery, politely cutting short all the small town gossipers he bumped into and all the well-wishers for Jenny. He felt a smidge guilty about his hastiness but he just didn't feel comfortable being away from the farm, even if it was only a few miles away.

Slowly opening the screen door, so it wouldn't squeak and slam waking Jenny if she was dozing, Fred slowly crept into the kitchen. Jenny was in the lounging chair and it looked as if she were asleep.

Softly walking over to the stove, Fred spied the hot steaming lasagna which Jenny must have just pulled from the oven. Wow, it smelled good and Fred stood over the pan waving his hand to his nose to delight in the flavorful aroma.

"Unh . . . Unh, Unh . . . Keep your hands off of that!" announced Jenny.

Fred jumped. He thought for sure Jenny was sound asleep and he turned to see her looking at him out of one eye and displaying a big grin.

"Sorry Hon . . . Thought you were zonked out."

"That's okay . . . As a matter of fact I just laid down as you were pulling up the driveway . . . Thought I'd snag ya sneaking some Lasagna!" and Jenny laughed.

"Not this time Dear . . . Not this time!" Fred exclaimed.

Fred chuckled and patted Bailey on the head who now rose to greet Fred.

"Everything Okay Pal . . . . I sure feel much better with you around. But don't get too lackadaisical. After I change I have a date with a big pile of _____!"

"Fred . . . Watch your language. You don't want Bailey picking up any bad habits!"

Fred chuckled, "I'll be right back. Let me go transform into Super Farmer . . . Ha!"

Jenny giggled and closed her eyes. "I'll be here. Not going anywhere . . . I just need a little nap."

Fred returned to the kitchen and just as he was leaning over to kiss his wife on the forehead he

*noticed out of the corner of his eye, a huge cloud of
dust whirling up the driveway . . .*

"What the heck?" Fred muttered softly.

It was Roger, making a grand entrance as he
always seem to do. Fred quietly snuck out the door
to see Rogers's car sliding to a screeching halt.

Roger slowly opened his door and straggled out and
Fred held his finger to his lips, "Shhh . . . Jenny's
sleeping in the kitchen."

"Ah . . . Sorry Fred. Guess I should remember
things like that?" Roger shrugged.

"That's okay Rogg. Lately she can sleep through
anything but . . . What are you doing here this
morning?"

"Well . . . If you must know, things are starting to
slow down a little. Winter coming and all . . . So Ben
and I decided . . . Well I mean Ben gave me the rest
of the day off soze I could come up here and help
you fertilize."

"Thanks Roger but it's not necessary . . . I was just
heading out to start it . . . And . . ."

"And I will help you then!" exclaimed Roger.

"Besides, the two of us can do it a lot quicker!
Mmmm, See you got the loader ready!" Roger said.

Roger beamed up to the cab of the old Trojan,
"She's still a beauty eh Fred!"

"Yeah the tractor and spreader are already down at the field. Roger this is awful nice of you but . . . Well, I can pay you what Ben pays you."

Fred didn't want to start paying out for labor yet; at least till the farm fund had been built up a little more and maybe after the first crop turned in a profit. But he felt guilty and made the offer to his friend.

Roger stood with his hands deep in his pockets and looked directly into Fred's eyes and with authority answered, "NO . . . Won't have it Fredster."

"But Rogg . . . It's only . . ."

"The answer is NO!"

Fred was humbled but Roger immediately walked up to Fred and took his big burly hands and lightly grabbed Fred's shoulders.

"Listen here Fred. If it wasn't for you Fred why . . . Why I'd probably be in an insane asylum. The way you watched over me after the fire! The way you stood up for me and took all those bruises when Ben and the other guys jumped all over my case. Well I never told you this Fred but . . . You're a better friend than a guy could ever ask for. And that's you Fred . . . You!"

Roger pointed his finger firmly into Fred's chest and continued, "And I guess I never had the nerve to tell you this but the best thing you ever did for me was to kick me in the butt over the Fairbanks thing! It worked. I see things different now Fred! I'm happy now . . . Why Ben has been so nice to me it's not funny . . . And guess what Fred?"

Fred was smiling now, "What Roger?"

I'm really likin this farming thing . . . How do you like that? Roger the Farmer . . . Ha!"

Fred grabbed Roger's arm and shook his hand, "Thanks Rogg . . . It's a big lift with . . . What's going on with Jenny and all."

Roger nodded his head, "Yeah I know . . . The whole town knows. But I should be thanking you Fred. For giving me the opportunity to be the kind of friend to you . . . that you have been for me."

Roger looked a little swollen in the eyes but immediately perked back up and slapped Fred on the back, "Let's do it . . . I'll ride the bucket down . . . I like that . . . You drive Fredster!"

And with that Fred started the loader and tilted the bucket back. Roger jumped in and the two headed down the hill with Roger singing his own silly version back in the saddle again!

Fred and Roger managed to almost finish the last 100 acres of the fields which Fred had not yet completed. Fred would continuously meet Roger at the end of the rows with the loader in order to keep the spreader full of manure. The job went very well as the soil was rather firm, absent of any recent rain fall.

Ben and Fred decided that the lower fields along the Shuntook River might be some of the best fields to get ready as the natural run off from the North Mountains always provided great natural irrigation.

Only once, back in the 1930's did the Shuntook ever over flow it's banks and his Uncle Harry said, only half the fields were flooded. But it was always the lower acres which produced most of the famous Goodman sweet corn so that was where Fred decided to re-inaugurate the Goodman legacy.

It was late afternoon when Fred and Roger made their way back to the house and Roger, figuring that he didn't smell his best, decided to leave instead of stepping into the house with Fred for a cup of coffee.

Fred removed his boots on the rear porch remembering how Aunt Ruthie's biggest pet peeve was having Uncle Harry and Rube track manure all over her kitchen floor when they came in from the fields. Fred chuckled over the thought and tip toed into the kitchen just in case his wife was napping. But to his surprise she was up and she looked like she had just done her hair.

"Wow . . . You look pretty good Mrs. Goodman!"

"Well . . . I'm a little tired but I got up and decided to take a shower for dinner with my husband. Ah . . . Um . . . Speaking of which, a shower may be a good suggestion for my husband . . . . Shew . . . You smell."

Jenny held her nose, waved her hand, and in jest said, "Go get cleaned up Mr. Goodman and I'll get a coffee ready for you. I was just going to have a tea so go . . . Please." And Jenny giggled.

Fred did as she asked and when he returned to the kitchen he found his wife sitting at the table holding her head in her hands.

Bailey was leaning up against her chair with his head resting on the table and Fred rushed over to her, "Are you okay Sweetheart?"

"Just a little dizzy . . . I guess . . . It'll pass . . . It always does." Jenny weakly said.

"Mmmm . . . See, this does happen a lot. You don't tell me all the time. I have to be here to see it!" Fred sternly replied.

"I just don't want you to worry sweetheart. You have enough to do and besides . . . Bailey's here, remember?"

Fred still would not be comfortable with that. A few moments ago Jenny looked bright, full of color in her face but now she looked pale and feeble. Fred helped her to her chair and she sat quietly for a while.

After about ten minutes Jenny looked a lot better and Fred put the lasagna back in the oven to reheat it for dinner. As Fred walked back to the kitchen table he crouched over and intently gazed out the window . . .

"What you looking at Fred?" Jenny asked.

"There's a car slowly coming up the drive."

Fred now leaned on the kitchen table peering to see who it might be.

"Who is it Fred?"

"Can't quite make it out dear."

But Fred suddenly stopped and jerked his head over to his wife and with a little astonishment in his voice answered, "It's Ellen Crenshaw."

"Good Lord" Jenny started to stand up and probably exit the room and continued, "I don't need to deal with that old witch!"

Fred went over to his wife and gently put his hands on her shoulders and coaxed her back down on to the kitchen chair. He then dropped down on one knee and rubbed her arms as he tried to reason with her.

"Listen, I know how you feel about her. . . Don't blame ya. She is kinda hard to take but this is the Goodman Farm . . . And everybody in town is concerned about you Hon. It's the way it is in an old country town Jenny. At least we should hear her out. It's the polite thing to do."

Jenny had her smug pout look upon her face.

"Well just see what she wants and send her on her way Fred. I'm not feeling up to this . . . Get rid of her as quick as you can . . . Goodman Farm or not! She's just an old buzzard Fred. I'm not looking at forward to talking with her."

Fred stood and reflected one last thought to his wife, "And that's what you said about Darcy, remember . . . And now look!"

Jenny sighed and looked up to her husband, "Ohhh, Okay but please try and keep it short . . . Please Fred?"

Fred stood up quickly and patted his wife on her back, "I promise." And then he rushed over to the kitchen rear hall and foyer.

"I'll just let the old buzzard . . . Ahem . . . I mean Mrs. Crenshaw in."

Fred chuckled out loud and Jenny tried to smile but it looked more like a grimace of pain rather than an approval of Fred's levity.

Just as Fred approached the rear door, Ellen Crenshaw was creeping up the rear steps, cane in hand.

Fred swung the screen door open for the older patriarch of the town.

"Well Mrs. Crenshaw . . . How nice to see you!" Fred had to keep a real straight face with that one.

Ellen looked up, "Hi Fred . . . How you doing. Hope this isn't a bad time to come calling?"

"No, no . . . Not at all . . . Come in please."

The older women paused for a second right in front of the door as Fred had his arm extended still holding the screen door for her.

"Actually I was hoping to speak with your dear wife." ruffed the elder.

"She's right here in the kitchen . . . But she is a little tired." Fred said as he tried to lay some ground work for a quick visit as he promised Jenny.

Ellen Crenshaw walked by Fred and headed into the kitchen, "Like I said young fellow . . . Won't stay long."

Fred held his breath as Ellen turned into the kitchen, wondering how cordial Jenny was really going to be.

Mrs. Crenshaw took no time in walking right up to the table, slid a chair over so as to be directly in front of Jenny, and sat. The older women groaned a little as she seated herself, holding her cane between her knees while cupping her wrinkled hands on the top of the old hand carved staff.

Ellen smiled but immediately put back on her typical uncompromising look which she was so famous for.

"Hi Jenny dear . . . Won't keep you long so I'll get right to the point dear."

Fred quietly took a seat at the other end of the table hoping not to disrupt Ellen's thoughts. Fred was extremely curious himself and he noticed that Jenny was trying to be cordial but she wasn't quite pulling it off. Jenny sat motionless with almost a blank look on her face.

Ellen could notice Jenny's apprehension as well, as Ellen was no dummy, so the older woman maneuvered the conversation carefully.

"Look dear . . . I know I haven't been the most pleasant person to you dear. But I would think of you kindly if . . . If you would hear me out. But I wouldn't blame you if you just asked me to leave."

Now Jenny was of course a very well-mannered and caring person and it was in Jenny's nature to respond to the old cackled hen with a respectful response to a comment like that.

"Oh don't think of it . . . I wouldn't ever throw you out Ellen! And you aren't that bad of a person."

Jenny almost choked when she heard herself saying that to the old wretch.

Mrs. Crenshaw knew exactly how to control a conversation when she wanted to and she continued, "Ah . . . You're such a darling liar dear! But if the truth of the matter be known . . . I know that most in this town just loathe me!"

All of a sudden a smile came across Jenny's face and she stopped the older women in mid-sentence.

"That's not true . . . You shouldn't say that about yourself. Why I'm sure you have a lot of great qualities?" Of course Jenny couldn't think of a single one at that moment.

It was Ellen's turn to interrupt and she sighed and with her normally obnoxious snort, "Oh Bolder dash dear . . . I know people can't stand me!"

Then Ellen leaned over to Jenny and with a cynical whisper, "To tell you the truth dear . . . Don't tell a soul this dear . . . But . . . Half the time I can't stand myself. . . . Hmm!"

And then breaking into a roar of laughter Ellen went on.

"I'm just a miserable old women . . . Don't know why I am . . . But it gets on my nerves too."

Fred was fascinated. As he noticed that Jenny was now showing some warmth and tenderness in her eyes, and the old cagy women knew it too.

Up until now, Bailey had remained lying on the floor next to the lounge chair. Maybe sensing Jenny's displeasure over Ellen Crenshaw's unexpected visit, Bailey didn't even extend his normal greeting to the guest. But Bailey, perhaps now realizing a softening of Jenny's attitude, lurched up and sluggishly approached the senior women.

Apparently Ellen hadn't noticed the large dog lying on the floor when she first entered, but she was certainly caught off guard when Bailey stuck his nose in her lap nudging her cane to one side.

Ellen Crenshaw turned quickly at Fred and with what seemed like a sincere concern in her voice exclaimed, "Oh Lordy . . . Fred . . . Since when do you keep your cows in the house!"

Fred couldn't help but to laugh as he rose and stood next to Bailey and explained, "Ah . . . This is Bailey, our loveable canine guardian!"

Ellen shrugged, "Land O Sakes . . . Dog you say? Why he's as big as a Guernsey!"

Jenny didn't realize it herself but she was ear to ear with a smile and she womanly giggled and said, "He's been a good dog and a good friend! But you said you wanted to ask me something?"

"Oh yes . . . Almost forgot . . . Well I was talking to that Smithfield girl . . . What a Darling . . ."

Jenny looked confused and chimed in with, "Smithfield girl?"

Fred jumped in with, "Darcy Honey . . . That was her maiden name."

Ellen looked up at Fred.

"Thank You . . . Darcy . . . She's really a sweet girl. Anyway, she came by my house last night and . . . Well . . . She told me about your problem with the people you work with and that you have a big medical piece to edit . . . Or something like that? Anyway, I stopped by to see if maybe I could be of some help to you with that."

Now Jenny looked even more perplexed. What would this woman know about editing medical texts and how could she possibly be of help to Jenny? Just because her husband is a Dentist? Jenny was baffled and so was Fred.

"Well that's very kind of you Ellen but what . . . I mean how . . ."

Jenny didn't quite know how to ask the woman how she could possibly help, without perhaps insulting her?

But of course Ellen knew what the concerns were that Jenny was puzzled over and she rapidly let Jenny off the hook.

"Dear . . . Being in the field you are in you must have heard of Allied Publishing?"

"Of course . . . They publish all sorts of medical texts for medical schools." Jenny answered.

"That's correct dear . . . Well at one time . . . Well I guess you could say I owned Allied Publishing."

Jenny looked thunderstruck and really didn't know what to say but she tried, "Ah . . . Wow I didn't know that . . . Did you Fred?"

Fred shrugged his shoulders. This was news to him but what was more bewildering is that, how could have Ellen kept something like that a secret in a small town like Oak Grove?

Jenny stuttered a little, "Gosh, I mean . . . Nobody has ever mentioned anything like that . . . Wow!"

Ellen reached out and patted Jenny on the knee, "Well that's because nobody knows besides Doctor Crenshaw . . . And of course that Smithfield darling."

Jenny's next question was, "How does Darcy know anyway?"

Ellen chuckled, "That's cause she was snooping one day when she was cleaning at my house. I hire her to help with the housekeeping and things like that. And one day she came across some documents and such. She felt bad I guess and I made her promise not to tell a anyone. And I guess she never did . . . Bless her soul."

Ellen sat back in her seat and rested one hand on the top of Bailey's head and continued, "Actually it was my Fathers business. He was a very . . . Very intelligent man, but a demanding Father. I grew up in the business and by the time I was 22, he had me editing text books. I got pretty good at it I might say. Hated it . . . But good at it."

Jenny's interest was certainly heightened and she started bursting with questions. "If you hated it so much . . . Why did you stay?"

"Good question my dear. Well I hate to say it, but I tolerated it because I knew that one day the business would be mine. My Father was grooming me for that, and I dare say . . . He never hesitated to dangle that thought over my head with threats of casting me out from his will. Listen to me babble on.

I should be more considerate and let you folks relax."

"Nonsense . . . Please go on." Jenny was insistent and Fred could tell that Jenny was becoming enthralled with Ellen Crenshaw. Who would have imagined that!

It was starting to be apparent that this wretched old coot, the legendary witch of Oak Grove, the most despised person in this town, was nothing more than a lonely old Lady who was craving love and attention. She just didn't know how to receive it. And Fred could see Jenny's gradual transformation from repulsion toward this woman, to a captivated interest.

Ellen decided to indulge Jenny's request.

"Well I thought about leaving . . . At least a thousand times."

She cackled and continued with another sigh, "But I guess I was in love with the prospects of having all that money someday. I grew to worship the thought of all that money and how it would free me from all the worries of the world . . . Ha! I wasn't what you would call an attractive women. The Gentlemen never paid too much attention to me. I even began to believe that the money could love me back but of course that was just the disillusionments of a young uninviting girl I guess?"

Jenny sighed in a compassionate manor. "Well, don't be too hard on yourself."

Jenny leaned over and patted her hand on the top of the old lady's hands that now once again were perched atop her cane.

Fred leaned back in his chair and smiled. He was not only amazed at Jenny's about face attitude toward Ellen Crenshaw but it was also the warmth she was starting to show toward the old gal.

"So I take it you did inherit the company." Jenny asked.

"Oh yes . . . My Father passed away when I was twenty four . . . God rest his soul. And I found myself running the whole shootin match!"

Ellen smiled and chuckled and gently slapped Jenny on her knee and continued, "With a big pile of money to boot."

Jenny couldn't help to smile, "I take it you don't own Allied anymore?"

"Gosh sakes, no . . . I told you I detested that business and I couldn't wait to gather up all that loot and set out to see the world. Oh I ran it for about two more years."

Ellen cleared her throat. "Listen to me babble . . . Would it be too much trouble to ask for a glass of water . . . I haven't talked this much since who knows when."

Fred jumped up and poured a large glass of water for Ellen. She patted him on the arm when he handed it to her. She took a large swallow and Fred moved back to his seat.

"Well go on . . . Go on . . . I'm dying to hear the rest!" Jenny insisted.

"Like I said I found a buyer but there was a longer transition period than I thought . . . Good thing, I guess, cause that's when I met Doc Crenshaw."

Jenny was hooked, "Wow . . . How'd you meet him there?"

"Well he was working on a book . . . With three other Doctors. Handsome fellow he was back then! Anyway, well he swept me off my feet."

Ellen started laughing now and Jenny couldn't help to smile and laugh along with her.

"So . . . You fell in love . . . But what about your plans to travel the world and all that?" Jenny was real curious.

"You dear sweet girl . . . I never received so much attention from a man and well . . . I guess I couldn't resist all that attention. Anyway . . . I sold the Business, gathered up all my loot and I married the young Doctor."

Jenny was bursting with questions, "How did you end up here in Oak Grove?"

"The Doc and I first moved to New Jersey where he joined a firm there. I wrote a few drama novels while he did his Doctoring and . . ."

Jenny cut Ellen off quickly. "You mean you are an author?"

"Oh yes . . . Wrote eight books in all. Used a ghost writers name however . . . Still collect the royalties too! Made out very well for myself."

You could tell Jenny was impressed. Jenny sat back in her chair a moment trying to load her next barrage of questions.

"But how did you come to settle in Oak Grove?"

"Oh yes . . . You asked me that didn't you?"

Ellen laughed, "Guess I'm getting a little senile dear? Let me see . . . The Doctor got tired of working for this group of Dentists so on one of our little vacations, we were traveling through Oak Grove and wouldn't you know it? Our car broke down. That nice John Baker, Dave's Dad, had just started his garage and he fixed our car. He and his wife even put us up for a few days while we waited for parts. They told us how the nearest Dentist was in Shuntook some thirty five miles away and well . . . Here we stayed and set up shop."

"Wow . . . Who would have known? Did you know all this Fred?"

Jenny turned toward her husband and Fred just shook his head indicating that he didn't have a clue.

Jenny sat back in her chair, smiling, totally taken back and engrossed in Ellen Crenshaw's story.

"Wow . . . That's all I can say. I guess you would think living in a small town like this . . . Somebody would have known?" Jenny sort of threw her hands up in bewilderment.

Ellen smiled, "I know . . . But I made the Doc promise not to tell. Everybody just figured I was some young floozy who chased a young handsome Doctor around for his money."

Ellen giggled and continued as she leaned over to Jenny slapping her on her knees, "To tell you the truth, it was the young Doctor who was chasing the money! But he has been a good man and a good husband but . . . I guess I miss talking with the girls! Guess that's my own fault I guess."

Ellen was in the middle of her sentence when the buzzer on the stove went off indicating that the lasagna had finished its job in warming up.

Ellen stood up quickly tapping her cane once on the floor, "Tied you up long enough . . . Don't want to keep you folks from your supper . . . but you haven't answered my question dear?"

Jenny stood up and took the older women's hands, "That's so sweet of you Ellen but I wouldn't feel right unless I could pay you, but we . . ."

"Bolder Dash . . . I don't want your money Dear. Gosh o Sakes I have more than I know what to do with . . . If anything, I should offer to pay you for keeping me from dying from boredom."

And of course Ellen could resort very quickly back to her aggressive attitudes, "Well . . . Will you let me help you dear or not!"

Jenny smiled and gave Ellen a hug and while holding her hands on the older woman's shoulders answered, "Of course . . . I was going to start working on it the minute they send me a draft."

"Call me when you get it Dear . . . Now let me get going so you can have your dinner in peace."

Ellen let out a gruff and started shuffling toward the door. Jenny walked her to the door with Bailey accompanying the two and Fred just sat quietly with his hands folded on the table raising only one of them briefly to wave and bid Ellen Crenshaw a good evening.

Jenny slowly walked back into the kitchen to see Fred leaning back in his chair, one leg crossed over his other knee, with a huge smile upon his face.

Probably embarrassed over the outcome of this startling encounter with the witch of Oak Grove and sporting a slightly defensive attitude, Jenny placed her hands on her hips and stammered, "Go ahead smart guy . . . Go ahead and say what your dying to say! I know exactly what you're thinking . . . Go ahead."

Fred smiled and stood. "Whaaaat . . . I'm not thinking anything!"

"Riiiight . . . Don't try and con me Fred Goodman. You're gonna say things like . . . See how wrong you can be about people! Or how about this . . . I told you . . . wait to call Pearson and tell them I can't do the project! See, I told you something might come up . . . Go ahead Fred . . . Say it."

Fred walked over to his wife and placed his arms around her and laughed.

"Don't have to say a word. You said it all . . . And I'm still madly in Love with you."

Jenny leaned back a little and smiled, "Did you know about any of this Fred . . . I mean about Ellen's past?"

"Nope . . . I'm just as surprised as you are Sweetheart."

"Gosh, I feel so foolish with the way I felt about that woman." Jenny hung her head down a little and stroked the top of Bailey's head.

"Don't feel bad Hon . . . There was a reason for this to happen now!"

"I know . . . I know . . . Everything happens for a reason . . . Is that what you're going to say?"

Fred laughed again and kissed his wife on the cheek, "Something like that . . . Something like that. Now can we EAT! I'm starving!"

Well, well, well . . . What do you know? What other surprises were waiting around the corner for the Goodman's?

Chapter Seventeen
Thanksgiving Approaches

Jenny had been holding her own for the most part. She still encountered severe fatigue and intermittent dizziness but she was remaining stable without any further symptoms which Doctor Chapman was concerned about.

Fred remembered what the Doctor had said back in September; the closer Jenny gets to full term without any severe changes in her health, the better the chances are of a uncomplicated delivery. But it was a major chore for Fred. Jenny could see the fatigue in his face but Fred refused to slow down.

Still a mystery to Fred, Ellen Crenshaw and Jenny were becoming great friends. Ellen was extremely helpful with the Pearson assignments, making short work of what Jenny would take hours to do. Ellen was courteous and would let Jenny review them for accuracy but Jenny could never find anything wrong with them! Ellen was also helpful around the house and provided great company for Jenny. Fred came back one day from Bens and found Ellen vacuuming the floors! Fred didn't mind. It was one less assignment Fred had to deal with and besides, Fred liked knowing someone was close by to Jenny if he couldn't be.

Darcy turned out to be a Saint. Darcy Shiff no doubt was bonded to Jenny and she too was at the farmhouse every day, and for several hours a day. She did all the shopping and laundry for Fred and Jenny and She and Ben often would come over for dinner, bringing the dinner with them, and then did all the clean up afterwards. Amazing, if you had asked Fred six months ago if he would of guessed life would be this way with Darcy and Ellen Crenshaw, he would of said, 'What are you Nuts!'

Thanksgiving was only a week away and Fred returned from the Town to find Ellen and Darcy busy at work in the parlor.

"Hey . . . What's going on girls?" said Fred with a big smile, as he stepped through the French doors.

Obviously Fred could see they were getting ready to close the parlor up for the winter and Jenny, in her wheel chair, was directing the show.

Now normally, Fred wouldn't close up the house till after Thanksgiving but it didn't appear that they would be doing any entertaining this year. Jenny took advantage of the offered help and decided to do it a little early.

Jenny was using her wheel chair quite a bit now and Fred felt better that she was. Jenny was very prone to getting dizzy and with all the extra weight she was carrying now; it was safer for her to maneuver around the house. Bailey still escorted Jenny everywhere she went!

Darcy was unfolding a sheet to cover the old sofa, "Fred, do you know where the rest of these are . . . I only could find a few!"

"Yeah sure . . . I'll go look for some more!"

Fred went over to Jenny and patted her cheek, "How you doing Sweetheart?"

"Okay I guess." She answered.

She looked very tired and Fred leaned over and whispered in her ear, "I'm glad they're helping but I feel so guilty . . . They do so much for us Jenny."

Jenny sighed, "Yes . . . Me too . . . But I'm so tired all the time. And look at you Mr. Goodman . . . You look exhausted!"

And Fred was. It was only 10 o'clock in the morning but Fred was ready for a nap. Fred went up to one of the spare rooms where he remembered stacking a bunch of covers which he put there last spring for storage.

"Here you go Darcy. . . This should be enough." Fred dropped the sheets on a chair.

"You guys look like your almost done . . . We can't thank you enough for all your help around here! I'll go get some coffee and tea going!"

"Make sure you put saccharin in mine Fred!" Ellen shouted as she finished up with the dusting.

Fred smiled and went into the kitchen as Jenny and Bailey started to follow.

"You ladies have this under control . . . Think I'll give Fred a hand" Jenny said. "Fred's right, I don't know what we would have done without all your help."

Both Darcy and Ellen just smiled at Jenny and Ellen quipped, "Just run along dear . . . Were almost finished."

Only fifteen minutes had passed by . . .

Fred just put a plate of Danish's down on the table when he and Jenny heard the rumbling noise of the large French doors closing.

Both Darcy and Ellen came into the kitchen and took a seat.

"All set Fred . . . All you have to do is turn the heat off and you're all ready for winter. I closed all the doors upstairs as well and the French doors at the end of the hallway." Darcy said.

Fred stood and walked in between Ellen and Darcy who were seated side by side. He placed a hand on each one of their shoulders and leaned over and gave each a kiss on the cheek. "I mean it ladies . . . Jenny and I can't thank you enough for all your help.

We'll never forget it . . . And some way, somehow, I'll find a way to make it up to you!"

Ellen snipped, "Oh Bolder Dash Fred . . . We are glad to be here. . . You know . . . That's what neighbors and friends are for Fred!"

"Yeah but you guys have gone beyond the call to duty!" Fred smiled and sat back down.

It was Jenny's turn. She stood up and she too managed to lean over and hug her two new found friends.

"Well . . . I'm not sure I can take you away from your families much more. I've decided to give my Mom a call and see if she can come out for a while and help us as well." Jenny laughed and continued, "Give you guys a break for a little while!"

Now Fred wasn't aware of Jenny's intentions but at this point, he wasn't going to argue with his wife. The extra help would be appreciated.

Darcy stood up and gave Jenny a big hug, "We don't mind helping. And Jenny, I never told you this before but . . . I always wanted a sister and if I had one . . . I would want her to be just like you."

Darcy smiled but you could see she was holding a tear back, "But I do have to run now. Got to pick up a few things for Ben's Mom and Dad . . . I'll call you later!" With that, Darcy waived to Fred and scooted out the rear kitchen door.

"Good Lord." Ellen said as she struggled to lift herself out of the chair. Jenny grabbed her arm to help the older women up.

"Ah . . . That's better . . . These old bones . . . I've got to run as well. I have a date tonight with the Doc and if I don't get home and get a nap in . . . I'll end up sleeping through it!"

Jenny placed both her hands on Ellen Crenshaw's shoulders and spoke softly, "Ellen, at one time I thought you were the biggest witch in town. But now I have seen something entirely different. I was wrong for prejudging you. You are the sweetest, most compassionate, funniest women I ever met! Not to mention the best editor I have ever seen . . . My talents are minuscule next to yours."

"Oh poppy cock . . . I can't call you the sweetest liar I ever have known . . . Like I did my very first visit here. Because now I've grown to know you too. But you are the most darling woman!"

"Jenny smiled, "I'll walk you to the door."

Well Ellen still could be a forceful woman now and then but Jenny had learned that it was only a façade. A part of this women's unique personality.

"You'll do no such thing . . . Look at you . . . You're as big as a house!" Ellen gently patted Jenny's tummy. "Now you go back and sit in your Wheely ma jig over there . . . I'll let myself out . . . See ya later Fred."

With that, Ellen shuffled toward the door and Fred waved good-bye.

Both Fred and Jenny knew it was time to call in some extra help . . .

Jenny took a seat in her lounger and Fred asked, "So you think we should call your Mom?"

"Yeah . . . I think it's time . . . We can't keep taking advantage of our friends!"

"Your right . . . When do you want to call?" Fred murmured.

"Now . . . If you hand me the phone Sweetheart."

Fred rose from the table and grabbed the portable phone from the kitchen counter and handed it to his wife. As he did she stroked his arm and said, "Fred, I love you. You have been a real sweetheart too . . . Just thought I'd tell ya again."

Fred smiled and took a seat this time in Jenny's Wheely ma jig, as Ellen referred to it. He sported around the kitchen playfully chasing Bailey who was dodging Fred's maneuvers.

Jenny laughed but firmly said, "Will you knock it off! I'm trying to make a phone call here!"

Fred realized he was being a little annoying so he parked Jenny's wheel chair and coaxed Bailey to quiet down.

Jenny tried her Moms house several times but there was no answer. And what was odd as well, the answering machine was turned off.

"That's strange Fred . . . Hope everything is okay?"

Fred, in a confident tone answered, "I'm sure everything is okay. Probably went out and forgot to turn the machine on. But if it will make you feel better. . . Why don't you try one of your sisters?"

"Good idea . . . I'll call Samantha!"

Jenny wasn't real close to her sisters. She maybe talked with Judy, her older sister, two or three times a year but she always got along better with Samantha. Judy was five years older than Jenny and fell into the same kind of life style as Jenny's Mom, marrying for money rather than love!

Jenny and Samantha were closer in age and would write each other back and forth often. And normally they spoke on the phone a couple times a month. Jenny was only a year older than Samantha and Samantha still lived in Columbus only five miles from their Mom. She might know better than Judy, what might be going on with her Mom.

Jenny had a short conversation with her sister . . .

Fred listened intently and could tell by the course of the conversation that Jenny was not too happy with the phone call.

Jenny hung up the phone and in a dejected voice looked up at Fred and sighed, "I should have known better to count on my Mom being around when I need her!"

"What's wrong Sweetheart. . . You look sad!"

"Well apparently Mrs. Bachman is off to Europe with Mr. Bachman . . . And they are not expected to return till February . . . Hmmm! Nice of her to tell me. Nice time to go to Europe when she said she would come out and help her pregnant daughter!"

Fred listened as he stood up from the table and then knelt down in front of Jenny who was still seated in the lounger. "Gosh . . . I'm sorry Hon. Why did Samantha have to go so quickly?"

"Oh she said the kids were acting up or something? Who cares anyway. . . I never could count on them for anything . . . Not like Darcy and Ellen!"

Tears came to Jenny's eyes and Fred did his best to console her but he knew that Jenny never did have a good relationship with any of her family. And Fred knew why as well, Jenny's Dad.

A few minutes went by and then Jenny reluctantly said, "Maybe you could call your Mom?"

Fred hesitated a little, "Yeah . . . But that could have some problems as well. Mom would come if Dad will accompany her. She won't go anywhere without Dad. And he won't step a foot in this house!"

"Oh yeah . . . I forgot about that. " Jenny answered.

"You know Jenny . . . I could never quite understand that. There must be more to that story than what he says!"

"What do you mean Fred?" Jenny answered inquisitively.

"Well . . . What I mean is . . . I know he didn't like Grandpa Sebastian much. And He didn't like Farming. But why would that be a reason for not wanting to come into this house? Sebastian's been gone a long time now . . . And even at Uncle Harry's funeral . . . He didn't come back to the house? I remember Aunt Ruthie making excuses for Dad when Mom and I were the only ones to show up?"

Jenny listened and Fred shook his head and became more puzzled over this mystery. It had bugged Fred for many years, yet he never approached his Father with it.

Jenny remained quiet and Fred eventually spoke again, "Tell you what . . . I'll give them a call tomorrow. Let me think on how to handle this before I call."

Jenny replied, "That's fine Fred . . . How about we get some lunch and maybe lie down for a little bit? I'm really tired!"

Fred rose off the floor where he had positioned himself to console Jenny. "Okay . . . How about a salad and some of that chicken soup Darcy's Mom sent over?"

"That would be great Fred . . . But you better hurry before I fall asleep!"

The day finally ended but just as Jenny and Fred were about to leave the kitchen and head off to bed, Fred's Mom called . . .

"Hello" Fred answered.

"Well Hello Fred!"

"Mom . . . Believe it or not I was going to give you a call tomorrow."

"That's nice dear . . . I talked to Jenny last week and I just wanted to see how she was doing?"

"Well, about the same as last week but things are getting hectic around here!"

Fred's Mom cut him off, "I can imagine Fred . . . You do sound run down . . . And Jenny has been telling me about everything you have been doing for her and how this ordeal has been running you ragged."

"Yeah, I don't like to admit it Mom but . . . With my freelance stuff and Jenny, and the Farm . . . Gosh! I didn't think it would be this hard."

Jenny patiently listened and she knew Fred must really be feeling the strain because he never admitted it before and never, ever, complained.

"Well listen Dear . . . Last week Jenny mentioned she was thinking about seeing if her Mother would come on? Any word yet?"

"Yeah . . . Not good news . . . Her Mother is over in Europe with her Father!"

"Europe . . . Gosh sakes . . . That poor girl . . . She must be heartbroken?"

"Yep!" Fred didn't want Jenny to feel any worse than she already did so he changed the subject a little.

"Darcy and Ellen Crenshaw have been great but we kind of feel like maybe we are taking too much advantage of our friends!"

"Yes I can understand. Isn't that something about Jenny and Ellen . . . Who would of thought!" Fred's mother chuckled and Fred did the same.

Fred's Mother was a kind women and she didn't want to make her son ask so her next words were, "Listen Fred, I spoke with your Father about coming up for a while . . . Would the first week in December be okay or soon enough?"

Oh Yeah . . . That would be great but . . . But what about Dad? You know . . . About him being on the Farm. Or is he going to leave you here and stay with somebody else?"

Fred hated to bring that subject up but he thought he better get it out in the open.

Fred's Mom paused a moment or two and then she responded to Fred's concerns, "You know your Father Fred . . . Stubborn as they come. Hopefully it will be enough for him to be there but I think he needs to discuss this issue with you directly!"

"Mom . . . You know something about that situation with Dad, which I don't . . . Don't you Mom?"

Fred's Mom cleared her throat and with a little more firmness in her voice stated, "Fred . . . I'm surprised you never talked to your Father about this? Why Fred, you're a grown man now?"

With a slight hesitation Fred answered, "I always had my suspicions that there was more to tell . . . But I guess when I was younger, I was afraid Dad would get mad. Then when I got older . . . I guess I felt like it was none of my business."

Fred's Mom laughed, "Oh you Goodman boys . . . You are all great guys but none of you know how to be open and honest with each other! Especially your Father! By the way . . . Your Brothers said Hi! Lord, if I didn't call them, I don't think I'd ever hear from either one of them!" And then she laughed again.

Fred spent a few more minutes on the phone and then gave Jenny the good news but she probably already figured it out . . .

"Your Mom's coming?" Jenny blurted no sooner than Fred placed the phone back in its cradle.

"Yes . . . Sometime in the first week of December. Is that okay?"

"Of course. You know how much I like your Mom. But what about your Dad?"

Fred shrugged his shoulders, "Don't know?"

Jenny smiled and got up from the lounger and sat back down in her wheelchair and motioning with her hands, "You can fill me in as you chauffer me down to the bedroom."

Bailey lumbered up from the floor and Fred laughed as he flipped the lights out as he moved through the kitchen doorway.

The last words heard that evening were. . .

"Hey will you slow down Fred . . . This isn't the Indianapolis Five Hundred!"

Chapter Eighteen
Fears Realized

Thanksgiving went by in an uneventful way for Fred and Jenny.

This was out of the ordinary for them as Fred would usually invite his Aunt and Uncle and Cousins, from his Mother's side of the family, over for Holidays. Roger would of course be there and at least last year, Claire attended.

Although Fred and Jenny received many invitations, they felt that the best thing for Jenny, would be to have a very quiet Thanksgiving. Everybody who normally was part of the Goodman Thanksgiving Day festivities certainly understood the change of plans this year.

Roger actually was invited and accepted to have Dinner with Howard and Mildred Shiff and of course Ben and Darcy were there. Fred still chuckled over the unexpected friendship between Ben and Roger and the gossip in town had it, that Roger was elevated to a Dairy Manager. Who would have imagined!

Believe it or not, Fred had actually found the time in the last few months to clean out the room next to Jenny's office where they intended to have the nursery. The new Goodman's expected arrival was projected toward the end of December. Fred painted the walls, the color Jenny wanted, which wasn't the blue Fred had suggested! It ended up being, as Jenny put it, a neutral color suitable for a boy, or a girl. Darcy found a great used crib and dressers and Ellen hung some new curtains. The room looked fantastic.

But Fred always felt a little ominous leaving the room every time he was in there. He was worried that something might go terribly wrong with the pregnancy and there was no way for him to completely rid those haunting thoughts from his mind.

But that wasn't the only room Fred now had to get ready . . .

Fred struggled as he moved through the doorway holding the last three cardboard boxes he needed to move upstairs. He couldn't see in front him too well and didn't notice Jenny in her wheelchair.

"Hi Hon", Jenny announced her presence.

Fred jumped, stumbled, and all three boxes careened to the floor.

"Jeez . . . I could of almost hit you with these boxes. Let me know a little sooner when your around Hon!", Fred Grumbled.

Jenny tried to smile but Fred could see she wasn't feeling too good.

"Sorry Sweetheart . . . Didn't mean to jump all over you for my clumsiness." Fred apologized.

"That's Okay Fred . . . When did you start moving all this stuff out?"

"This morning . . . Right after my Mom called and said they decided to drive up and they were on their way!"

"That's good. When do you think they'll get here?" Jenny asked.

"Couple days anyway. Dad isn't exactly a speed demon when it comes to driving. I just have these boxes to bring up stairs . . . And clean up a little in here."

Jenny wheeled closer to the door and peeked in, "A little . . . Whew . . . You better open the windows and air this room out!"

"Yeah . . . I'll get it all set and besides . . . You know my Mom . . . She'll probably clean it again after she gets here!"

"Is this room going to be okay for them . . . I mean your Mom . . . Or what's happening with your Dad? Is he going to stay here too?"

Fred stuffed his hands in his pockets.

"Don't know what Dads going to do? Guess we'll wait and see when he gets here. Yeah this room should Okay. It's large, has two closets, and is close to the bathroom and kitchen. This was Harry and Ruthie's Room"

"Yes I know . . . You only mentioned that about a hundred times. C'mon . . . Let's go get a coffee." Jenny smiled and started wheeling toward the kitchen.

Fred gave Bailey a playful slap on his backside as Bailey accompanied the wheelchair to the kitchen. Fred followed the procession.

The Day went by slow and easy . . .

Fred prepared a roast for an early Dinner as Jenny appeared to be in better spirits, than usual and had a hearty appetite this day, which wasn't always the case lately.

"Fred that was delicious and before you clean . . . Do you think we could go out and sit on the porch? Like we used to?"

Since late September, Jenny hadn't felt much like meditating and chatting with her husband like they always did after dinner. It was their normal routine, sort of a ritual which got lost in the shuffle of Jenny's poorer health.

"What are you nuts?" Fred exclaimed as he looked over to his wife as if she was crazy. "It's December, it's cold out!"

Jenny giggled in her trademarked manor when she thought Fred was acting too over protective of her.

"I'll be fine . . . Besides it's not that cold and I'll put on a coat."

Fred sighed, and looked out the kitchen window. The daylight hadn't quite disappeared yet and he groaned a little.

"I'll be right back." And Fred left the kitchen and returned holding a wool blanket.

"C'mon if you're going . . . It's getting dark!"

Fred helped Jenny from the chair and they went out to the porch and sat in the glider which was here since the days of Harry and Ruthie.

Jenny sat on the glider and motioned for Fred to come sit next to her. Fred threw the blanket over her and sat down.

Jenny held the blanket up and said, "Scoot over and snuggle!" and Fred did.

It wasn't as cold as Fred thought. Winter was moving in with a gentle change rather than a drastic one and there still was no prediction for snow.

Jenny grabbed Fred's hand, "We are almost there Sweetheart . . . The baby is due at the end of the month."

"Gosh Yes . . . It's been something else around here though hasn't it?" Fred let out a sigh.

Jenny laughed, "Yes it has and you've been terrific Fred."

Fred patted Jenny on her hand. The couple slowly gazed out over the back of the farm.

Realizing that her husband looked content, a look she hadn't seen in a while, Jenny remained silent for a minute or two before she spoke.

"So . . . In the spring you will officially start the Goodman Farm again, Eh Fred!"

Fred smiled, "Yeah . . . Guess so. . . With the help of Ben that's for sure!"

"Well everybody has been terrific! Darcy, Ben, Ellen, Mildred and Howard Shiff, Roger, Dave and Tony down at the garage . . . Wow . . . Can't name them all. Now your Mom and Dad." Jenny ran down a large list of people who had been very supportive.

Jenny reached out to pet Bailey's head, "And last but not least, my sweetie pie Bailey."

Bailey leaned over when he heard his name and gently poked his nose into Jenny's neck.

Fred nodded but Jenny continued, "Maybe I should tell you this more . . . Besides the fact that I am still madly in love with you . . . I love living here in Oak Grove. I like the people here and it is so much different than Columbus Ohio."

Fred laughed, "Well. . . We'll see if you still feel the same way when you get cow pucky all over your shoes and clothes. . . Or I track it all over the house!"

Jenny giggled and the couple spent the next hour, even after it got dark, sitting and talking about the recent past and the prospects of the future. Bailey of course just stood next to Jenny and often she would reach from beneath the blanket and stroke his head.

The Evening finally came to a close . . .

Fred was feeling fairly content as he prepared the house with his final inspection for the evening. Maybe because it was getting closer and closer to Jenny's due date or perhaps it was that Pearson had lightened the load on Jenny. Jenny told her employer about her pregnancy and they were glad to grant Jenny a leave of absence. Whatever it was Fred, couldn't believe he was so calm that evening?

When Fred returned to the bedroom, Jenny was still awake but reading something in bed. Fred changed and went into the bathroom and while he was brushing his teeth, he nonchalantly peeked around the corner of the doorway to the bedroom. His eye caught something peculiar looking which drew his interest.

Bailey was walking in circles on Jenny's side of the bed, occasionally whimpering, and once or twice putting his front paws up onto the bed.

"Ah C'mon Bailey . . . I'm trying to read." Jenny said several times to her companion.

Fred finished brushing his teeth and quietly stood in the doorway watching Bailey's unusual performance.

After a few more spins by Bailey, Fred walked over to the dog and gently held his face and spoke, "What's up Bailey . . . What's wrong with you tonight? Never seen you do this before Boy!"

Fred looked to Jenny and shrugged and Jenny said, "Fred, did you let Bailey out for his walk?"

"Yeah . . . . Right after we came in from the porch, remember?"

"Oh yes . . . Maybe he's just trying to play or something." And Jenny just went back to reading her book.

Bailey finally calmed down and Fred crawled into bed but he had a very hard time falling asleep after Jenny shut her reading light off.

Occasional through the night, Fred would see the silhouette of Bailey looking onto the bed at Jenny, as if he were checking on her. The calmness and contentment that Fred had felt earlier in the evening was now replaced with concern.

The next morning arrived . . .

Fred groaned as he struggled to wake up. He felt like he was up all night, which he practically was, dumbfounded over Bailey's actions the night before. He waved his hand over to Jenny's side of the bed but she wasn't there. Fred sat up with a start. He quickly grabbed his robe and sped down the hallways to the kitchen.

When he arrived, he was stricken with awe. There stood Jenny, fully dressed, hair done up and make up on, frying up some bacon on the stove.

Fred scratched his head and stood there looking very confused, "Hon . . . What the heck!"

Jenny laughed, "Fred don't look so surprised . . . I feel great today! Don't know why . . . But I feel great!"

Fred slumped into a kitchen chair and Jenny rushed over a cup of coffee, "It's been a while since I felt good enough to serve my husband his morning coffee!"

Fred couldn't get over what he was seeing. He looked over to Bailey who was sitting, almost at attention, staring at every move Jenny made.

Fred scratched his head again looking for something to say, "You can't eat bacon Honey."

"That's right . . . But you can. Now why don't you go get dressed and I'll get the eggs going as soon as you get back . . . Now Shoo!"

Fred was in total refusal to believe in what he was witnessing . . .

When breakfast was over, Jenny even did the dishes. And she refused to let Fred help. This was overwhelming Fred's thoughts.

He still must have had a very bewildered look on his face when Jenny took a seat in her lounger.

"Fred . . . You look like you've seen a ghost or something?"

"Sort of." Fred answered. "A ghost from Jenny's passed!"

"Fred don't fight it. You should be happy that I feel so good today. It's unbelievable!" Jenny exclaimed.

Fred mumbled in a sarcastic tone, "That's the problem Jenny. This is not normal and maybe a little too good to be true!"

"Ah Fred. . . What ever happen to your famous philosophy . . . Everything happens for a reason!"

"Oh I didn't forget it . . . That's what I'm afraid of. What is the reason?"

Jenny held her hands up to her side, "Who knows Fred but I'm not going to let you spoil my good day!"

"Okay, Okay . . . Did you say that Darcy was coming up this morning?" Fred asked.

"Yes, about 10:30 . . . She has to drop something off at the barn to Ben and then she's coming up to the house. She has some baby clothes that she wants to give me. . . . Why do you ask?"

"Well it's just that I have to get those new Andross Schemas out in the mail by 11AM or they won't get back in time to Andross. So I'll wait till Darcy gets here."

"Fred, you have to stop being a worrywart . . . Suit yourself . . . Just don't screw up those whatever's. You need that work to carry us through the winter."

"I know . . . I know." Fred answered and with that he went up to his studio to get the papers ready to mail and Jenny picked up her book and started reading. Bailey stood right up against the lounger and refused to lie down.

About an hour passed . . .

Fred returned to the kitchen with three big envelopes in his hand and looked at his wrist watch, "Its 10:30, Where's Darcy?"

Jenny chuckled, "Fred relax . . . Just go and mail those envelopes. She'll be here shortly."

Fred was worried about something. He didn't know why but he was. He walked over to the kitchen window and looked down to the barn.

"Here she is . . . She's just pulling into the barn."

"Fred, you're going to run out of time, just go . . . Darcy will be up in a minute."

Fred had one hand on the window sill and the other on the table and he turned to Jenny. "Okay but . . ."

Fred stood and Jenny walked over to him and softly smiled.

"Fred . . . I don't know what's gotten into you today but . . . Thank you for caring. I love you Fred, Now go." Jenny then gave her husband a big hug and kiss.

With a lot of hesitation Fred walked to the door and turned to look at his wife. He then turned toward Bailey. He stopped a minute and tried to smile. Fred put his hand down to his belt where he wore his medical alert pager and he pushed the test mode. The beeper went off.

When the Med Alert people came in September, they gave Fred a pager as well, so he would know instantly if there were any problems. He tested Jenny's every morning but he didn't think to see if Jenny had hers close by.

Fred tried one more time to give his wife a smile but it just wouldn't come. Fred was sensing something but he couldn't put his finger on it.

Fred sped down the drive to the road . . .

He slowed down long enough when he got to the barn, rolled down the window and waved his hand out to Darcy, Ben and Roger who were standing next to Darcy's car.

About fifteen minutes after Fred left, Jenny got up out of the lounge chair and peered out the window. She looked at Bailey and said, "Come Bailey . . . I'll try and use the bathroom before Darcy gets here."

Jenny started walking down the front hall to the junction of the back hallway. Walking wasn't very easy for her lately as she had gained 56 pounds during the pregnancy. It was more of a wobble than a walk.

Bailey hugged her side to give her support. As Jenny turned the corner, she suddenly stopped. Bailey started going spastic. Jenny put one hand up to the wall and the other on her forehead.

"Oh Bailey I don't feel . . ."

With that Jenny turned her back up against the wall and sank to the floor with her legs outstretched. Bailey nudged her so she might stay upright and keep her back against the wall and whimpered loudly, maybe hoping somebody would hear.

Jenny started drooling and twitching and Bailey was frantic. Pacing one way and then scurrying the other.

Finally Bailey ran down the main hallway to the kitchen. He first went to the kitchen door which was closed, blocking the screen door which he jumped through before when Jenny was in trouble. He even tried to turn the door knob with his mouth but to no avail. Bailey went to the closed kitchen windows and started barking hoping to catch the attention of someone outside. But apparently Darcy, Ben and Roger had gone inside the barn and could not hear Bailey's distress calls.

Bailey would not give up. He then ran back down the hallways, passed Jenny, and went into the bedroom.

He looked around and finally spied what he was looking for, the medical alert pager which Jenny had left on her night stand.

It was amazing that Bailey knew what it was for. Jenny and Fred would go through the once a week tests with the communications division of the Medical Alert Team and Bailey always watched.

Running back to Jenny with the pager in his mouth, Bailey hoped Jenny would see it and use to call for help. But it was no use. Jenny was now lying completely on the floor tremendously shaking. Bailey shook the pager out of his mouth so violently; it slammed up against the wall.

Whimpering and crying Bailey ran back to the kitchen and stood on his hinds and peered out the window. Nobody was to be seen. Bailey stopped a second. Then he spied the French doors leading into the parlor. He darted toward them for a moment, then he turned around and backed all the way up against the far kitchen wall. Then, with a lurch, Bailey ran as fast as he could to build up speed and lunged through the glass section of one of the French door leafs sliding to a stop after knocking over two tables and a lamp.

But Bailey wasn't out of the house yet. There was only one more avenue of escape; through the big bay window on the front of the house.

Limping slightly, Bailey went to the other end of the parlor. Without hesitation, and with a big howl, Bailey ran through the parlor and leaped up and through the large Bay window careening shards of glass everywhere.

Bailey landed on his side of the gently sloping lawn tumbling over and over. Bailey was on the run before he even finished falling and raced toward the barn.

Darcy, Ben, and Roger who were now back out in front of the barn heard the sound of shattering glass. They watched Bailey leap through the bay window and run to them for help.

Darcy held her hands to her face, "Oh my God . . . Jenny's in trouble!"

Ben already was making tracks for the house and Darcy followed. Roger started to follow as well but just as he started, Bailey collapsed on the barn drive. Roger stopped, hesitated slightly and then ran back to Bailey's side.

Darcy and Ben found Jenny lying on the floor having severe seizures. Ben called 911 but the sound of sirens already could be heard. Bailey apparently triggered the Medical alert pager.

Darcy slid to Jenny's side trying to hold her enough to keep her from hurting herself and Ben dashed to the kitchen door to let the paramedics in.

Fred just got back into his car at the post office . . .

Fred jumped when the pager signal went off and the transmission came through.

"Medical Alert . . . Repeat . . . Medical Alert . . . Fred please return home as soon as possible . . . Emergency help in transit to your home."

"I knew it . . . I knew it . . . Oh God . . . Please let Jenny be okay!" Fred cried out loud and stepped on the pedal as he sped toward the farm.

Fred could see the red blinking lights up in the farmhouse drive and he nearly slid off the road as he rounded the corner at Rte. 16 and Pasture Lane and almost again as he turned in his drive leading to the house.

Fred saw Roger hovering over Bailey and both were covered in blood.

While Roger was kneeling over Bailey he shouted to Fred, "Go . . . Go . . . Go" as he waved his arm toward the house.

Sliding his car onto the grass so as not to block the Rescue Vehicles, Fred bolted from the car just as the paramedics exited the house with Jenny strapped on a stretcher.

"This is her husband" Darcy shouted as she followed the stretcher out of the house.

Fred quickly looked to Darcy and tried to rush to his wife's side but was cautioned away by one of the paramedics.

"Fred!" Darcy shouted, "Bailey" was all she could say and she started crying.

One of the paramedics turned to Fred, "If you're the husband you can ride with us to the hospital . . . But up front."

Fred could hardly talk as he was consumed with fear for his wife, "Is she okay . . . Is she Okay?"

Can't tell yet Sir . . . Let's get her to the hospital as quick as we can . . . They are ready for us."

Fred climbed in the front seat and as the ambulance slowly moved down the drive, Fred could see Roger, still leaning over Bailey. Roger was crying.

Fred turned to look at his wife through the small window between the cab and the ambulance.

Chapter Nineteen
The Worst Feared

The ambulance arrives at the hospital!

Despite Fred's fierce objections, the paramedics and ER Technicians urged and ushered Fred into a small family waiting room which was private and apart from the main ER waiting area.

A nurse stayed with Fred to try and comfort him and act as a liaison with the ER Staff who immediately rushed Jenny into one of the ER Surgery stations. Doctor Chapman was already down at the ER awaiting Jenny's arrival.

Fred sat on the edge of his chair, cupping his hands around his face, "Please oh please let Jenny be okay." Fred recited this over and over and the nurse gently placed her hand on Fred's shoulder rubbing it gently.

About twenty minutes had passed when Doctor Chapman opened the door and stepped in.

Fred immediately jumped to his feet, "Jenny. . . Is she. . ."

Dr. Chapman motioned both his hands for Fred to sit, "Calm down Fred and I'll let you know where we are at."

Fred sat and quietly heard Doctor Chapman out.

"I'm not going to lie to you Fred but Jenny is in tough shape right now!"

"Oh my Dear God!" Fred whimpered with tears seeping from his eyes.

The Doctor placed a hand on Fred's forearm and continued.

"Here's what we are going to do . . . We first have to stabilize Jenny's vitals and control her seizures. When we get that under control, we are going to move her up to the regular Surgery Center. Then we will see how the baby is doing through all of this and hopefully we can perform a cesarean."

Fred looked up to Doctor Chapman, "You don't sound very confident Doc?"

"I can't sugar coat this for you Fred . . . Right now it's a fifty, fifty chance that we can control this. All I can assure you of is that we have an excellent medical staff and facilities. We will do everything which we can Fred . . . Everything . . . Now I have to get back to Jenny and the nurse will keep you posted and show you where you can wait after we move Jenny."

With that, Doctor Chapman hurried away from the room.

Four hours had passed before Jenny was moved upstairs to Surgery . . .

This was a nicer waiting area compared to the others Fred had seen at the hospital before. There was a larger area in the center with several separate alcove areas off to the sides. Some had chairs and small tables and others had lounging chairs.

Only one older gentleman was there with Fred at the moment and he appeared to be sleeping in one of the loungers. But Fred was too nervous to sit let alone, fall asleep.

Continually pacing the whole width of the waiting area and often down the adjoining hallways, Fred made his rounds over and over again.

Often Fred, so full of anxiety, would forget where he was and cry out loud, "Oh my God . . . How could this be this way!"

Many times Fred would stop and bury his head onto the walls and bang his head a few times.

It was apparent to the two nurses on duty at the small reception station of the waiting area, that Fred was in a terribly frazzled state and offered to give him a mild sedative, but Fred refused.

It was now about 4pm and Fred was so exhausted that he had to sit. Leaning forward, resting his elbows on his knees and cradling his head in his hands, he stared at the floor. Fred didn't hear the chime when the doors of the elevator opened.

Darcy and Ben burst out of the elevator. Darcy first looked left and then right. She spotted Fred in the chair and rushed over to him and sat down on the floor in front of Fred. Ben came over and patted Fred on the shoulder and took the seat next to Fred.

"Fred . . . How's Jenny?" Darcy said softly but with sincere compassion.

Fred looked up at Darcy, "We don't know yet . . . Doctor Chapman told me about 5 hours ago they were trying to stabilize Jenny or something. . . Before they could do anything . . . Jeez . . . What's taking so long?"

"Well, were here for you Fred." Ben asserted.

"Thanks Ben but . . . I should have never left the house this morning!"

Fred slapped his knee and continued, "Damn it . . . If only I stayed I may have been able to get Jenny here sooner. Maybe this all could have been prevented."

Darcy quickly looked to Ben. Both Ben and Darcy realized that Fred didn't exactly know what happened that morning.

Darcy cut Fred off from rambling out over his guilt with the situation.

"Fred . . . Don't be so hard on yourself . . . You couldn't have gotten the Medics there any sooner."

Fred looked confused. "Yeah right . . . Seconds count for stuff like this!"

"I know Fred but even as Ben and I ran up to the house . . . We already could hear the sirens. The Paramedics were already on their way! When Ben called 911 they told Ben that the call had already come in."

Fred who was even more confused looked over to Ben who gave a nod of confirmation.

Ben then proceeded to give Fred some more of the details.

"You see Fred. . . Bailey made the call. Somehow, someway Bailey triggered the alarm on Jenny's device! As a matter of fact . . . The fireman I talked to after you left in the ambulance with Jenny, examined the device. He said he found it on the floor about 10 feet where Jenny collapsed and it looked like it had been chewed or dropped, or something. Anyway, it was badly damaged."

Ben paused a moment and then continued and Fred just stared at Ben in a very surprised way.

"Bailey apparently tried to get out through the kitchen door . . . The knob was really bent . . . I guess Baily then stormed through the French doors to the parlor and then again out the bay window to get us."

Fred just kept shaking his head in almost disbelief, "Whoa . . . That dog . . . That's the second time he came to the rescue for Jenny. Unbelievable . . . Amazing!"

Ben placed his hand on Fred's shoulder and Fred remained silent a few moments before he looked at Ben again and grimly said, "How's Bailey? How's he doing?"

"We don't know yet Fred? Roger took him over to Doc Wilsons . . . Bailey's in rough shape too. He took a whole bunch of glass in his sides and underbelly. Roger called us as we were on our way down here and said the Doc was going to operate on Bailey. Guess Roger's hanging out there for a while before he heads down here?"

Ben continued, "Hope you don't mind Fred but I sent a couple guys up with some plywood . . . To board up the window and put a new knob on the kitchen door. Ellen Crenshaw showed up with a cleaning crew to pick up the glass and straighten things up. I knew you wouldn't want to deal with that when you got home."

Again Fred shook his head, "Thanks Ben . . . Thanks. But how could this all happen guys? How could everything be going so good for Jenny and I and then all of a sudden . . . This happens . . . Why?"

Ben and Darcy sympathized and agreed with the nods of their heads

A few short minutes later . . .

The doors of one of the operating rooms, halfway down the long hallway flew open and Doc Chapman, dressed in scrubs, accompanied by a nurse dressed the same, briskly walked toward the waiting room.

Fred jumped to his feet but the Doctor motioned for Fred to stay where he was. The Doctor approached Fred and placed both his hands on Fred's shoulders.

"How you holding up Fred?" The Doctor asked.

Fred really didn't answer and the Doctor looked over to Ben and Darcy, "Are these guys with you Fred?"

"Yeah . . . This is Ben and Darcy . . . Very good friends."

The Doctor smiled, "Do you want them in on this Fred?"

"Of course!" Fred answered.

"Fine . . . Now follow me."

The Doctor showed Fred, Ben and Darcy into a little conference room off of the waiting area. He closed the door and lowered the blind on the door. Everybody took a seat including the nurse who was holding a clipboard and a pen.

Doctor Chapman remained standing. Fred, Ben, and Darcy sat there motionless expecting to hear terrible news.

"Thanks for your patience guys . . . It's been a rough day that's for sure! This is Eleanor . . . She is the nurse assigned to Jenny for the duration."

The nurse smiled and Fred, Darcy, and Ben said a quiet hello, almost in unison

The Doctor continued, "Fortunately we have been able to stabilize Jenny's condition but we have not yet received the results back on the condition of the baby. We should know shortly but I didn't want to keep you folks out here to long, without knowing something."

Doctor Chapman now directed his attention to Fred directly.

"Fred . . . We're not out of the woods yet. The next three to four hours will tell us the story. Eventually we will have to do a cesarean. It will be critical in trying to save Jenny but I can't tell you yet about what the condition of the baby will be after birth. The baby has undergone the same trauma as Jenny and Jenny had a sky high blood pressure along with some internal hemorrhaging, and of course serious convulsions."

"That doesn't sound good Doctor?" Fred murmured.

"I'm afraid it isn't the best news Fred but we are in better shape now, than we were a few hours ago. As soon as we do the cesarean . . . We will bring the baby to the maternity intensive care and give it a complete evaluation."

Fred, Ben and Darcy just sat dumbfounded, at a loss for words.

"Now listen folks . . . I will get word to you the minute I have something to report."

Doctor Chapman walked over behind Fred where he was seated and started rubbing his shoulders.

The Doctor leaned over Fred and said, "Fred, are you sure you won't let me get something for you to take. A mild sedative . . . It won't knock you out or anything like that . . . You are so full of anxiety and we need you to be strong for Jenny when this is all over."

Fred stood and turned toward Doctor Chapman, "Thanks but no thanks . . . I'm fine."

Nobody in the room believed that and the Doctor gruffed a little and said, "Okay Fred."

The Doctor headed for the door, turned toward the threesome, smiled in a reassuring way and left the room leaving Fred and his two friends still stunned and bewildered about everything which the Doctor had said and what had been going on.

Roger showed up at the waiting area at County Hospital at about 7:30pm . . .

The elevator bell announced Roger's arrival. Roger stepped out of the elevator and first looked to the reception window, but quickly noticed Fred.

Fred had gone through another round of pacing and now that he knew which operating room Jenny was in, he chose a new seat which, with a slight lean to the right, he could look down the hallway, hoping to see Doctor Chapman on his way back.

"Hi Fred . . . How's Jenny?"

Roger took the seat right next to Fred. Roger wasn't very good in situations like this and he really didn't know how to console his friend.

"Well Rogg . . . It's not going too well. We still don't have any real answers but the Doc says. . . Maybe in the next few hours!"

Roger lightly slapped Fred on the knee and folded his hands on his lap.

"Thanks Rogg for seeing to Bailey . . . How's he doing?"

Roger stammered a little, "Ah . . . Not so good Fred. Doctor Wilson said he had a lot of glass which pierced into his stomach and sides . . . One piece nearly got his heart. . . I'm sorry Fred. The Doctor operated on him but he won't know anything till morning. Right now Bailey's resting comfortably but!"

"That's okay Rogg . . . You did all you could."

Roger moaned, "Gosh I hope Jenny will be okay Fred."

Fred shrugged his shoulders and slumped back into his chair.

Roger sat back as well and decided to be quiet for a little bit. Then he suddenly perked up, "Hey Fred . . . Where's Ben and Darcy? I thought they were here?"

"They're here. They went down to the cafeteria to get something to eat . . . Before they close at eight."

Roger quickly looked at his wrist watch, "Ah Fred, would you like me to pick you up something to eat? Before they close and all!"

"No Roger . . . Thanks anyway, but you can go!"

Roger jumped from his seat and headed toward the elevator, "You sure you don't want something Fred? Maybe I should just stay here with you?"

"No. . . No you go Rogg . . . You must be really hungry. . . I'll be fine."

Fred chuckled as Roger disappeared into the elevator and whispered quietly to himself, "That Rogg . . . He will never give up the opportunity to eat . . . No matter what's going on!"

But Fred didn't mind, Roger had turned out to be a better friend than ever before.

The waiting game was still not over.

Chapter Twenty
Secrets Revealed

Fred dozed off in the chair!

Fred was obviously exhausted and as one might think; it would not be too easy to zonk off in an arm chair like Fred did. He had tucked his feet under the chair with his elbows resting on each arm of the chair, and his head was tilted back.

It was about 45 minutes before Ben, Darcy and Roger came back from the cafeteria. Fred didn't realize they had returned until Darcy softly rubbed the top of his head and whispered in his ear.

"Fred . . . Fred Sweetie . . . Wake up . . . Somebody special is here to see you."

Fred groaned and fought hard to open his eyes. He rubbed his eyes a little, blinked a little, and tried to focus on the people standing in front of him.

Fred finally came back to reality and tried to jump from his seat but it resembled a stagger.

"Mom . . . Dad . . . When did you guys get here?"

Fred's Mom smiled and wrapped her arms around her son.

"Oh Fred you look so tired . . . My poor Hon!"

Fred's Dad waited for an opening in his wife's affections and stepped closer to shake Fred's hand and then he gave his son a large bear hug.

"Good to see you Fred . . . Wish it was under better circumstances. We just got in about an hour and a half ago. We stopped at the farmhouse hoping to surprise you and Ellen Crenshaw was there . . . She filled us in on the news and . . . Ordered us right down here."

"Gosh . . . I knew you were coming Dad but I guess I sort of forgot." And Fred scuffed the side of his head a little.

"That's quite alright Son. We met Ben and Darcy down on the first floor and they filled us in on the details Son . . . We'll hope for the best Son. That's all we can do now . . . That's all we can do."

Fred's Mom coaxed Fred back into his chair and then seated herself next to Fred. She tried her best to console her son while she constantly rubbed the top of one of his legs.

Fred's Dad explained that he had to stand for a while since he was sitting down the whole ride up here. Mr. Goodman wandered through the waiting area occasionally making small talk with Roger and the Shiff kids, as he referred to them.

Everybody was quiet for the most part but Robert Goodman decided to go over to the receptionist window and he softly started talking to the Nurse. Then he came over to his wife and whispered something in her ear.

Robert Goodman stood in front of his son and took him by the arm, "Take a walk with me son . . . I want to show you something."

"Dad I can't leave . . . What if they need me for something or . . ."

His Dad insisted, "Fred I spoke with the Nurse over there. She gave me a pager . . . Besides it's not far and I think it's fairly important."

Fred hesitated but his Mother waved her hand indicating Fred should go with his Father.

"It's okay Sweetheart . . . We'll come get you quickly if need be."

Fred's Dad guided him to the next floor and up a small stairway to an outside Patio . . .

"Wow . . . Look at the view . . . I didn't know this was here Dad!" Fred was surprised.

Fred's Dad moved over to the handrail and leaned over slightly folding his hands to the outside of the handrail. Fred did the same.

"Well it wasn't here when your brothers were born. They put it in shortly after. But when your mother was bringing you into the world . . . I spent a lot of time up here."

Fred smiled the best he could and his Dad finished the story, "You gave your Mother an awfully hard time. She was in labor with you for 18 hours . . . Shew . . . I could hear her screaming all the way up here."

Fred laughed and tapped his Dad's side in jest.

"But that's not why I brought you up here son. I brought you up here to finally level with you . . . To be honest."

Fred had a very quizzical look upon his face and his interests heighten to the point which he temporarily forgot all about the real problem he was facing.

Fred's Dad cleared his throat and began.

"Ahem well here goes. I'm going to tell you the real reason why I haven't set foot on that farm since I joined the Navy. You see . . . Your Grandpa Sebastian was a real tough unreasonable man. I mean Fred, he was darn right nasty. I know you got along with him okay but he was an old man then and you were just a youngin. Apparently he seemed to favor you Fred but that wasn't the case for my brothers and I . . . Except Harry. Harry was his first born and obviously his favorite. Well when Douglas was old enough he joined the Army and as you know, he was sadly a casualty of Korean War. I guess I had enough guts to leave and join the Navy but . . . Michael . . . Well he was not a very strong kid. He was a little different than the rest of us. He liked to read and he was a small fry kind of guy. Michael couldn't take much to the hard work on the farm. If he had been older, I would have talked him into joining the service too, but he was only sixteen when I left. Well your Grandpa Sebastian was brutal on that boy . . . Always belittling him, criticizing, and even once or twice . . . Took him behind the barn and beat him up."

Fred's Dad got a little choked up and paused for a while.

Fred placed his hand on his Dads shoulder, "Gosh Dad . . . I didn't know . . . Now didn't Michael die in a car accident?"

"Well that was the story but it wasn't quite the truth."

Fred was patient to hear the rest of the story and mystified as to why his Dad waited till now to tell him.

"I was stationed out in San Diego when Michael died. But about 5 days before . . . I received a letter from Michael. He said that if Sebastian climbed on his case one more time . . . He was going to run his car at full speed into the old Milton Bridge abutment. And that's exactly what happened. I tried to call him and I sent Michael a letter telling him I would ask for a leave and come back home to help him . . . But he was never home when I called and I don't think he got the message. The letter arrived a day after his death."

Fred's Dad started to cry a little and Fred rubbed his Father's back.

The Senior Goodman slammed his fist on the handrail.

"That #@!!#! Sebastian . . . He killed Michael! I confronted Sebastian at the funeral. I showed him the letter and he tried to snap it out of my hand but I wouldn't let him. He even threatened me if I would dare say anything. Even at the Funeral, His last words to me were . . . Michael was an embarrassment to the Goodman name . . . Don't you dare smear my name . . . #@**%#!"

Fred and his Dad stood quietly a moment and then Fred spoke, "I'm sorry Dad . . . I didn't know. Harry never said anything."

"I know . . . I asked him not too . . . Thought it might damper your love for the Farm. I'm surprised Fred that you never confronted me about why I distanced myself from the farm."

"I guess when I was younger Dad . . . I was afraid to ask you because I thought you would get angry and not let me go to the farm. When I got older . . . Well I thought I might be prying. I understand now Dad . . . I won't pressure you to stay at the farm."

Fred's Dad laughed, put his arm around his son and said, "Let's go Fred. We've been up here long enough . . . Let's go join the others. We can talk more about this later."

Fred felt a new special feeling for his Dad and although this was not the most opportune time for Fred's Dad's heartfelt confession, Fred was glad his Father opened up to him.

The two arrive back at the waiting room . . .

Fred and his Dad had no sooner sat down when the two double doors near the end of the long hallway flung open and Doctor Chapman strode quickly down the corridor. This time the Doctor was beaming a big smile.

Doctor Chapman walked right up to Fred and slapped Fred's shoulders and at the same time spotted Fred's Dad and Mom whom Doctor Chapman knew very well.

He quickly shook Fred's Dads hand, "Good to see you Robert . . . We'll chat later."

"Good news Fred . . . Jenny's fine and in fairly good spirits considering what she has been through!"

The Doctor stopped a minute, placed his hands on his hips and laughed.

"Fred . . . Congratulations . . . You are the proud Father of a 6 pound, 8 ounce Baby ... Baby Boy!"

The whole waiting room went into euphoria. Even some visitors, who apparently arrived in the waiting area a short time before, for matters of their own, joined in the celebrations. Fred was in utter ecstasy.

Ben at one time screamed out, "Yes. . . A boy . . . The Goodman legacy lives on . . . Unbelievable!"

Everybody was hugging and kissing each other. Handshakes, high fives, and slaps on the back were passed around. It was quite the sight to see and the excitement took about ten minutes to fade.

Fred found Doctor Chapman in all the commotion, "Oh gosh Doc . . . Thank you . . . Thank you so much for saving Jenny. And my son . . . Wow I've got to get use to saying that . . . Wow . . . My Son!"

Doctor Chapman slapped Fred on the shoulders again, "I'll be back but I have to attend to Jenny now. Congrats again Fred."

The Doctor walked over to the Nurse at the reception area and slid some paperwork to her over the high counter and she looked up to him. "I take it everything went well Doctor!"

Doctor Chapman turned once more to the jubilant gathering and then back to the Nurse.

"Yes it did . . . Earlier today I would have only given that women and her baby about a 20% chance of making it . . . Unbelievable!"

The Doctor smiled at the Nurse, slapped his palm down on the counter, and briskly walked back to Surgery.

At the same time in recovery . . .

Jenny was brought into a little room off of the recovery unit. Groggy and very much out of it, she lay still but she had a smile on her face.

A large woman walked into the room.

"Hi Jenny . . . My name is Amelia . . . Congratulations. I'm going to clean you up a bit and then we will take you to a room up in Maternity."

"When can I see my Husband . . . And my Baby?"

"As soon as I get you presentable woman. You went through HECK today!" The Nurse's aide let out a hearty chuckle.

"Your baby is still being examined up in Maternity but the word is . . . He's in great shape. He'll be ready for you when you get up there. And Doctor Chapman is with your husband now. Now listen . . . I'll be right back young lady. I have to get a few more things . . . Now don't go anywhere!"

The aide let out a large round of laughter and left the room, closing the door behind her.

Suddenly, Jenny sat up in the bed. It was a strain but she managed to do it. She sat quietly as if she was trying to hear something. Now somehow, Jenny succeeded to remove the covers, swing her legs over the side of the bed, and slip to the floor.

Even with two IV's attached to her arm, she struggled to the large window which was only a few feet from the bed. Jenny placed one hand on the window sill, and the other on the bed. Jenny gazed out over the City lights.

A few seconds later Amelia returned and was shocked, "Oh my Gosh . . . What are you doing out of bed Woman . . . How'd you get there?"

Amelia rushed over to Jenny's side, "What on earth are you doing here . . . Let's get you back to bed before the Doctor comes in . . . And Fires us both!"

Jenny went to turn but stopped and strained to ask Amelia, "Is Oak Grove over that way?"

Amelia looked quickly out the window, "Yes but way out there . . . About thirty miles . . . Why?"

Jenny softly answered, "Oh I don't know . . . Thought I heard something?"

Amelia laughed. "Girl you're delusional . . .Too many Meds I think . . . Thought you heard something . . . Gosh sakes . . . Now let's get you back to bed . . . AND STAY THERE!"

Amelia kept chuckling even though she was frightened over finding Jenny out of the bed. Amelia started to wash Jenny up while muttering over and over, "Unbelievable!"

But the story is not quite over . . .

Back in Oak Grove, the elderly Doctor Wilson and his wife were lying in Bed doing a little late night reading before retiring. But they both dropped their books to their laps and looked at each other when they heard the loud constant howling coming from the kennel area.

"My Gosh George . . . What is all that racket for?"

"Don't know . . . Must be one of the dogs out in the back kennel!"

"Well don't you think you ought a go see George? Before the neighbors start complaining?"

The elderly veterinarian groaned and rose from his bed. While shaking his head, he threw on a T shirt, overalls, and his slippers.

"Well . . . We have had this Animal Hospital and Kennel here for nearly forty five years. Long before we had neighbors. If the neighbors call and complain . . . Tell em to MOVE!"

The doctor grunted as he walked out of the bedroom. The Hospital was attached to the far end of the house and the older Doctor slowly made his way over to the office and waiting area. The lights were always left dimly on all night in the hospital area. When Doctor Wilson opened the door, he was in disbelief as to what he saw.

Bailey had crawled off the mattress the Doctor had prepared for him after surgery as Bailey was too big to fit into one of the cages.

Covered with bandages, Bailey stood on his hind leg's resting his front paws on the window sill staring at something outside the window and incessantly howling.

The Doctor walked over to Bailey's side, stooped down a little, and peered out the window also. Bailey ceased his howling.

"What ya see Bailey?"

The Doctor expected to see a Deer or some other kind of animal wandering through the yard but there was nothing.

"Hmmm . . . Bailey we got to get you back to bed."

The Doctor was definitely surprised. He really didn't expect Bailey to make it through the night.

Just then, the Doctor's wife came through the door and she too stood in amazement.

"Is everything okay dear?"

"I don't know . . . Why are you here dear . . . I have it under control."

"Thought you should know. That Roger fellow, the guy who brought you this Dog . . . He just called. The Goodman girl just delivered a baby boy . . . Isn't that nice Dear?"

Doctor Wilson turned to Bailey and stroked the top of his head.

"Did you hear that Bailey? Jenny's going to be okay and you're going to have a new baby brother . . . Or something like that?"

The Doctor turned to his wife and shrugged his shoulders as he really didn't know what to say to Bailey and embarrassed that in fact, he did!

"Well get this beast back to bed so . . . We can." stammered the Doctors wife.

Doctor Wilson coaxed Bailey back to his mattress and Bailey flopped down but he was now wagging his tail.

Just before Doc Wilson left the room, he turned, looked over one more time at Bailey and mumbled, "Unbelievable . . . Simply Unbelievable!" He smiled and went off back to bed.

The End

Hopefully you will join Fred, Jenny and Bailey in Book II of this series to see what's going on. Oh Yes, and the opportunity to meet the newest member of the Goodman Family!

ABOUT THE AUTHOR

Philip Sorant is a semi-retired General Contractor who spends most of his time now as a Freelance Web Developer and an Author of several realistic fiction novels. He was raised in New England and resides in New Hampshire with his wife and two sons.